RED BEARD'S CLINIC

SHUGORO YAMAMOTO

Translated by
SHELLEY MARSHALL

SHELLEY MARSHALL

CONTENTS

CHAPTER 1
THE STORY OF A MADWOMAN

1

YASUMOTO NOBORU STOOD before the gate and stared lazily for a few moments at the guardhouse. Queasy from a hangover, his head weighed him down.

"I guess this is the place," he muttered to himself. "The Koishikawa Charity Clinic."

His mind filled with thoughts of Chigusa. As he stared at the guardhouse, he recalled Chigusa's face. The soft lines of her tall, lithe physique, her long pale face with sharp features. The instant flush of her cheeks whenever he touched her. Her glistening eyes. An invitation to him seemed to rise in those eyes.

"Has it been three years?" he said to himself. "Why didn't you wait, Chigusa? Why?"

He turned to see a young man walking toward the gate. He immediately knew from his clothes and hairstyle that he was a doctor. Noboru returned to his senses and followed the young man to the guardhouse. When he gave his name to the guard, the young man turned and came back. He asked, "Are you Yasumoto-san?"

Noboru nodded.

"I know about you," said the young man and turned to the guard.

"I'll escort him."

He greeted Noboru with a modest affected bow and walked beside him.

"I'm Tsugawa Genzō," the young man said amiably. "We've been waiting for your arrival."

Noboru looked at him but said nothing.

"Yes, well," Tsugawa smiled. "Now that you're here, I can leave. You're taking my place."

Noboru looked skeptical and said, "I'm only here because I was invited."

"So you studied in Nagasaki," said Tsugawa, changing the subject. "How long were you there?"

"Three years."

Noboru recalled Chigusa with the words *three years* and frowned.

"This place is awful," said Tsugawa. "You're wondering how awful? You'd never be able to understand if you weren't here to see for yourself. Anyway, the patients are riddled with fleas and lice and covered with tumors. They all stink and are ignorant poor people.

"The pay couldn't be lower, but Red Beard will work you hard day and night. I was cursed for wanting to become a doctor. It's awful. This place is the pits."

Noboru said nothing.

I only came because I was invited, thought Noboru. I have no intention of being shut up in a so-called *charity clinic* after being trained in Nagasaki. That fellow should have asked for references. He was mistaken.

After they walked only fifty steps from the gate down the slushy pebble path, they came to the building. The antiquated awning at the entryway was warped. The roof tiles were skewed. The two ward wings slammed by ocean waves were off kilter.

Tsugawa Genzō went to a side entrance, pointed out the cabinet for shoes, and stepped inside with Noboru.

Around the corner down the hall was the waiting room full of people. They were probably patients waiting to be examined. The middle-aged and older men and women and the children were all poorly dressed. A pungent odor like discarded garbage or rotten fruit filled the space.

"These are outpatients here for treatment," said Tsugawa while wiping the tip of his nose with his hand. "Everything from the examinations to the medications is free. For this bunch, dying would be better than living. He made a sour face and gestured to one side. "This way."

They went down a connecting hall and turned right. Tsugawa stopped in front of the first room in the hall and announced himself.

From inside the room, they heard "Come in." The deep voice was rhythmic and resonant.

Tsugawa whispered, "That's Red Beard," signaled Noboru with his eyes, and slid open the *shōji* door.

The long room had six tatami mats in two rows. Opposite the door was a waist-high window. Cabinets with three levels were on the left and right sides and solidly built from aged yellowish oak lumber. The top two levels were shelves and the bottom had a drawer on the left and right. Of course, the medicines were probably locked up. A card written with the medication's name was affixed to each concoction.

The window faced north. The stained shōji door was discolored in the cold light. The sturdy broad back of the older man and his unkempt gray hair reflected the light.

Tsugawa Genzō sat, gave a quick greeting, and introduced Yasumoto Noboru.

The old man, still silent, turned to a small desk and wrote something.

He wore *hakama* trousers of a strange dark gray color, the same color as his tight-sleeve, lined kimono. Rather than the usual flowing split skirt-like hakama trousers, he wore the pants-like *tattsuke* sewn to resemble leggings. Pleats circled his waist but were finer around his shins. The leggings were tightly closed around his ankles with strings.

This room did not have a wooden brazier. It faced north and received none of the sun's warmth. The air thick with a medicinal odor was frigid. The cold rose from beneath their knees and spread into their entire bodies.

Eventually, the old man put down his pen and turned to them.

He raised his bald head with its wide forehead. His features were angular. A thick beard grew from his mouth to his chin. Intense eyes gleamed below the long, thick eyebrows found in the common saying, "Long eyebrows, long life." His lips closed to form an upside-down U and his eyes simultaneously reflected the sarcasm of a cynic and the curiosity of a child.

Noboru thought, Of course, he's Red Beard.

His beard was whitish gray, but his headstrong expression gave the impression of Red Beard.

He was somewhere between forty and sixty years old. His masculine intensity of a man in his forties and the steadiness of one in his sixties were a little unnatural but seemed to come together in one body.

Noboru bowed and introduced himself.

Red Beard said, "I am Nīde Kyojō," and stared at Noboru. His eyes, as though trained by a drill, assumed a pointed, impertinent expression, and locked onto his face. As if taking Noboru to task, he said, "You will begin training today. You may have your luggage sent here."

Noboru stuttered, "But I ... Wait a minute. I'm only here because I was invited."

Kyojō interrupted, "We're done here," and said to Tsugawa, "Show him to his room."

2

Yasumoto Noboru lived at The Koishikawa Charity Clinic as an intern.

He objected vehemently. He planned to become a doctor of the shogunate. He would study in Nagasaki, return to Edo, and be assigned a post as a government doctor.

His father Yasumoto Ryōan was a town doctor with an office at 5-chōme, Kōji-machi. Amano Genpaku, a friend of his father who carries the title of Hōin, the shogun's lead physician, recognized Noboru's talent early on, arranged for Noboru to study in Nagasaki, and promised to recommend him for a post as a shogunate physician.

Noboru explained this to Tsugawa Genzō.

"You had that support, but this happened anyway," Tsugawa started to say, but his smile insinuated, What happened?

"Well, I give up. I knew you were coming about two weeks ago because, for some reason, Red Beard seemed to be interested in you."

Tsugawa took him to his room.

On the right side of the hall after turning left from Nīde's room were three similar small rooms. Tsugawa went to the first room and introduced Mori Handayū, a fellow intern, to him. Handayū was a thin man, twenty-seven or -eight years old. He looked miserable and listless from exhaustion.

After introducing himself, Handayū said, "I heard rumors. This place is fairly tough, but if you're serious, many subjects are available for you to study that will be of great use in the future."

Handayū's voice was gentle but felt like a razor wrapped in cotton. A razor also seemed to be hiding deep in his bright, peaceful eyes.

Noboru realized Handayū ignored Tsugawa, never responding to anything he said or looking at him.

"He's the second son of a wealthy farmer somewhere in Sagami," said Tsugawa after they went out to the hall. "He doesn't care for me, but he is a prodigy."

Noboru ignored him.

Tsugawa's room was next to Mori's, and the last room was Noboru's. All the rooms had an area of six tatami mats covering slightly less than twelve feet by nine feet. The interior was dim with a window facing north. Only a thin *beri* rush mat covered the wood floor. The room felt bleak. A small old-fashioned desk was placed below the window. Its seat was a round straw mat woven from cattail. One wall was cracked. A closet with a heavy wooden door occupied the other.

"They haven't gotten around to laying down the tatami yet?"

"Not anywhere," said Tsugawa, spreading his arms wide. "The medical staff's rooms are all like this. The ward also has thin beri mats spread on the wood floor for the bedding."

Noboru grumbled in a low voice, "It's like a jail cell."

"Everyone says that, especially, the patients in the wards," said Tsugawa sarcastically. "They are poor people and feel inferior for having to be treated at a charity clinic. Even the kimonos conform to this style."

Noboru recalled what Red Beard wore and Mori Handayū wearing the same clothes.

He asked and was told the medical staff wore the same colored outfit in winter and summer, all the time.

The ward patients, both men and women, wore white tight-sleeve kimonos with attached strings, like the kimonos worn by children. These uniforms could be quickly untied for examinations, but the patients didn't like them. They constantly complained about the construction of the rooms with thin mats on wooden floors and the kimonos resembling jail uniforms.

"Has this been the rule for a long time?"

"It is Red Beard's reform," said Tsugawa with a shrug. "He's the dictator here. He's skilled at performing any treatment he is enthusiastic about. Men as reliable as he are rare even among daimyos or wealthy men. Too many decisions are tyrannical and made without consulting anyone else. Most people hate that."

"It looks like the braziers aren't used."

"At least, outside of the wards. He claims the coldness of Edo benefits one's health. The budget only includes coal for the wards. Let me take you on a round," said Tsugawa, and they left the room.

First, they saw the cramped room of on-duty doctors, then the front room where outpatients were examined, the room for preparing medications, the reception area for admitting patients, and the doctors' dining hall. Tsugawa put on his garden *geta* sandals and went out the south door.

This door was at the corner of the connecting hall. Once outside, they were across from the kitchen.

The one-story, tile-roof building was close to one thousand square feet. Beside it was a roofed water well. Four or five women were washing vegetables, probably for pickling, and building a mountain of washed vegetables. The white stalks and the greens bathed in the morning sunlight and looked strikingly fresh and vibrant.

3

Tsugawa pointed out one woman.

"See the young lady second from the right with her sleeves pulled back with the yellow *tasuki* sash. The one stacking vegetables. That's Yuki. She's Mori-sensei's girlfriend."

Noboru looked at her with indifference.

An eighteen- or nineteen-year-old woman came from the ward and called to Tsugawa. She could be a maid in a prosperous merchant's home given her elegant features, personal appearance, and speech. She probably ran here and was trying to catch her breath. Her face was flush and tense.

She impatiently said, "She's getting painful spasms again, but the medicine is gone. I'm sorry, but could you please make more right away?"

Tsugawa answered, "You have to ask Nīde-sensei. The other doctors aren't allowed to touch that medication. He's in the front room."

She glanced at Noboru. Perhaps she felt his gaze on her and shot a quick look sideways at him. While her cheeks blushed, she bowed and trotted back through the south door.

Tsugawa prompted Noboru to walk. They hurried to the South Ward beside a wide, empty lot measuring 7,000 square feet. At the far end of the lot, a fence surrounded the medicinal garden.

Originally, the garden was called Koishikawa's Medicinal Garden. Medicinal plants were cultivated under the direct control of the shogunate. Two eight-acre gardens were planted and spread to the north and south divided by a road.

The clinic was located in a portion of the southern garden. That area was on a high hill on the western end. The medicinal garden was in the highest part and provided an enjoyable panoramic view extending to the west.

The garden was bland during the winter. Most of the medicinal trees and herbs were withered. Small placards written with the product names were set up on the sides covered by straw to protect against frost.

They walked down the raised path slushy from melted frost. Several official gardeners spreading out dirt and replacing the straw covering greeted Tsugawa, who introduced Noboru to them. They politely introduced themselves to Noboru.

The huge, fat, older man was Gohei. The expressionless young man, lanky like a withered tree, was Kichitarō. Noboru remembered the other names: Jisaku, Kyūsuke, and Tomigorō.

Tsugawa asked, "Gohei, how are you feeling? Can you do it, yet?"

"Maybe soon," said the old man. While his fingers scratched his fat double chin, his eyes narrowed as if spellbound, and nodded. "Yes, maybe it will be soon."

"I'll stop at the end of this month. I'd like to taste it by then." He cautiously added, "I think maybe it's for the best. I wonder how it is."

"We should go to the shed," said Tsugawa and started off.

As they walked, he said, "I'm making sake from Korean grapes. It's black and feels too thick on the tongue but tastes good. Red Beard had me make it for medicinal uses and plans to use it someday."

When they left the medicinal garden, Tsugawa headed to the North Ward.

Woods of large beech trees, Mongolian oaks, camellias, pine or cedar trees, and a deep bamboo grove were planted as a windbreak. A new home was built and surrounded by the bamboo grove. Tsugawa started toward the house but seemed to change his mind and walked by while shaking his head.

"Sugi from earlier, the woman we met at the south door," said

Tsugawa, still walking. "She lives in that house and is the nurse to the sick lady of the house."

"Is that house part of the clinic?"

"The young lady's parents built it with their own money. Their daughter is a special patient."

Tsugawa's voice sounded dry.

No one knew her identity, which was a strict secret, but she seemed to be the daughter of a comfortably wealthy man. She was around twenty-two or -three. Her name was Yumi, and her looks were striking.

She fell ill when she was sixteen. From the beginning, no one knew she was insane. She was engaged to a man, but he broke it off and married another woman. She fell into a melancholy that lasted a year. Around that time, we thought she could be cured, but then she killed a shop clerk.

Seventeen or eighteen men worked for her father's business. Over a short two years, she attacked three of them. One was saved from danger, but she killed two young men.

"She did not simply kill. She seduced them and killed them after robbing them of their freedom as men," said Tsugawa and licked his lips. "This is the story of a man saved from danger. At first, she loved the man and snuck him into her bedroom. She seemed filled with sensuality and drove the man crazy. When he could no longer resist, she stuck him with an ornamental hairpin."

Noboru frowned and quietly muttered, "The origin was betrayal by a man."

Tsugawa licked his lips again and said, "Red Beard's diagnosis is different. He said it is a variety of innate sex mania. More than madness, Red Beard says it is the physical manifestation of insanity."

The phrase *sexual pleasure from murder* floated into Noboru's head. During his studies in Nagasaki, he learned about a case like this from a Dutch medical book. It said this condition had been in Japan for a long time and mentioned several similar cases. He took notes.

The daughter's crime disappeared through her parents' power. The murdered man was a shop clerk who snuck into the bedroom of the proprietor's daughter and tried to rape her. That was what it looked like. A dead man tells no tales. That was how it ended.

However, when she stole the life of the third man, a clerk, others understood what was happening for the first time and summoned Nīde Kyojō. He said to build a confinement room and to shut her in there. Otherwise, she would surely kill again and again.

Unlike other types of insanity, this one originated from lust. Not at all different from a sane person, he emphasized there is no way to prevent this crime other than imprisonment. However, the public objected to the plan to build a confinement room in a home with a family and many servants and to imprison her there.

The parents claimed she was being treated at the clinic because the house was built on its grounds. They donated the building to the clinic and would spare no expense to treat the madness of their daughter who would die a lunatic if no cure were found.

In the fall of the year before last, the house was built. The young woman accompanied by her maid Sugi moved in.

Tsugawa said, "The entire building is a prison. Inside is a two-room kitchen. Sugi does all the cooking and washing. Necessities for daily use are brought in from the parents' home once every three days.

"Sugi has a key. No one is allowed inside the house. The daughter lives alone and never goes outside. Only Red Beard goes inside."

"Is there a treatment protocol?"

Tsugawa shook his head. "Well, more than treatment, the problem seems to be intermittent attacks. Therefore, the medication especially compounded by Red Beard is collected by Sugi. Red Beard never allows anyone else to prepare the medication. The medicine seems to have an extremely positive effect."

Noboru pondered sexual pressure from murder. When it is a physical manifestation and congenital, the daughter's transgression is no more her crime than the repulsiveness of an ineptly carved wooden statue is the crime of the wooden statue... But Chigusa's situation is different. Chigusa is a sane young woman.

Noboru bit his lip.

"I feel bad for Sugi," Tsugawa continued. "She's a live-in servant and has no choice but to live in a house built as a jail to care for the young madwoman. She has no idea when this will end."

"If she's a servant, she can quit."

"No, she can't. From the bottom of her heart, that young woman has compassion for her employer. It may be love more than compassion."

Tsugawa shook his head and sighed. "I may not be the least bit reluctant to leave this place but have lingering regrets about no longer seeing Sugi."

Noboru recalled Sugi's blushing face a short time ago.

4

Sugi's face did not blush because of Tsugawa. He seemed to talk amiably with Sugi but did not think about her at all. When Noboru first met her outside the south door, Sugi's cheeks flushed. She shyly gave a slight bow and noticed Noboru staring at her. He heard this from Sugi after they became closer friends.

Eventually, Noboru and Sugi got to know each other well and didn't hide their meetings from others. Thinking about it later, it was not from pure feelings. He fell into various situations, repressed feelings of desperation, and wanted a companion to hear his grievances. This might have happened because he was curious about the affliction suffered by the young woman Yumi. Thus, Sugi became his best companion. Noboru talked about his dissatisfaction with joining the clinic and even about Chigusa. This confidential talk made him feel tender warmth and serenity.

"I never thought that," he said to Sugi. "What kind of crafty plan is that? If I annoy him and break his patience, I intend to find a way to ask him why he asked me to come."

"Can you?" Sugi did not sound convinced and tilted her head. "But I think Yumi's situation is not related to your joining this clinic."

This was the first time Sugi expressed her opinion. Noboru looked doubtfully at her.

"Why?" he asked. "If it's as you say, Amano-sama should pay compensation. Even if compensation is not paid, the promise of an appointment as a government doctor for the shogunate must be forcefully protected."

This first unhurried talk Noboru had with Sugi happened one evening at the end of February.

A bench was set up in front of the bamboo grove about sixty feet from Yumi's home. Seven benches for patients being admitted were set up in sunny places. The bench in front of the bamboo grove was for Yumi. A garden alcove with a roof was built. No one went near it at night.

That evening, after an argument with Nīde Kyojō, Noboru had the gardener Kichitarō buy the sake he was drinking in his room. He couldn't stand it and went out. He was drinking the sake from a gourd at that bench when Sugi appeared.

She had prepared Yumi's rice gruel and was surprised to find Noboru there. She said she was there to look around.

A short time ago, Yumi had an attack. Sugi gave Yumi her usual medicine. After she fell into a deep sleep, Sugi said she locked the door and came outside. Noboru asked her to speak slowly because he was drunk. This was the first time they talked like that.

He said, "You're good-natured. Are they that honest? I have problems in this world. I think if I joined this place, this job wouldn't be worth the trouble. I know it was a trick."

"I believe Nīde-sensei called you here."

Noboru took another drink from the gourd.

"For a long time, the sensei has wanted better doctors to work here. He said he wanted a skilled doctor at this clinic who would do his best to cure the patients better than anywhere else."

"So he shouldn't have called me. You don't become a good doctor only by studying. Time and experience are also required. Of course, I'm still a beginner."

He gave a quick nod for emphasis. "Yes, that's the only reason he called me here. That's what I was arguing about with Red Beard."

"Oh, so you're a Red Beard."

"There are many Red Beards," he said like he was spitting.

After dinner that evening, Nīde Kyojō summoned Noboru and told him to submit notes and diagrams from his time studying in Nagasaki.

Noboru refused. He studied every subject of Dutch medicine but labored to learn internal medicine. He devised methods for diagnosis and treatment. They were his achievements understood only by him.

Those notes and diagrams would promise him a grand future. If made public, their value would sink.

Isn't there a doctor who gained fame from a treatment for cataracts and made a fortune?

Noboru said, "My medical techniques are newer, have great value, and were achieved through my hard work and at my expense. I can't show it to others. I shouldn't be obliged to."

However, Kyojō disagreed and took him to task.

"You refused, but I will not listen to your babbling. Hand over all your notes and diagrams. That is your only business."

Noboru told Sugi he had no choice but to do as he was told.

"If Red Beard summoned me here, that was the only reason," said Noboru, while licking the gourd. "So he didn't bother me until now. I won't wear that uniform. Even if I do nothing and goof off, he acts oblivious to it all."

"You're drunk."

"I'm drunk? I only drank this much," said Noboru and took another swig. "I drink because it's prohibited. Anything forbidden here, I will do."

"Please stop," said Sugi and tried to take the gourd. "I hate drunks."

Noboru roughly grabbed the hand she reached out. Her hand was soft, cool, and warm. Sugi didn't try to move away but stared while still being held. On the bright starry night, the air was warm. The fragrance of winter daphne drifted in from the medicinal garden.

"Do you hate me?" Noboru whispered.

Sugi calmly said, "I hate you when you're drunk."

Noboru was silent for a short time and then released her hand.

"Well, go home."

"Please give me that gourd," said Sugi. "I'll keep it until tomorrow."

"Leave me alone," said Noboru and took another drink. "You're probably satisfied taking care of that batty daughter. Don't worry about me."

Sugi took the gourd from him. She snatched it with such force Noboru couldn't stop her.

Sugi stood. "You'll get this back tomorrow," she said and returned to the house.

Noboru said nothing and listened to the sounds of Sugi's *zōri* sandals growing faint.

5

After that night, Noboru and Sugi got closer.

He intended to never become an intern. He had observed that life here was messy, listless, and boring.

A village official managed this clinic, commonly known as a charity clinic. The hereditary post was held by Ogawa-san. The shogunate assigned an assistant.

Ogawa-san had a separate estate, but his office was in the front building. He did the accounting and conducted other business there with the assistant.

There were five on-duty doctors on the medical staff. Their office was a part of the wards and connected by a corridor to the front building.

The on-duty doctors were Nīde Kyojō, the medical director; Yoshioka Itetsu; Ida Goan; Ida Gentan; and Hashimoto Genrōku. They worked in the fields of internal medicine, surgery, and gynecology. The Idas were father and son and also worked as town doctors in Shitaya Okachi-machi. Three to five town doctors commuted to the clinic and worked on commission.

There were two interns. This pair and Medical Director Nīde were the only full-time staff doctors. These three were mostly responsible for treating the admitted patients. The other doctors were not enthusiastic about the outpatients and often careless in their treatments.

The two wards were the North Ward and the South Ward. Each ward had three ten-tatami-mat sickrooms, two eight-tatami-mat sickrooms, and two six-tatami-mat sickrooms for seriously ill patients.

More than thirty patients were admitted. Most were elderly people, women, and people who were carried in with external wounds or had collapsed.

As Tsugawa Genzō said, all the sickrooms had thin, bordered mats on the wood floors. The bedding was laid on top. The thin mats were changed every five days, and the bedding every seven and exposed to sunlight and wind.

The patients, whether young or old, male or female, were given white, tight-sleeved cotton kimonos that were tied using attached cords. Even women were not allowed to tie their kimonos with obi sashes or wear colored kimonos.

"They call this a charity clinic, so we should at least be allowed to sleep on tatami mats."

"Since I brought one, they should let the women wear colored kimonos because the white ones make us look like convicts."

The patients' discontent never ended.

All their discontent and dissatisfaction were directed at Nide Kyojō. These were decisions made solely by him. Even the way he handled the treatments was gruff. His coarse language upset the patients, repelling not a few of them.

Kyojō often went out to visit various daimyos and wealthy families, as well as, his private patients he treated on house calls.

At those times, the two interns were left in charge. Although that was fine while an on-duty doctor or a commissioned doctor was present, they lived elsewhere and commuted. If an emergency patient appeared at night, unforeseen events the interns could not handle were common.

Immediately after Tsugawa Genzō departed, Noboru was called by Mori Handayū and was treating his third admitted patient. He was called and went with Mori to the sickroom, but Noboru only watched and did nothing.

It could not be said Handayū forced him to be a helper, but probably the third time, when he finished the treatment and left the sickroom, he stopped Noboru in the hallway. Handayū was breathing heavily and asked, "What are you doing?" and glared at him. "How long do you intend to continue behaving like this?"

"What are you talking about?"

"Your passive resistance," said Handayū. "How long do you intend to carry on with that stupid resistance to draw attention to yourself? Do you think anyone sympathizes or is Nīde-sensei wrong?"

Noboru was so angry he couldn't speak.

"Please, carefully consider this," whispered Handayū. "No one else is harmed but you, Yasumoto-san."

Noboru wanted to slug him.

He quickly guessed Mori Handayū was devoted to Kyojō. Tsugawa told him Mori was the second son of a wealthy farming family in Sagami. Maybe to a man from the countryside, the charity clinic administered by the shogunate and its medical director Nīde Kyojō are splendid and should be revered.

Oh, that's stupid, thought Noboru. Handayū has hardly spoken to him, but when he unexpectedly did, a burst of scathing sarcasm poured out. Noboru had to use all his might to keep from punching him.

He never told Sugi about that incident. Handayū had the sincerity of a man raised in the countryside and was liked by his colleagues and patients. Once in a while, Sugi praised him.

A young woman named Yuki lived at a cookhouse called Makanai-jō. Tsugawa told Noboru she was Handayū's girlfriend. However, Sugi said Yuki's love was unrequited, and Handayū avoided her.

"She seems to be head over heels," said Sugi one evening while seated on the usual bench. "It's kind of pitiful to watch. Mori-san's reliable nature is impressive, but when I think about Yuki-san, I hate him."

"Stop talking about Handayū," interrupted Noboru. "I want to hear about Yumi-san. Have you been with her for a long time?"

Sugi took on a cautious tone.

"Why are you asking about her?"

"Because I'm a doctor," he said, "Unlike Mori, I came here with formal training in Western medicine. I know diagnoses and treatments unknown to Red Beard."

"So why won't you become an envoy of that knowledge?"

"At a dump like this?" he asked, waving one hand. "I won't become an intern in this sort of charity clinic. I have no intention of training to become a doctor here."

"You're drunk again."

"Don't change the subject," he said. "I refuse to be an intern and am not interested in any old disease contracted by anybody. However, if a person with a rare illness appears, as a doctor, of course, I'd like to become involved. At this place, Yumi-san is that case."

"I don't believe you."

"You don't believe me. What don't you believe?"

"Everybody's feelings," said Sugi. "When Yumi's story is mentioned, your eyes take on a lascivious and obscene expression. But Tsugawa-san is the worst, no one other than Kyojō-sensei is serious."

6

Noboru looked at Sugi in the darkness.

"I didn't know about that. What did Tsugawa do?"

"I'm not talking about that."

"It's all right, Sugi-san," he said in a different tone. "I'm a doctor who came here to learn the latest medical techniques. If I know details about the symptoms, my treatment may be different from Red Beard's. Tell me and we'll see. Do you think it's a waste?"

Sugi looked back at him. "You sound so serious."

"You should know me better."

"You're drunk," said Sugi. "Goodnight. We'll talk the next time we meet."

"Why won't you tell me?"

Noboru tried to grab her hand. She avoided his hand and stood. While stifling a laugh, she said, "Because you act like that."

"This and that are different."

Noboru quickly stood and embraced Sugi. She stared at him. He placed one hand on Sugi's back and the other rounded her back in a tight embrace.

"You love me, don't you?" he asked.

Sugi said, "You —"

"You love me," said Noboru and pressed his lips to Sugi's. "I love you."

He felt the power drained from her body, which became supple and heavier. Noboru was about to pull her back to the bench, but Sugi slipped from his arms and jumped back while suppressing a smile.

"I hate you when you act like that," said Sugi, "Goodnight."

"Do as you like," he said.

He didn't see Sugi again for five or six days.

It was probably the middle of March. The cherry blossoms on the grounds were in full bloom. The late-blooming medicinal trees and plants in the gardens had all budded. And early ones bloomed into flowers. Passing winds left the air laden with the strong fragrance of these flowers.

After lunch, Noboru took a walk to the medicinal garden and met Sugi on her way back from doing laundry. While walking a slight distance apart, he asked, "Why didn't you come in the evenings?"

Sugi answered, "I caught a cold. I've gotten better and intended to go tonight." She lightly coughed as she spoke and sounded hoarse.

"Are you still producing mucous?" he asked. "You must take care of yourself. It may be better if you don't come out tonight."

Sugi was smiling when she said, "What?"

"You can't hear me well," he said and moved a little closer to her. "What happened?"

Sugi answered, "I'll come tonight."

"Don't overdo it. Are you taking any medicine?"

"Yes, Kyojō-sensei gave it to me."

"Not overdoing it is best. I'll prepare a medication for your throat."

Sugi nodded and smiled.

That day, when he ate dinner in the dining hall, Noboru was notified of a visitor at the entryway. Kyojō had gone out and hadn't returned. Mori Handayū pretended not to know anything. Since he was forbidden to leave during a meal, Noboru asked what sort of visitor. He was told she was a young woman named Amano Masao.

Amano Masao?

Noboru did not recognize her name but made a quick guess. Chigusa had a younger sister who was still a girl. He hardly knew what she looked like but knew her family name, Amano. He was sure this younger sister had come here to see him.

I guess she's that young woman.

Noboru wondered why she came. He couldn't figure out whether she came on her own or did someone else push her to come. He couldn't carelessly meet her.

"Tell her I'm not in my room," said Noboru to the receptionist. "Please, ask if she'd like to leave a message because I can't see her now."

When dinner ended, the receptionist came and told him she wanted to see him and waited but eventually went home.

She didn't leave a message and said she'd come again. Mori Handayū heard this answer from across the way. Noboru realized Handayū had been nonchalantly listening, stood up making a racket, and left the dining hall. He would make the gardener Kichitarō go buy sake. The tall, lanky young man was weak-spirited and stuttered. He was reluctant to buy sake.

As usual, Kichitarō wanted to say something when he was discovered and yelled at, but his severe stuttering prevented him from saying what he thought. When Noboru shouted, he stopped speaking and left scratching his head.

Noboru grumbled to himself, "She sent her younger sister. What is she planning this time? This trick isn't clever."

The sake came. Noboru drank it cold. After he was fairly drunk, he left carrying the sake bottle with the remaining sake.

On the hot, cloudy night, no moon was in the sky, and no stars could be seen. The air smelled of dirt and flowers, slightly sweet, steamy, and humid. At those times, he could feel the strong aromas. It was dark, and he was probably drunk. He passed in front of the bench without noticing her, and Sugi called from behind to stop him.

He said, "You came?" when he went back to her.

"Yumi-san is asleep," said Sugi. She spoke in a barely audible, hoarse voice. "What happened?"

"I stumbled," he said and staggered to the bench and sat. "Come here."

Sugi sat apart and said something.

"I couldn't hear you," he said and shook his head. "I can't hear that voice well. Come a little closer."

Sugi slid a little closer.

"Here," he said, took out a medicine bag from his sleeve, and passed it to her. "Infuse it in tea and drink it. I wrote down the directions for infusion. It should help your throat get better."

Sugi thanked him and asked, "Did you bring sake?"

"A mouthful is left."

"I brought something, too."

"What?" He moved his ear closer to her.

"Your gourd," she said, displaying the gourd. "I've had it for some time and forgot about it. Yumi-san drinks this delicious sake. I brought a little."

"Ah, this sake is probably brewed from the fruits of shrimp grapevine grass."

"You know about it?"

"Red Beard has me make medicines from it. I've tasted it several times in Gohei's hut," he said and took the gourd. "I'm amazed you brought sake."

7

Noboru drank from the gourd. It was dark, faintly sweet, and had a medicinal scent. When Tsugawa was still there, he tasted it when he visited Gohei at home. He only had a teacup's worth; he couldn't drink anymore. Its flavor was too rich.

This time he was drunk. The sake felt differently on his tongue and seemed more delicious than before. While listening to Sugi, he was oblivious to the large quantity he drank. She talked about Yumi.

"It's true. I think it's different from Kyojō-sensei's diagnosis. Yumi-san is not insane. I am sure of that. Please, listen carefully to what I'm saying."

"Honestly, you're not telling me everything," he said. "But tonight, that's all right."

"Because you are drunk."

"Your voice sounds strained."

"I'm fine. On the other hand, you're talking like a stranger." To remind him, she said, "Please, listen carefully."

Noboru reached out a hand and grasped Sugi's hand. Leaving her hand in his, she said, "When I became a live-in maid, Yumi was fifteen, two years older than me. She was the eldest of three sisters. The middle sister was twelve or thirteen. The youngest was seven.

"Yumi had a different mother. Her mother didn't die but was divorced for some reason and seemed to leave on her own. No one I asked knew the details. Since she was a little girl, Yumi knew her mother was different but brushed that aside.

"Yumi was much prettier than her sisters. She had an unyielding spirit and tomboy traits but was deeply compassionate. Her stepmother, two sisters, relatives, neighbors, and even the employees liked her and depended on her probably because she was the heiress.

"When Yumi was fourteen, a year before I became the live-in maid, she was engaged to marry.

"On the surface, everything was fine. She grew up normal and happy. From a young age, Yumi experienced misfortunes she shared with no one. They were all related to sexual matters. The first time was when she was nine."

Sugi whispered in her raspy voice, "I can tell you because you're a doctor. Please understand that if you weren't a doctor, I wouldn't say a word."

"I understand," he said, feeling a little dizzy. "Sexual play between children is not uncommon."

Sugi said, "Yumi's situation was different.

"When she was nine, a sales clerk in his thirties molested her. He threatened to kill her if she spoke a word to anyone.

"Despite being so young, she thought the queer sensation she felt in her body was a sin. The words 'I'll kill you' if she told anyone paralyzed her.

"That clerk left the shop after six months, but he did the same thing several more times before he left. Each time, he made the same threat. This seemed to leave a deep scar in her mind.

"Nearly two years after the clerk left, a neighbor, a young man of twenty-four or -five, molested her in a different way than the clerk.

"Next door was a large merchant's house with a storehouse having thick earthen walls and three doors. Sugi never said what type of merchant.

"The young man was an uncle of the daughter. He was staying at the house because of some trouble.

"The daughter was the same age as Yumi, who often went over to play. One time, they were playing hide-and-seek in that house. Yumi hid in the storehouse. Usually, unused objects, such as antiquated dressers, oblong chests, and wicker clothes hampers, were stored and stacked in there. Four tatami mats were laid out in the center.

"Yumi had been hiding for a short time in a gap between a clothes hamper and an oblong chest. The young man entered carrying a paper-covered lamp with a wire mesh stretched over it.

"Yumi thought it was the seeker and relaxed when she saw who it was and quietly called to him. The young man jumped in surprise."

"'It's me,' whispered Yumi. 'We're playing hide-and-seek. Be quiet or she'll find me.'

"The young man played along. He took something out of an old dresser and lay on the tatami. He drew the lantern close and began reading a book. The seeker came to look around one time but quickly left. Eventually, the young man called over Yumi.

"He said, 'The seeker won't come back again. Come here. I want to show you something funny.'

"She went over to him. He made her sit beside him and showed her the opened book. There were pictures, but Yumi didn't under-stand what they meant.

"He asked, 'Do you understand this one?'

"'Come closer to get a better look," he said and unexpectedly pulled her to him. Yumi forgot about the picture but didn't realize what he was doing. She felt he was acting like the clerk once did. She stopped breathing, more from fear than surprise. She heard a voice say, 'I'll kill you if you tell anyone.'

"The voice was like the clerk's and the young man's. The mesh sliding door of the storehouse was closed. She looked at the wire screen stretched over the sliding door. The metal screen of the sliding door closed Yumi in there. She thought it blocked her escape route.

"When she felt the eyes of the metal mesh blur and her limbs shrink, Yumi was delirious.

"'You're going to kill me,' she said.

"He laughed. That laugh was scarier than the threat to kill her. She could not forget his callous laugh. He said, 'Come back here tomorrow. '

"Yumi did as she was told. She thought he'd kill her if she didn't.

"After the young man left until her engagement, three men molested her. Each time, Yumi thought she felt the eyes of the metal screen blur and heard a voice say, 'I'll kill you.'

"Her good looks, boisterousness, and deep compassion made her adorable and treasured by all. However, these terrifying experiences were the underside.

"Then there was her future husband. They exchanged nuptial sake cups in a private ceremony. Although her adoption into the groom's family was set for the following year, the other party broke the promise. Her husband-to-be went off with someone else. Although she did not understand the reason initially, she soon heard rumors.

"The reason for breaking off the marriage was her birth mother."

Her mother was famous for her striking good looks and accomplishments in traditional performing arts. However, the year after Yumi was born, she ran off with another man who murdered her in Hakone.

One story was it was supposed to be a lovers' suicide, but the man survived. The other, she was supposed to marry this man but was killed by him out of malice for marrying Yumi's father.

It didn't matter which story was true. Yumi's heart was bewitched by the sin of the secrets between a man and a woman, and the accompanying inevitable deaths.

Sugi said, "The thought, I'll be killed. He'll kill me, stuck in Yumi's head. Sometimes a woman must be that way with a man. But when she did, she would be killed. Yumi always believed that she would be killed like her mother."

Noboru shuddered. Sugi's voice changed. His ears caught the change a little while ago, but he ignored it. Her voice was no longer hoarse and didn't sound like Sugi's normal speaking voice.

"You probably understand," she said in a voice that wasn't hers. "If the man does something like that, I think I'll be killed. I'm not bad and do not wish that, but later I'll be killed."

Noboru's head was spinning.

She's Yumi, he thought. He tried to let go of her hand but was paralyzed. She slid closer to him and wrapped one hand around his neck. Noboru screamed, but his voice made no sound, and his tongue did not move.

This isn't Sugi. This is Yumi.

He was gripped by terror that seemed to make his hair stand on end. The woman held down Noboru, embraced his neck with one hand, and brought their chests together. While speaking, she gradually forced him onto his back and gently got on him.

She said, "The first time, the shop clerk snuck into my bedroom, I thought the same thing. Eventually, he would kill me. The next time, he'll kill me. Then I took out this hairpin. See. Look at it."

She showed one hand holding a glittering, flat ornamental hairpin to Noboru. The hairpin gripped like a knife in her hand looked like silver. He could see its shiny two legs with sharpened tips in the dark.

She whispered, "I waited silently."

Her hot breath and hushed voice drunk on a secret pleasure were right next to his face.

"The shop clerk came in, lay by my side, and extended his arms to embrace me."

She made that action as she continued speaking.

"Like this. Do you know what I did with the hairpin? I thought, I'm going to kill the man who was going to kill me. I wasn't the only bad person. It was not my wish to do that. If he was going to commit that crime, that man must die. That's what I thought."

Noboru saw her face spasm. He saw her facial expression twist and her lips pull back exposing her teeth. He tried to push away her body, but his entire body was limp and numb. He felt like he couldn't even move a finger.

It's a dream. This is a dream.

Noboru thought, I'm having a nightmare. She quietly pushed the hairpin gripped in her hand behind his left ear.

"I did it like this," she said. "Before the shop clerk realized anything, I extended my hand and was free. While muttering lies, I put all my might into that hand. Like this."

She showed how she killed the shop clerk. Noboru went blind, but her voice filled his ears. She shouted triumphantly.

"That time, I pushed this pin in deep, right here. I relied on my strength. I left it to my strength."

Noboru felt a violent shock somewhere on his body, heard a woman's scream, and passed out.

8

Noboru saw Red Beard seated before him, beside him sat Mori Handayū. He could hear Red Beard talking to Handayū.

Am I still dreaming? he thought. The two figures right in front of his eyes looked to be far, far away. Their voices did not resonate and sounded like he was listening through a wall. It felt surreal.

I'm sure this is a dream.

He shut his eyes, then carefully opened them again. Mori Handayū was gone, and Nīde Kyojō sat alone.

"Sleep. Go to sleep," said Kyojō. "It'd be good to sleep one more day. Don't think about anything, just sleep."

Noboru tried to speak.

"Don't worry," said Kyojō, shaking his head. "She made you drink medicinal sake, a medicine I compounded and mixed in sake. It was a special medication to quiet the young lady's spells. She heard about you from Sugi and looked for a chance to do this.

"You were drunk like a fool. If you hadn't been drunk, you would have immediately known she was a different person."

Noboru shook his head. He wanted to say he was drunk, but it was also dark, and her hoarse voice fooled him. He tried to speak but could only shake his head. His voice didn't come out, and his tongue didn't move.

"If I had been a little delayed in going home, you would be dead," said Red Beard. "Sugi was at home asleep. She unknowingly drank the same medicinal sake. When I saw that, I rushed to the bench. Now, Yumi's head is wrapped in bleached cloths, but she's fine otherwise. I had no choice. Look at my arm. She was crazed like a beast."

He rolled up the sleeve of his left arm to show Noboru. Bleached cloth wrapped his arm from his wrist to his upper arm.

"She bit me in five places here," said Kyojō and lowered his sleeve. "No one knows about this incident, including Handayū, so don't feel ashamed when with others. You've learned from this mistake, haven't you?"

Noboru felt tears well up and fall from his eyes.

Kyojō took paper tissue from his pocket, Noboru thought he would wipe away his tears but didn't. He wiped around his mouth. Noboru was embarrassed, thinking he might be drooling, and closed his hardened eyes.

"You idiot," said Kyojō. "Go to sleep. We'll talk after you recover."

Kyojō stood and left. Noboru's ears followed the sounds of his footsteps and whispered, "Red Beard's not a bad guy."

CHAPTER 2
AN URGENT PLEA

1

Too much happened that day.

Around ten in the morning, an elderly man died in the North Ward. Soon after, a seriously injured woman laborer was carried in. Yasumoto Noboru was present at the elderly man's death and assisted Nīde Kyojō when he sutured the wound of the woman laborer. This was his first job as an intern.

Despite the madwoman incident, Noboru's attitude did not change. He had no desire to be an intern, remained intent on leaving the clinic, and sent a letter to his father. However, a change occurred deep in his heart. He surrendered to Red Beard.

When he saved Noboru from the hands of the madwoman Yumi, Noboru was facing imminent death. If others knew, he would be defenseless, mortified, and stigmatized. No one else knew. For that, he owed a great debt of gratitude to Red Beard.

This may sound strange, but Noboru felt at peace. By owing a debt to Red Beard, the wall between them crumbled. He could imagine closer connections in unseen places.

Later, he came to understand their relationship, but he hadn't realized that yet.

After running headlong into the embarrassing incident with the madwoman, he knew nothing about the responsibilities to the people confined in a charity clinic. Despite being needed, he kept the defiance in his heart to leave this place.

Nīde Kyojō seemed his usual self. He saw through to the bottom of Noboru's heart and might have been waiting for the coming of the time to persevere. He was reminded of something, but he changed little on the surface and never attempted to speak to Noboru.

One morning at the beginning of April, Kyojō called Noboru to the North Ward. Mori Handayū responded to the call. Noboru didn't immediately stand.

"I'll tell you this one more time. Please, get up and go immediately to Room No. 1 in the North Ward."

"Is that an order?"

In an indifferent tone, Handayū said, "Nīde-san has summoned you. Is something wrong?"

Noboru reluctantly stood.

"You should wear a jacket," said Handayū, trying to be patient. "Your kimono will get dirty."

Nevertheless, Noboru went out as he was.

Room No. 1 in the North Ward was the room for seriously ill patients. Kyojō sat at the bedside of the patient, without looking, gestured for Noboru to come over when he entered, and told him to examine the patient.

An unpleasant air filled the room. It seemed to be a bitter grassy smell like pulverized mugwort. Of course, that smell came from the patient. Noboru sat at the bedside while screwing up his face.

In a glance, he knew the patient was dying. Following the protocol, however, Noboru searched for a pulse, listened for breathing, lifted the eyelids, and looked into the pupils.

Noboru said, "He may live for half an hour. He's unconscious, does not seem to be in pain, and may last half an hour."

He pointed to purplish specks that appeared on both sides of the patient's nose.

"This is his case history," said Kyojō and handed him a sheet of paper. "Read this and make your diagnosis."

Noboru took the paper and read. The fifty-two-year-old patient's name was Rokusuke. He was admitted to the clinic fifty-two days ago.

Initially, he complained of weakness in his entire body and slight abdominal pain. After around twenty days passed, the pain increased, and he began vomiting and lost his appetite.

His vomit was a liquid and gave off a foul smell in a dark brown ribbon of liquid. A tumor was found in the lower part of his stomach in the center of his abdomen. After fifty days, the pain spread throughout his entire abdomen. The frequency of his vomiting increased. The weakening and exhaustion in his entire body were apparent. Noboru committed these important points to memory and then opened the patient's kimono. All his bones seemed to protrude under his skin full of dry, bluish-black wrinkles. Only his abdomen was unnaturally bloated.

Noboru touched the tumor; it felt hard as a rock. As he confirmed the entire tumor did not move, like it was attached to a bone, he recalled the name of a disease to tell Kyojō.

"No, that's not it," said Kyojō, shaking his head. "This is a rare example of a medical case written in your medical notes. Obviously, it is a tumor, but there is another distinct symptom. Read the notes about his medical history one more time."

After he read it, Noboru suggested another illness.

Kyojō said, "This is an enlarged gland, a tumor grew in the pancreas. The pancreas is under the stomach and between the spleen and the duodenum. Because this organ does not move, the person does not feel pain even if cancer develops. By the time the tumor is discovered because of pain, the cancer has already spread to many other organs. Thus, the wasting away is severe and death is quick. This medical case is quite rare, so you should remember it."

"This condition has no treatment."

"None," said Kyojō, shaking his head with a wry smile. "Not only this disease, every disease does not have a treatment."

Noboru slowly looked at Kyojō.

"That may change as medical techniques progress. But even then, the life force in that body probably can't endure," said Kyojō. "Medical technology is in a deplorable state. Even after the passage of many years, you can feel the sorry state of the medical field. When an illness occurs, a body may defeat it, but another body is beaten and succumbs. The doctor can confirm the condition and the progression of the illness. A body with a powerful life force can provide slight assistance. But that's all. Greater ability in medical techniques does not exist."

Kyojō shrugged one sturdy shoulder to express self-mockery and sadness.

"At the current level of our ability, we must first fight poverty and ignorance. Beating poverty and ignorance is the only way to compensate for the lack of medical techniques. Do you understand?"

Noboru thought in his heart this was a political problem. Kyojō spoke forcefully as if he heard Noboru say that.

"You may say this problem is political. Everyone says that. However, what have governments done so far to address poverty and ignorance? Look at poverty. The Edo shogunate issued laws and ordinances but not thousands. Among them, however, can you find one example where people were not abandoned to wallow in poverty?"

Kyojō's lips tightened into a line. He sounded exasperated and probably aware that was fairly childish. But Noboru raised his eyes and looked at Kyojō like he was lured in by his tone.

"But Sensei," he countered, "Wasn't this charity clinic ... this facility for recuperation established at government expense?"

2

Kyojō shrugged.

"A charity clinic?" said Kyojō. Again, his expression was mocking and sad. "You'll understand this place if you stay here. Dispensing free medicine and medical treatment as we do here is better than no medicine or treatment. However, the problems began long ago. If poverty and ignorance were handled properly, most illnesses would never occur."

Mori Handayū appeared and announced an injured woman had been carried in.

"The young woman is a laborer who had an accident at a construction site. She has serious wounds to her waist and abdomen.

"Makino-san examined her but can't handle this case alone and asked for the sensei."

Kyojō looked exhausted. Makino Shōsaku was a full-time surgeon. Noboru looked at Kyojō.

"Very well," said Kyojō. "I'll go now, but tell him to treat her as much as he can."

Handayū left right away. Kyojō stared at the patient's face, closed his eyes, and gently dropped his head. He tried to bow low but only looked down.

He quietly said, "Rokusuke was a gold and silver lacquer master craftsman. He's fairly well known among his fellow craftsmen and has sold several writing stands and jewelry boxes to the Kishū and the Owari clans. He has no wife, children, or close friends. He was carried in from a cheap lodging house but has had no visitors. He's quiet, doesn't talk, and neither asks nor answers questions. I never heard him say one word until today."

Kyojō sighed. "This illness brings on agonizing pain. It's so painful, the patient doesn't speak. Perhaps he says nothing until he takes his last breath. This is the way a man wants to die."

Kyojō stood. After sending Mori back, he said, "Care for this dying patient."

"Nothing is more solemn in a man's life than his last hour. Take a good look at him."

Noboru said nothing and changed where he sat.

First, he stared at the patient's face. It was repulsive and already revealed the shadow of death. His flesh had wasted away. His face during his life was probably gone. His eye sockets, cheeks, and chin were sunken as though the flesh had been scraped off. His skin was covered in dry, dirt-brown wrinkles with purple bruises and stuck to protruding bones. More than a man's face, it was mostly a skeleton's skull.

Noboru muttered, "I didn't know Red Beard talked so much."

He was unconsciously talking to himself and thought someone else was speaking. He looked up and to his left and right, but, of course, no one was there. His eyes returned to the patient, and he mumbled again.

"He had the habit of saying, 'Don't chatter idly here.'

"Don't I talk too much?"

The patient's breathing became short and urgent. From time to time, he groaned and panted painfully.

He was unconscious. The little remaining life was slipping from his body.

"This is ugly," Noboru said in his mouth. "Is death solemnity? Death is hideous."

Eventually Mori Handayū came. He was holding a rice bowl, a chopstick with cotton wrapped around the point. These might have been used by the old man. He sat near the pillow of the patient and without looking at Noboru said, "I'll do this. Please go to Nīde-sensei."

Noboru looked at Handayū.

"He's in Room No. 3 in the front," said Handayū, still looking away. "Go now. He's about to suture the wound."

Noboru recalled the words of Tsugawa Genzō who said, "Red Beard works people hard night and day." He felt Genzō's wink was cynical.

The people who come for treatment are examined in the front. Room No. 3 specializes in surgery. When Noboru entered the room, the white flesh of the naked body caught his eyes. The space was only eight mats wide. A thin bordered mat was laid on the wood floor wiped to a bright shine, and bleached cotton cloth covered the mat. A woman's naked body lay on top. She was asleep facing up.

Right after Noboru entered, Makino Shōsaku turned around the folding screen to hide something from his eyes. He was called by Kyojō and went behind the screen. This time he had to look at the exposed naked body before his eyes.

The body of the woman he believed to be twenty-four or -five was well built, had sturdy, suntanned arms and legs, and beauty with surprisingly white smoothness. The dark nipples of both voluptuous breasts and the obvious swelling of her broad abdomen partially covered by bleached cotton cloth confirmed an early stage of pregnancy.

Noboru averted his eyes. During his training in Nagasaki, he examined and treated a few female patients but never saw a woman's naked body in this condition, full of youth and strength.

"Hold down her legs," said Kyojō. "I gave her a drug, but she may become violent. Make sure she doesn't jump up."

At that moment, Noboru noticed her hands were spread wide and tied at the wrists with cords to posts. He followed Kyojō's instructions, sat between her extended legs, and pressed his hands on her kneecaps. He didn't know where to look and felt his face redden. This position was indescribably absurd and embarrassing.

"Don't look away," said Kyojō. "Closely watch the suturing technique."

He removed the bleached cotton cloth covering a part of her abdomen. The tip of the needle held in his right hand curved into a small hook. More than two cotton strands passed through the eye of the needle. When the cloth was removed, the wound was visible. It was from the left side of her torso to below her navel and longer than six inches. The surface of the wound was irregular.

Of course, after sterilization, the open wound looked like it burst open vertically because of thick subcutaneous fat. A small amount of blood trickled out when Kyojō removed the cloth. Her entire abdomen spasmed, and she groaned. In that instant, her intestine bulged from the wound.

The fat, bluish-gray large intestine pushed out, squirming like a living being and meandering like a snake outside the wound.

Noboru fainted. Everything blurred in an instant. He felt light-headed and thought, Oh, I'm gonna fall over and black out.

3

He was unconscious for a moment. He came around immediately when someone slapped his cheeks but felt he had been out for a long time. Of course, he was in Room No. 3 in the front. Makino Shōsaku was holding him and probably slapped his cheeks. Across from them, Kyojō looked upset and said, "Go back to your room."

Noboru looked away and stood. If he saw the woman's body, he'd pass out again. He should have been stubborn but didn't dare stay.

Noboru laid down in his room. He looked on the verge of vomiting when he remembered and tried his best to think of something else.

However, today's failure right after the incident of the madwoman Yumi overwhelmed him with humiliation beyond salvation.

"What an undisciplined mess."

Noboru fell asleep with his arm covering his face.

"How can I even say I was trained in Nagasaki?"

He recalled how good he felt and proud when he told Sugi, the madwoman's companion, about his formal study of Dutch medical techniques and his knowledge of treatments unknown to Kyojō. Slowly shaking his head, he groaned.

Noboru didn't eat lunch.

Mori Handayū peeked in on him and suggested they eat together. Noboru refused and stayed in bed. He still felt queasy and had no appetite.

Handayū said, "You should eat. Nīde-sensei said you'll be going on house calls with him this afternoon."

"House calls?"

"He goes on a round of house calls to treat patients. Depending on the situation, you won't get back until evening."

Noboru said nothing.

"The old man Rokusuke died," said Handayū and closed the shōji screen door.

Red Beard had two house calls. One was by invitation. Many

homes of lords and wealthy people have patients. The other was charity treatment for poor people.

The Koishikawa Charity Clinic, commonly called the free medicine dispensary, originally aimed to provide diagnoses and treatments for free to sick poor people. Depending on the illness and other circumstances, the listed patients couldn't go to the clinic or had previously been admitted and treated at the clinic. Nonetheless, people hated being treated at a charity clinic. Even if recommended by the head of the household or people in town, those who would not go to the clinic were not few. Red Beard visited those people and forced an examination and treatment on them. However, few thanked him or were pleased. Noboru often heard stories like these.

Noboru whined like he was tired, "The attendants from the clinic can't enjoy this? But shouldn't there be a reason to refuse after a failure? Shouldn't Red Beard acknowledge the refusal?"

A half-hour after lunch ended, Handayū came to tell him again. Noboru went out with Kyojō.

Kyojō noticed that Noboru had changed out of his uniform and back into his ordinary clothes. He glimpsed Noboru and looked displeased but said nothing.

Noboru wasn't the only one accompanying Kyojō. A young servant carried the medicine chest. He wore leggings to his shins and straw sandals. His short overcoat was the same gray as the medical staff's coats. The characters of Koishikawa Charity Clinic were undyed on his collar. The servant's name was Takezō; he was nearly twenty-eight. He had a severe stutter and was called Stuttering Take. For close to five years, he had been carrying Kyojō's medicine chest.

He was short in stature and thin. His face was burned dark. He gave a friendly response to anyone who spoke. His eyes had a look of impatience. Of course, they never conversed. It was only "Good morning. It's a nice day."

He stuttered so much and seemed to use all his nerves and physical strength to speak. A cordial reply to leave a good impression was an impossible task for him.

Nearly four and a half hours after leaving the clinic, they neared the back of Dentsū-in Temple and called from the back. A man about fifty years old ran to them and faced Kyojō. He hurriedly bowed as he told them he was about to go to the clinic.

Kyojō said, "Rokusuke died."

"Oh," said the man, sounding confused.

"He took his last breath two hours ago. We've readied his body. Do you know if he had any relatives?"

"Uh, what do we do now?" The man was flustered and gulped. "It's a little complicated. I know the old man had a daughter, but a child fell ill and was brought here by the landlord Tōsuke. The mother flew away."

"I don't understand what you're saying. Is there something you need?"

"Well," the man looked doubtfully at Kyojō. "That's true, but will you come in?"

"I must go to Nakatomi-zaka. A seriously ill patient is waiting," said Kyojō. He turned to Noboru. "Yasumoto, you two will go to Kashiwaya and see about the situation there. I'll be back in half an hour."

Noboru looked at Takezō. Stuttering Take shook his head while looking up. That seemed to mean, You have no choice. Kyojō left with him.

Kashiwaya was a rental inn in Nagi-chō right behind Dentsū-in Temple. A man named Kinbei owned the inn. Rokusuke, the gold and silver lacquer master, lived there for two years and entered the charity clinic after his illness worsened.

From the time he gained a fine reputation as a gold and silver lacquer master, close to twenty years ago, he came to Kashiwaya and lodged there. Sometimes he stayed for two or three days, half a month, or even forty days.

At first, no one knew what sort of man he was and guessed he was a yakuza or gambler. His appearance wasn't bad. He had a calm personality but hardly spoke during his stay. He only drank small amounts of sake and listened silently to the stories of the worlds of the other guests. Then he vanished and did not reappear for two years but then showed up every other month.

They discovered he was the gold and silver lacquer master, Rokusuke, six or seven years ago. At that time, his reputation had dropped. He barely had any work. If in the mood, he did repair work. He was hard to please. Even when he came to Kashiwaya, he shut himself away in his room and no longer listened to the stories of other people.

"He hardly ever spoke," Kinbei said to Noboru. "He stayed at the inn for close to twenty years. I don't know if he had a wife or children. I knew nothing about him when he was admitted to the charity clinic. Nobody did."

Four children were waiting at Kashiwaya.

4

They were probably the children of Rokusuke's daughter. The oldest daughter was ten-year-old Tomo. She had come down with a high fever and was confined to bed. The younger three children were the oldest son, eight-year-old Sukezō; the second daughter, six-year-old Tomi; and the three-year-old youngest son, Mataji.

Their clothes were full of patches. All were thin and had sickly complexions. Except for the youngest Mataji, they looked ill.

Tomi was hugging her baby brother Mataji. Sukezō moved closer to them like he was trying to cover them with his body. His eyes mingling fear and hostility darted around.

Rokusuke had stayed in this 4-1/2-mat room that faced north. The sliding doors covered in thick paper and the shōji doors were old and full of patches. The sliding door had a large tear that flapped endlessly each time the wind blew in.

The tatami was worn. The straw stuffing oozed out in places. The walls were peeling. As in any cheap lodging house, it was good enough. This place behind the Dentsū-in Temple had few lodgers and looked bleak and rundown.

While Noboru examined Tomo, he listened to Kinbei's story. Tomo had a severe cold. She had a high fever and sometimes coughed up phlegm but no other serious symptoms. Her nutrition, however, was terrible. A situation shared by her younger brothers and sister. Kinbei thought if this continued, she would be in great danger of contracting pulmonary tuberculosis.

Noboru advised him to cool Tomo's forehead, warm the room, keep the wind from entering, and change her bedclothes because she was sweating.

"They say garbage piles up in sunken places in the ground," said Kinbei and sighed. "For years, business here has been bad. My son is a day laborer. My wife and daughter must take in side jobs to get by. We're always burdened by troubles like this. Others say there are ways to prosper and pile up money, but I don't understand why pitiful souls like us bring trouble to this place. Oh, what did you say?"

Noboru said, "I'll ask after you finish."

Kinbei returned to his story.

His tale became more complicated. He believed Rokusuke did not have a wife, children, or relatives.

"However, early that morning, an old man arrived with those four children and said, 'These are Rokusuke's grandchildren.'"

At first, Kinbei could not believe him but listened to what the old man had to say.

"His name was Matsuzō, the sixty-two-year-old manager of a rental house called Gorobei-dana in Odawara-chō, Kyōbashi. The man spoke plainly."

"I was born in the 37th year of the sexagenary cycle and am exactly sixty-two years old. My name is Matsuzō. My wife died three years ago."

"He seemed to have a pleasant personality."

"Five years, three months, and fifteen days ago, the family of a man called Tomisaburō moved into a row house I managed. Tomisaburō said he worked as a cabinetmaker. His wife's name was Kuni. They had three children. Tomi still had not been weaned.

"He said he was a cabinetmaker, but Tomisaburō was a lazy bum and often wandered around. He had money problems and was in deep debt all over the neighborhood.

"Kuni had a personality so pleasant it was irritating, never complained, did piecework when staying indoors, and cared for the children. Of course, she never opposed her husband. But Tomisaburō took his anger out on Kuni and punched and kicked her when drunk. Before the day ended, he didn't simply take his violence out on her."

"Matsuzō didn't know the details and had to guess. He thought when Tomisaburō got drunk, he repeatedly screamed, 'Go to your father. He's got a load of money. Ain't you his only daughter? Dammit, your father's a bastard who doesn't have blood or tears. His only daughter and grandchildren have a hard time getting food. He acts like he's got nothing to do with that and does what he wants. He's not human.'

"Kuni said nothing.

"She was silent despite being punched and kicked. She didn't even cry and held on until her husband was drained of anger.

"Of course, the tenants in the row house wondered, Who is that *father*? What is his situation? The manager Matsuzō had no idea, either.

"One time, Matsuzō summoned Kuni and asked her. That happened on October 9 of last year. Kuni dodged his questions and wouldn't say.

"She only said, 'I have a father, but he had a reason to disown me,' and wouldn't introduce him to Matsuzō and said no more.

"Tomisaburō made bad friends, began to stray, and never had a job. He continued to disappear from home for three to five days. During this time, Mataji was born, and life became harder. Around ten at night seven days ago, Kuni came to the manager's home.

"Matsuzō was sleeping and didn't want to talk. Kuni entered, and he listened. First, she asked, 'Was a bulletin recently issued by the shogunate?'

"The bulletin stated *twenty-five pieces of silver will be given* to informants about a robbery. A gang of three robbers invaded Nanzō-in Temple in Atagoshita, Shiba, and stole several temple treasures. The stolen goods included a gilt copper statue of Buddha made by a famous Buddhist statue sculptor one thousand years ago. Only several of these precious statues exist in all of Japan.

"It would be lost forever if the robbers stupidly melted it down.

A reward was offered to the informant who knew about the where-abouts of the Buddha statue."

"Do you know something?" asked Matsuzō.

Kuni nodded.

"About two weeks ago, Tomisaburō came home. I saw him hide something in the ceiling. He had been with his crooked friends. It seemed strange, but I pretended not to notice.

"When he was out, I secretly took it out to look. It was a Buddha statue wrapped in a *furoshiki* cloth and treated paper.

"The statue was a little more than a foot high. I thought it may be that Buddha statue from the Nanzō-in Temple."

Matsuzō said, "Then she came to see me. I thought if she received the twenty-five pieces of silver, it would help out with her money problems at home and be good for Tomisaburō. If his crimes piled up, he'd eventually be banished or appear at the prison gate. If he were arrested and learned of the hardships of a jail cell, he would reform and become a serious man."

She said, "Should I become an informant and have him arrested?"

Matsuzō immediately told Kuni, "Of course, that would be good. Since you've seen the Buddha statue and believe it's the one, take it out and keep it safe."

He made her talk to the town official with the statue and make her last-minute appeal. He didn't go with her to see the town official or the landlord. She had to inform them by herself.

Matsuzō met with the town official. If the town magistrate summoned him, he intended to put in a good word for Kuni in his statement.

He was immediately called in. Matsuzō appeared with the town official. They declared they knew nothing, Kuni worked hard in her poor life and faithfully raised her four children. Her husband Tomis-aburō was a yakuza, and Kuni alone provided for the family.

"At the magistrate's office, this month, the official-in-charge in Kita is Shimada Echigo no Kami, but he's awful."

Noboru looked suspiciously at Kinbei.

"Yes," said Kinbei and nodded at Noboru. "They say he's

awful," he insisted. "Even if the husband is a thief, the process is not for the wife to focus on the reward and inform on her husband. She's a terrible woman who goes against human relations. He'll probably order her to jail while a careful investigation is conducted.

"This result was unexpected; Matsuzō and the officials were speechless. After they left court, however, a police officer informed the men of Kuni's message."

> In a place called Nagi-chō behind Dentsū-in Temple in Koishikawa is an inn called Kashiwaya Kinbei. An old man named Rokusuke should be staying there. Please take the children to him and explain the situation. He should take them because they're his grandchildren who share his blood.

5

"Then the manager Matsuzō, went home," said Kinbei. "I told you about Rokusuke-san's circumstances because he is now at the charity clinic. And I think I've already done what I could.

"Kuni wished the children to be entrusted to him. Now, what should I do? And this poor child has a terrible fever. Do I have any choice?

"I scolded my wife for complaining. After putting this child in bed and Nīde-sensei examining her, I went out when I thought about borrowing his wisdom."

One of Kinbei's children came to ask about dinner.

"Mama wants to know."

Kinbei sighed and stood like he was exhausted.

"I don't understand why I'm burdened by this trouble," lamented Kinbei. "Once a fortuneteller stayed here for ten days. This fortuneteller said all the nails in this house are driven in backward. They're upside-down nails. He called that bad luck.

"I asked, 'What does driving nails in backward mean?' That wasn't a common saying I had in my head. He probably wasn't a perceptive fortuneteller with his lack of insight. 'That may be so,' he said, 'But you can't pull out all the nails in this old house and hammer them in the right way.'"

As Kinbei stood, he added, "That fortuneteller skipped out without paying his fee for ten days of lodging. That was probably his proof of the upside-down nails. It's horrible."

More than a half hour passed when Kyojō returned.

He immediately started to examine Tomo, as Noboru told him what Kinbei said. Kyojō said nothing and finished the examination. While sipping the tea brought by Kinbei, he pulled the medicine chest closer and took out ten bundles of two types of medicine, which were already compounded. Several times, he explained the treatment and the instructions on how to administer the medicines.

"Then what is that for?" Kinbei said, sounding confused. "Why do we have to look after these children?"

Kyojō said, "I don't know why, but talk to the town magistrate. It's fine if they are taken back to the row house in Odawara-chō. Otherwise, you will care for them until living quarters are decided. Do you object?"

"Well." Kinbei made a throaty sound and swallowed. "I told the sensei here that business is bad, and my family is scraping by. So having to keep caring for them—"

Kyojō interrupted. "Rokusuke left money. He asked it be used to settle matters if he died. I was entrusted with five *ryō* and two *bun*. I've heard the lodging fee has been paid. Is that true?"

"Uh, well, yes," said Kinbei and quickly raised his head. "Did you say Rokusuke-san left money?"

"If he didn't, I'll cover your losses," said Kyojō. "But if you object, the children will be placed with someone else."

Kinbei agreed to take care of them.

Kyojō asked, "What about the husband, Tomisaburō? Has he been caught, yet?"

"Uh, I wonder what happened. I think I heard he was arrested, but maybe he wasn't. He's the last thing I'm thinking about."

Kyojō looked at the children and asked each one's name and age. They were sweet but pitiful. He didn't seem to honestly see them. Kyojō's stern face and beard terrified the children. The three younger ones, frozen in place and huddled together, could not give satisfactory answers.

"Everything is fine. Don't worry," said Kyojō in an angry tone. "Your mother will come home soon, and your older sister will get better.

"Hey, when you get big, what do you want to do?"

He tried to put them at ease, but his stupid question came out of the blue. The children said nothing and only widened their eyes. He was probably mad at himself for asking a dumb question. As he blushed and stood, he said, "Don't worry. Your mother will be back soon."

Kyojō, who earlier sent Takezō back to the clinic, walked past the front of Dentsū-in with Noboru. He hailed a street palanquin and told the bearers to go to Kodenma-chō.

"Hurry," he shouted. Noboru watched one of the palanquin bearers fly off.

"What are you starting?" muttered Noboru from inside the palanquin. "What are you up to?"

When he arrived at the jail in Kodenma-chō, Kyojō sought a meeting with the magistrate.

Although well-known here, the greeter was too formal. He said the magistrate, Shimada-dono, was in attendance at the castle. In his place, a sympathetic Okano came out to politely greet him.

Immediately after Kyojō passed through to the reception room, he asked if a woman named Kuni from Gorobei's in Odawara-chō was jailed. Okano nodded and said, "She's in jail."

"I'd like to examine her," said Kyojō. "Of course, I'd like to speak to Shimada Echigo-dono. She has a rare illness and is being treated. I'd like to study the effects of the medicines prescribed."

Okano stared at Kyojō's face and asked, "Will it take long?"

"I don't think it'll take half an hour."

"That's not up to me but to Nīde-sensei."

After thinking a short time, Okano said, "Please, come to the medicine room."

He escorted them. They turned down a hallway to see a row of several rooms facing the courtyard. Okano led the two to the room at the end. The room was about six mats wide. One side was a built-in closet. The other was a wall. Objects wrapped in treated paper were stacked close to the wall. One he removed from its wrapping had the powerful scent of sunshine that filled the room.

"Fortunately, the man in charge was Shimada Echigo," said Kyojō to himself. "If this were Tsutsui, that pigheaded man wouldn't act even as an assistant. If it's Shimada … Did you say something?"

"No," said Noboru, shaking his head.

The expression in Kyojō's eyes looked like he woke from a dream. He frequently looked at Noboru's face and seemed to want to say something. He looked indignant and said nothing.

Soon Okano returned with Kuni and said to call him when they were finished. He sat Kuni down and left.

"Come here," Kyojō said to her. "I am Doctor Nīde Kyojō. I treated your father Rokusuke and am here to try to get you released. Come closer and tell me about yourself."

6

Kuni said, "I'm thirty-two," but she didn't look a day younger than forty. Her hair was tied back by a straw stalk. Her hair lacked luster and half of it was grey. Bruise-like blotches darkened her thin, bony face. Wrinkles covered her dry skin.

A half-width obi sash with many patches closed a lined kimono made from sold swatches sewn together. She looked more wretched and pitiful than any beggar.

Despite Kyojō's enthusiasm, Kuni's expression stayed blank. She sat there, unresponsive.

She's like a bottomless sake bottle, thought Noboru. Her figure was pleasing, but nothing was inside. It's like she's cast off skin.

"You take over, Yasumoto," Kyojō said as he ran out of patience. "I'm going to see Okano," he said and went out.

Noboru thought about the late Rokusuke and the children at Kashiwaya. A grandfather and his grandchildren. The grandfather died alone in a charity clinic. The children were shivering in a strange, cheap travelers' inn. While pondering this, Noboru started talking about the children. Kuni trembled and opened her eyes wide.

Nearly shouting, she asked, "Are the children safe? Did their grandfather take them?"

Noboru explained that Rokusuke died and the children's situation. Rokusuke left money and died. Kyojō had decided to help her. He told her she had to explain her circumstances in detail because she had to think about their future and how she would care for them.

"My father died?" she muttered lazily. The words seemed to spill from her mouth, then she was silent. She was dumbfounded and stared blankly for a long time. Eventually, she whispered, "He probably suffered."

Noboru shook his head. "No, he died peacefully."

Kuni's unfocused eyes gazed at Noboru. Her voice was feeble and without spirit. She seemed to be talking to herself more than to him. Her awareness of his presence appeared to be vague and distant.

Kyojō returned and Noboru signaled with his eyes. Kyojō said nothing and sat. However, Kuni seemed not to notice.

Although Kuni was Rokusuke's only daughter, from the age of three to ten, she was a foster child in a farming family in Tamagawa. Her father came for her when she was ten. They lived together for two years until her birth mother showed up and took Kuni away.

She later found this out, but her mother had run off with Rokusuke's young pupil—he was Tomisaburō. That is why Kuni became a foster child.

Her mother wanted Kuni and secretly contacted her when she was twelve. When she asked if Kuni would run away with her, Kuni didn't object.

"I didn't know my mother, but it was the year I wanted my mother. She said, 'I'm your mother. Please, come with me.'

"She said, 'I'm so happy you want to come with me.' It felt like a dream for us to be together.'"

Her mother said Tomisaburō was a relative. Of course, Kuni believed her.

They lived on the beach in a charcoal house in Kyōbashi. Rokusuke's shop was in Maki-chō in Nihonbashi, so we moved to a backstreet no Kamiya-chō in Shiba and started a small general goods store. Tomisaburō ran the store. Her mother apprenticed in a teahouse.

"Later I also found out my mother eloped with Tomisaburō when he was seventeen. She was seven years older, took care of Tomisaburō for a long time, and made him lazy.

"After Kuni came, Tomisaburō let Kuni be the sales clerk while he fooled around all day. He began drinking at noon and then fell asleep."

She knew nothing about the relationship between her mother and Tomisaburō. She thought he was simply a relative but had questions. Why doesn't he work? Why does he wander around? Why doesn't my mother say anything? Nothing made sense.

Kuni worked alone as a sales clerk for close to a year when her father appeared without warning. She knew he was her father and thought she'd escape but was so scared she couldn't move.

"My father said to me, 'Come home.' Even now, I remember. My father's face was pale. While he forced a smile, he said, 'We'll go home together. Kuni, you are my precious only daughter.'"

Kuni's voice cracked, and she shook violently.

"'My precious only daughter,' he said."

Tears fell from her eyes. She didn't wipe them away but kept talking through the tears.

She looked at her father, and her fear was gone. She was already thirteen. From three years old, she was a foster child and lived with him for two years. She still did not keenly feel the love between a parent and child.

"No, I'm staying with Mother," declared Kuni.

Rokusuke looked at Kuni for a moment and said, "If you have any problems, I'll do anything for you."

Kuni said nothing about this to her mother or Tomisaburō. She thought her father wouldn't come again, in fact, she didn't see

Rokusuke for ten years. In the summer of Kuni's sixteenth year, her mother forced her to marry Tomisaburō. She couldn't stand that awful idea and cried to her mother.

"If I didn't, I would no longer be able to live with my mother."

Kuni explained her mother kept asking her to agree for her mother's sake. Kuni probably felt good. Not knowing what it meant to be married, she became Tomisaburō's wife.

A storm erupted in the house.

This is not a remarkable tale. Her mother secured her tie to Tomisaburō by making him marry Kuni. She was close to forty and didn't believe she could find any other man to rely on. To her, this was the only way. As a woman in her prime, at the same time she secured her connection to this man, she suffered from intense jealousy.

7

One winter evening two years after Kuni married Tomisaburō, for the first time, Kuni understood the relationship between her husband and her mother.

Their home in Kamiya-chō was only one six-mat room inside the store. The couple and her mother slept separated by a bedside screen. Even then, Kuni still had no understanding of the conjugal bed and put up with the revolting acts.

That night after the usual thing, she did not fall asleep right away. As her body was on fire at her core and feeling irritated she didn't know what to do, her mother called to Tomisaburō.

He was sleeping. Her mother called several times. Kuni crouched her body and held her breath. Her mother snuck in and woke him up. He grumbled in his sleepy voice and clicked his tongue.

While Kuni held her breath, she shrunk her body inside the bedding. Soon Kuni had a realization. This was not the first time she heard her mother's voice escaping her throat. So far it might have been several dozen times. She remembers hearing it when half asleep and half awake.

While her eyes were half closed, she thought she heard dozens of times the sounds of grinding teeth, husky pants in the throat, anguish-filled screams, and the moans of her mother watching a dream.

However, that night, Kuni understood everything. She understood the relationship between her mother and her husband. For these past two years, her mother had been angry for no reason and found fault with everything about her.

Since she didn't have the least bit of love for Tomisaburō, she felt no jealousy. Seething with disgust, she had a sudden attack of nausea. In an instant, she was out of her bed and throwing up.

Kuni said this much and then firmly pressed both hands to her mouth.

Perhaps a revived memory brought on the nausea. She kept her hands firmly pressed on her mouth for a long time.

"That's enough," said Kyojō. "What happened to your mother?"

Kuni dropped her hands from her mouth and looked lazily at Kyojō.

"She died," said Kuni listlessly. "I left home right after that and became a live-in servant at a teahouse."

Kuni gave birth when she was twenty-three, six months after her mother died but wasn't with her when she died.

Tomisaburō, who told her that her mother was on the verge of death, said her mother didn't want to see Kuni and wouldn't see her if she came. Kuni wondered if that were true.

"For nearly five years after leaving home, her mother did not come home once. I didn't know where she was. But she seemed to be with Tomisaburō. He often spent time away, sometimes, as many as three days."

They couldn't make a living from the small shop selling household goods. From seventeen or eighteen, Kuni did piecework. They barely survived by combining her and her mother's earnings.

"So after my mother left, the household budget was tight, but Tomisaburō didn't complain much. Sometimes, he handed over a few sen coins."

He told her, "Take it. Last night, I got into a little mischief with some friends. I won a little."

However, she suspected he saw her mother, and that was her money. He was that important to her mother. When she was dying, she only wanted him to take care of her. If she saw Kuni, she would die with regret and jealousy. Kuni believed her mother knew this.

Kuni said, "I didn't go to her funeral. Even now, I don't know where her grave is. Because my mother would not enjoy a memorial service, I never set up a Buddhist altar. If she has a soul, I think my mother still hates me."

The back of Noboru's neck chilled. He pondered the deep-rooted sin of blind love and the awful obsession found in Kuni saying her mother, dead for ten years, still hated her. This was vividly revealed in her expression, which he had difficulty understanding. She continued speaking but Kyojō interrupted.

"I know what happened after that. Rokusuke sent news to you."

"Yes, soon after my mother died, he came to the house in Kamiya-chō."

"That was the first time, I heard that man was my father's pupil. He did bad things with my mother and ran off. My father said, 'Come with me. Staying with that man will only bring tears.' He said to leave, come home, and live with him. I was cruel on purpose and refused. I'm horrible. I asked him to leave me alone."

Kuni got pregnant but didn't love Tomisaburō. She didn't want to be cared for by her father and the care ended. She thought the gods and Buddha did not approve.

"That's what I thought. When my mother ran off with that man, I went with my mother. When my father came for me and I refused to go home with him, I wondered what my father felt. How miserable was he? How painful was it for him?"

Kuni told Tomisaburō they were moving to Kanasugi. Later, she gave birth to Tomo and Sukezō.

Her father found her again and left behind silver coins.

At that time, her father closed the Maki-chō shop. He said if something happened to notify him at the lodging inn called Kashiwaya behind Dentsū-in Temple.

Rokusuke left behind these words.

"I have no interest in working. It's all boring. My whole life is meaningless."

Noboru recalled a story heard at Kashiwaya. They said he appeared from time to time over the past twenty years. He did something, stayed, time passed, and he came to stay again. That corresponded to Kuni's blunt refusal to live with Rokusuke at the Kamiya-chō house.

He probably wanted to hide from the world and himself. The old, dark, cheap lodging inn in the desolate town on the outskirts was suited to him. This scenario seemed to float before Noboru's eyes.

His name known throughout Edo as a master of gold and silver lacquer was forgotten. He threw away the skills that created products bought by the three branches of the Tokugawa family. As an unfamiliar old man living alone in a cheap inn, he silently drank sake while listening to the conversations of the shabby guests.

"I understand," whispered Noboru to himself. Rokusuke's sorrow and pain were so deep that he was inconsolable. While afflicted by a painful disease, until his death, he never groaned with pain, perhaps because he already experienced deeper pain. As he thought this, Noboru shut his eyes and sighed.

"No," said Kuni. "I don't believe that."

8

Her loud voice startled Noboru.

"I don't think, even a little, that someone making accusations is bad; that person is pitiful," stressed Kuni. "He is not a human being and doesn't earn anything. Even when food was a problem for the children and me, he didn't care and acted badly. He told me to go get money from my father and to speak without swearing.

"I can't talk about that. He's the reason why my father had such a hard time. That's why I can't say anymore."

"But you should talk. If he is arrested and suffers in prison, he may change for the better. Isn't that what you told the manager?"

"No, I didn't," said Kuni, shaking her head. "The manager said that, but I didn't think that or say that even in court. Can I be honest?"

"Please do," said Kyojō, nodding.

"If I could," said Kuni, biting her lip. "If I could, I would want to kill him with my hands. Even if we didn't have children, I would kill him. Today, I'll do it. Tonight, I'll do it. I thought this dozens of times. These are my true feelings."

First, Kuni wiped her eyes. Her earlier tears had dried. Her wiping hands spread the tracks of her tears. She resembled an angry kabuki actor in *kumadori* makeup.

Eventually, Kyojō said, "I understand. I understand. Is it good to keep it bottled up? Tomorrow, you'll surely be able to leave this place. However, if you tell the official what you just told me, he will crush you. Be quiet and lower your head. If you say anything, it should simply be 'I'm so sorry.' You have to think about the children. Do you understand?"

Kuni answered, "Yes," quietly to herself, and slowly bowed, lowering her head almost to her lap.

When Kyojō left the jail, he silently walked north. At Kashi-waya, he asked about preparations for the evening meal.

He had various experiences since the morning. He thought the day was coming to an end, but outside, the setting sun was bright. The streets were lively with people and palanquins.

Kyojō looked tired. He was stooped over and walked dragging his legs. He shook his head while grumbling to himself. He heard that people are fools. People are idiots. Some are good but are fools and idiots.

When they arrived at 2-chōme, Koku-chō, Kyojō slowed his pace and asked Noboru, "What do you think about what she said?"

Noboru struggled to answer. "About killing her husband?"

"No, about everything she said." Kyojō shook his head again. "It's wrong. It's a mistake to blame only Tomisaburō. If you ask Okano, he should have been arrested already. Perhaps he's only a weak-spirited, lazy man. But the one reason for what happened was Rokusuke's wife. She seduced him when he was seventeen. After they eloped, he got used to being a kept man. Once he got used to it, slipping away was extremely difficult. In time, he would step onto the wrong path. Many examples like this exist. He's nothing more than another sorry example."

Noboru started to speak but shut his mouth and blushed. While having a relationship with her mother, he made her daughter his wife. He wanted to point out the repulsiveness of that man but before speaking he remembered his mistake.

The humiliating mistake with the madwoman Yumi. Kyojō probably didn't notice, quickened his pace, and continued speaking in the same tone.

"Life is filled with lessons. However, not one lesson applies to everyone. Even the rules of do not kill and do not steal are not absolute." In a quiet voice, he said, "I will say this to Shimada Echigo. 'You don't want to do that. That is no condition for cowardly behavior but is unavoidable when something must be done. Now is the time to turn away from those lessons.'"

When they came out next to the canal in Koku-chō, Kyojō turned to Noboru and said, "Go back to the clinic.

"I'm going to see the town magistrate and intend to have a nice dinner. Please tell them I'll be a little late getting back."

Noboru agreed and left Kyojō.

The next day, Kuni was released from jail but did not receive the reward of silver. Of course, that was probably Kyojō's doing. She didn't care if she went back to her old neighborhood as long as she would be with her children now at Kashiwaya.

The next day, Kyojō ordered Noboru to accompany him to Kashiwaya for Tomo's examination. At that time, Kyojō gave Noboru a small package containing five ryō in silver.

"This is bequeathed to Kuni. Ten ryō are left. I will hold on to that for emergencies. Tell her I'll visit soon to discuss this."

"But this much?" asked Noboru. "Did Rokusuke bequeath this money?"

"The small five ryō was bequeathed. The other ten ryō are different," said Kyojō with cheerful eyes looking at Noboru. "They are a gift from Shimada Echigo."

Noboru looked puzzled.

Kyojō continued, "Echigo no Kami is a husband and has a deeply jealous wife at home. For some years, she has complained of depression. Once a month, I was called to examine her. She never ran out of the usual medications compounded by me. That's why I said it was good that Shimada was in charge."

Noboru still looked puzzled but said nothing and looked at Kyojō.

"They say keeping quiet doubles the meanness. Echigo no Kami hides a mistress in his villa," said Kyojō with eyes open in amazement. "It's no surprise he keeps a mistress, but his wife's jealousy was unusual. You could say I'm scum and intimidated him.

"Yasumoto, I'm well aware that my way is cowardly."

However, Kyojō looked pleased and showed little self-reproach.

He said, "Kuni's release was appropriate. Ten ryō was the fee for his wife's treatment. Moreover, there was no change in my cowardice.

"If in the future I look pleased with myself, please don't hesitate to mention this incident. Well, that's it. Now, we should go to Kashiwaya."

CHAPTER 3
THE MUJINA ROW HOUSE

1

NOT LONG AGO, the rainy season began. Yasumoto Noboru wore his medical coat. Its tight cotton sleeves dyed a faint dark gray and close-fitting hakama trousers were starched. He felt embarrassed the first time he wore them like everyone was staring at him.

Nīde Kyojō and Mori Handayū were silent and seemed indifferent to their first sight of Noboru wearing the medical coat. None of the other medical staff said a word but gave a mocking look or sneered each time they saw him.

Only one of them was happy for him and honestly said so. She was the young woman Yuki who worked in the kitchen. Yuki saw Noboru wearing his medical coat.

"My goodness."

She clapped her hands and beamed a smile. She said, "You finally put on the medical coat. That's wonderful. That means I won."

"You won?" questioned Noboru. "Did you make a bet?"

"Yes," said Yuki, slightly panicked, she crafted a smile. "If you can call it a bet, I made a bet hoping Yasumoto-sensei would feel this way."

"Feel what?"

"Feel comfortable at the clinic," said Yuki bravely. "It may be funny for me to say so, but talented doctors need to work here. If a doctor seems like a real doctor, he should want to work here."

Noboru realized something.

She was repeating what Mori Handayū said.

He heard Yuki loved Handayū from Tsugawa Genzō and Sugi, the attendant to the madwoman Yumi.

Handayū seemed indifferent to her, but Yuki was crazy about him.

Sugi said, "The strait-laced Mori-san is a fine man, but when I consider Yuki-san's feelings, he's horrible."

Once in a while, Noboru saw them talking. Handayū passing by called over Yuki to talk, usually while standing. One time, he noticed Yuki crying at the fence around the medicinal garden.

He thought it happened at dusk one late spring evening. Handayū's arms were crossed. He was standing straight like a rod and looking up at the sky. Beside him was Yuki hiding her face with her sleeve and crying. They were fairly far away. Noboru looked away and left.

The silhouettes of their figures looked surreal in the light mist lit by a single lamp.

She's certainly mimicking Handayū.

As Noboru thought this, he casually said to Yuki, "Is that Mori-sensei's opinion?"

Yuki gracefully nodded and smiled, "Yes, Mori-sensei says that."

"I have an opinion, too," Noboru said and frowned. He sounded furious. "Mori is fooling himself. The truth is anyone wants to rise in the world. Winning fame and amassing a fortune are the most powerful and honest desires of human nature.

"Red Beard is doing fine. He is already a well-known physician. Daimyos and wealthy families welcome him with great respect. His fame is probably enhanced by working at a charity clinic anywhere. But we're not like that. We are no-name interns. If we stay here forever, we'll only end up unknown at the end of our lives. That is not what I want."

"You're tired, Yasumoto-sensei," said Yuki kindly. "Saying something so spiteful is proof you're tired. Please, go rest."

Noboru dropped his hands and walked away.

He was embarrassed, not only by what Yuki said but also by the contradiction he sensed in what he was doing and what he said.

Yuki's words weren't exaggerations or pigheaded. She always was honest and spoke her mind. On the other hand, he was fascinated by the work at the clinic and by Nīde Kyojō. This was the reason he was willing to wear the hated medical coat. However, if Noboru's mind hadn't been changed, he wouldn't have these feelings. The reason did not change. Simply, the words of a single patient changed him.

A plot of land called The Mujina Row House was on the hill called Nakatomi-zaka that rose in front of Dentsū-in Temple. It was known as a home for extremely poor people.

Noboru often accompanied Kyojō there to treat patients. One was named Yaya Sahachi. He was a stout man around forty-five or -six who suffered from pulmonary tuberculosis. In contrast to his sturdy appearance, he was weak and exhausted.

"Please tell me how can he get better?"

Who knows how many times the manager Jihei said those words? Kyojō turned around and sternly ordered, "Rest!" Sahachi obediently agreed.

When he experienced severe fever and bouts of coughing, he took off from work and slept. However, the moment he felt a little better, he would immediately get up and work. When discovered and reprimanded, a smile lit up his huge face. While sheepishly scratching his head, he kept bowing and said he would change his ways.

"I'll clear this away. I'll go to bed right after I'm done."

The manager Jihei heard that Sahachi married once while young but divorced a short six months later and has stayed single. Although he was skilled and made a good living, he was exceptional in having no desires. He sent his earnings to others. Even now, he lacked adequate household furnishings.

One time, Sahachi eyed Noboru's outfit suspiciously and asked, "Why aren't you wearing the clinic's medical coat?"

Noboru answered, "Because this is not a government facility. Kyojō arbitrarily decided on the uniform. It's not compulsory. So one can choose to wear it or not."

2

Sahachi avoided Noboru's gaze and muttered to himself.

"That coat is an act of mercy."

Out loud, he said, "When I see that coat, I know right away that is a doctor from the clinic. Poor people like us have a hard time getting to a clinic, but if we see a sensei pass by, many people will approach him for treatment. I'm grateful for the medical coat.

"That medical coat has different meanings.

"It doesn't constrain movement and is hygienic. If contaminated by a patient's bodily fluids or feces, the coat can be instantly changed. Even if not soiled, the rule is to change the medical coat every day in the summer and every other day in the winter."

Perhaps Kyojō began using the coats for these reasons. Noboru listened to Sahachi's words and secretly acknowledged their meaning.

"It's a good thing."

When he left Yuki and returned to his room, he shook his head like he was ridiculing himself.

"What is the strongest, most basic, honest desire of human nature?" he said, twisting his lips. "Wearing this fine medical coat."

When he came to Kyojō's room, he heard what sounded like Kyojō moaning on the other side of the shōji door. However, his moans more closely resembled the howls of a clipped voice. Noboru felt like he had been doused with water and rushed past. When he turned the corner to his hall, Mori Handayū opened the shōji door to his room and gestured for Noboru to come in.

"What is it?"

"I have to talk to you," said Handayū.

"I haven't eaten breakfast yet."

"Neither have I. Please, come in."

Noboru reluctantly went in.

"Where did you go?"

"Nowhere in particular," said Noboru and shrugged his shoulders. "I took a walk before breakfast. Why? What's wrong?"

"I ..." Handayū nearly shouted but checked himself and spoke quietly. "Nīde-san is upset. I've been wanting to talk to you about it."

Noboru said nothing.

"Earlier, Nīde-san was summoned by the police. He asked me to go to the station with him and I did," said Handayū quietly. "Matsumoto Sanzaemon-dono summoned him and Ogawa-san, the village chief, was there, too. They told him to stop outpatient treatments and to reduce expenses by a third."

Handayū explained the officials stopped outpatient treatments a long time ago. At the same time, an annex was built onto the clinic; the number of admitted patients increased; and outpatient treatments were no longer permitted officially. In reality, however, that was impossible.

The number of admitted patients increased from over seventy people to more than one hundred fifty. The patients who came for outpatient treatments numbered at least three hundred fifty people each year. At its height, the number exceeded seven hundred.

Most of them are poor and can't afford a town doctor. If they made a tearful appeal, a doctor might give in and treat them. Naturally, the number increased by one or two more people, and in time, we were back to the previous situation.

"Soon after Nīde-san became the chief doctor, he gave not-so-secret permission to provide treatments," said Handayū. "But now, it's being halted. And the total expenses of the clinic reduced by one-third."

"But ..." Noboru responded, "What's the reason?"

"A joyous event for the shogun. The reason seems to be various rising costs."

"What do you mean by a joyous event?"

"Some love affair gave birth to a princess. The shogun was overjoyed and held various festivities in celebration. No one said what exactly, but the police suggested a hidden meaning, and that angered Nīde-san."

Kyojō wanted to say, "If a joyous event happens to the shogun, isn't the usual course to free a criminal or give gold nuggets to charity?"

That was why he got angry, but he wasn't in a position to speak up. His words would have been seen as criticizing the government.

"Nīde said he agreed to the cost reduction. However, he could not stop outpatient treatments—" said Handayū and then stopped talking but continued in a quiet voice like a growl.

"I said, 'They are poor and sick. Stopping free treatments means they will be driven into their graves. I can't accept that and request a re-examination,' and then I left."

While they were talking, the wood blocks clapped to signal breakfast. Neither man stood. After Handayū finished, they remained seated for a short time.

"What about Ogawa-san?" Noboru eventually opened his eyes and asked, "Where does he stand? Whose side is he on?"

"Maybe neither. He should negotiate because he's responsible for the clinic," said Handayū. "But he only sat in his seat and never said a word. Perhaps he's not on either side."

Handayū stood and said, "Let's eat," and looked at Noboru. "Please be careful not to anger Nīde-san."

Noboru was quiet, as if he lost all confidence.

Kyojō was in a bad mood all morning. Of course, he didn't show anger or raise his raspy voice, but his anger was obvious from his grumpiness and irritability. Handayū and Noboru were with Kyojō from the examinations of admitted patients until he finished writing prescriptions. Each time something happened, the two exchanged warnings with their eyes.

Everything's fine, isn't it? Noboru whispered in his heart. He soon felt close to and liked Mori Handayū. He was surprised it didn't feel the least bit unnatural.

At least, he seems to be more human than Tsugawa.

He remembered Tsugawa Genzō's contempt for "the country

bumpkin" and had forgotten his similar views, and felt he could give Mori a few lessons.

When he finished writing the prescriptions, Kyojō looked at Noboru as he prepared to go out.

"What is the condition of Sahachi at The Mujina Row House?"

"There have been no changes."

"I have to go on rounds. Please, come with me."

Handayū and Noboru went out to the hall. As he was about to go into the dispensary, Handayū turned to Noboru and said, "Take care."

Noboru smiled and nodded.

3

Kyojō's destination was the estate of Matsudaira Iki no Kami. The entrance through the Ushigomi Gate was about two city blocks in front of the fire station. Until they arrived there, Kyojō talked constantly to himself.

"Do they have that right? If they do, who has it?" asked Kyojō and turned the wrist of one hand. "In troubled times, the world is tranquil and provides order. The authority of the shogunate unrelentingly suppresses the world. The four social classes of samurai, farmers, artisans, and merchants fear for their lives. Anything can be done to them. No matter how unjust or cruel, it could be officially forced through by the shogunate's reputation. That's how it is."

"I can't be tricked," said Kyojō, biting his lower lip. "I may be good-natured, like a senile old fool, but can't close my eyes to this contempt for people. I cannot be good-natured, even as an old fool who says nothing and lowers his head when the government mocks and shows contempt for the people."

For a short time, he stopped talking to himself. He was taking long strides but slackened his pace. One hand scratched his beard.

"It's injustice on injustices," Kyojō muttered. "Cruelty on cruelties. How much despair and pain must powerless people endure?"

He continued talking to himself for a long time with these distasteful words. His heart seemed to be angry, hateful, and boiling black. He cursed the shogunate and his inability to confront this power. However, when he eventually entered Ushigome Gate, Kyojō feebly shook his head while trying to rub something off with his right wrist.

"No, that's not it," muttered Kyojō, sounding exhausted. "They can't do that to me. I may be a doddering, good-natured guy but believe they're also humans. Their crimes have no capacity for truth despite having the seat of power and not knowing what they should know."

Kyojō's mouth turned down.

"They are the poorest ones and dumber than the most stupid and ignorant people. They are people to be pitied."

Carrying the medicine chest on his back, Takezō accompanying Noboru stuttered from behind, "This is Iki-sama's mansion."

Kyojō stopped as if startled, looked at his left hand, and stared at Takezō. The confused Takezō looked at Noboru who walked toward the guardhouse at the gate.

Kyojō and Noboru entered from the side entryway.

Tea and cakes were provided in the reception area. The chief retainer, Kawamoto Yukie, came out to greet them. Kyojō declined the tea. Immediately after the greeting, he formally said, "I'd like to ask for payment of the medical fee today."

Yukie heard fifty ryō in gold and stuck out his chin like someone poked his forehead.

"If you please, I'd like ten ryō to be in nuggets," said Kyojō with a calm face. "Now, I will see about the matter from the other day."

"The consultation."

"I will check the schedule."

Yukie hurried out.

"Iki-dono is worth 32,000 *koku* but looks richer than he is because he worked as a performer for a long time," said Kyojō.

Noboru wasn't sure whether Kyojō was talking to himself or him. His way of speaking left an impression of ridicule. "There's no reason for me to earn fifty or one hundred in gold. He's probably not in pain or itchy."

He sounded irritated when he muttered to himself, "What is fifty or one hundred in gold?"

Soon, the chamberlain named Iwahashi Hayato came out and presented a scroll with something written on it. It was a menu for five days. These meals were for Iki no Kami's tray. Kyojō picked up a portable brush-and-ink case and crossed out one item after another and added several lines of other items.

"Please feed him these foods for one hundred days," said Kyojō, returning the scroll to Hayato. "Chicken and eggs are banned. Only seafood and seasonings noted here are allowed. As before, cooked rice should be firm because polished rice will only shorten his life-span. Please maintain the ratio of three parts rice to seven parts barley."

Without waiting for Hayato's response, he said, "I will examine his veins."

Noboru joined him in Iki no Kami's examination.

Iki no Kami looked about forty-five years old and was fat like a walrus seen in pictures. For him, sitting seemed to be an ordeal.

His abdomen was unbelievably huge. Waves hit each time he moved his body. The flesh on his chin folded three times and hung down to his chest. His neck was not visible. The cheeks on his round face swelled to the point of bursting and closed his eyes to small dots.

Kyojō did nothing but stare from the lower step. He didn't move to check his pulse. He stared with sympathetic eyes but said nothing.

Iki no Kami did not gradually relax. Each breath was labored. He loosened his collar. His throat made strong guttural sounds as he wiped his mouth with tissue paper from his kimono.

Eventually, Kyojō said, "I've examined your menu. As I've told you, Lord, you are not sick and came to this condition that is far worse than illness. If there were a disease somewhere, I could treat the disease. However, your body often consumes meals rich in flavor. Therefore, fat has accumulated in all your internal organs and weakened them. All harmony in breathing and excretion is lost."

Around four-thirty, Kyojō threatened Iki no Kami in an unforgiving tone. Noboru, who was listening, noticed the intimidation in his words but was surprised by the severity of the meal restrictions. He heard about meals of three parts rice and seven parts barley and no chicken or eggs in the reception area, but when he heard it repeated to the chamberlain in front of Iki no Kami, the amounts and contents were inferior to the meals of a destitute man.

Movements resembling facial expressions were rarely seen on Iki no Kami's face bloated like a white leather pouch. However, his tiny eyes reflected the fear of a frightened child and sadness.

"A poor man falling ill is mainly caused by the crudeness of his meals." After returning to the reception area, Kyojō said to Noboru, "The illnesses of rich men and daimyos are determined by overeating delicious foods. The people in this world have no shame in killing the body through gluttony. When I see his figure, I am sickened."

Kyojō looked like he would spit.

When the chamberlain, Iwahashi Hayato, brought the money, Kyojō explained the prescription and pulled the medicine chest closer.

When the chamberlain left, Kyojō said to Noboru, "Wrap two of the ten ryō nuggets in paper and take it to The Mujina Row House.

"I will go to Ōkaku-dō and then make my rounds. To reduce expenses, I must first deal with the medications. Cajoling the proprietor of Ōkaku-dō may be part of my job.

"Well, that's all right. Now, go to Mujina Row House and give this to Jihei."

Noboru slipped the package into his sleeve and left.

4

Shortly before he arrived at the row house in Nakatomi-zaka, clouds covered the sky and thunder rang out. The moment he stepped into the manager's home, a severe evening downpour broke.

Jihei was making a straw sandal. When he saw Noboru, he stood up like he was going to throw it away and said, "I was about to go to the clinic when Sahachi threw up blood."

As he opened an umbrella, he asked, "Did you meet the messenger?"

"No, I was somewhere else," said Noboru and handed Jihei the package. "Nīde-san asked me to give this to you."

Jihei put the umbrella down, reverently took the package with both hands, and placed it on the Buddhist altar.

They shared the umbrella as they entered the alley, stepped on the boards covering the ditch, and entered Sahachi's home. The land on the lot rapidly sloped down to the bottom, and water over-flowed instantly during heavy rains.

The drainage was poor to a large ditch passing to the Koishikawa Canal. Heavy rains slightly floated the boards covering the ditch and forcefully swept away garbage at the drainage mouth.

Sahachi's home was not connected to the row house. Originally, it was a part of the row house, but about seven years ago, a landslide destroyed a section of the row house. Only this building at the end remained.

The huge pile of dirt that was deposited convinced the landlord to abandon the idea of rebuilding. Working alone, Sahachi detached this remaining wing and made it livable.

Over seven years, water washed away much of the dirt deposited by the landslide. Now, the lot was mostly flat, empty land. He explained the landlord became interested again in rebuilding the row house, brought in old wood, and started leveling the ground.

Jihei's wife Koto was in Sahachi's home.

"He's sleeping well."

Koto greeted Noboru and then whispered to her husband, "He says strange things sometimes. It's probably the delirium brought on by fever talking, but he seems to be in less pain."

"The sensei went on his house call rounds," said Jihei, as he sat. "If the messenger returns, please tell him the sensei came. If he's using an umbrella, bring me one right away."

The moment Koto went out, earsplitting thunder clapped in the sky directly above them. They heard Koto scream. The entire house seemed to tremble. Jihei rushed out the door and looked in the direction of the alley.

It was probably nothing.

"She's like a child," he muttered, went back inside, and sat. Noboru was looking at the sick man.

Jihei said, "A short time ago, I had my wife bring rice gruel. Well, he's been sleeping since yesterday afternoon. She prepared gruel and was bringing it to him, but he had collapsed in the workshop over there."

The workshop with a wood floor of ten square yards was attached to the living space consisting of a six-mat room and a two-mat room. Sahachi probably built it. The workshop was like a hut with wooden walls and no foundation or ceiling. The materials and gadgets for making wheel spokes were scattered around a single thin mat.

When Koto came, Sahachi was moaning, lying where he fainted. His blood flowed on the wooden floor. Koto told Jihei when he rushed over what happened. When Sahachi got into bed, he vomited blood again.

"His vomit filled half of a metal basin," said Jinbei in a hushed tone. "Holding him, I felt like I was going to throw up. I knew I had to leave."

Sahachi's eyes popped open.

"Naka," he said and looked around. "Naka, why have you come?"

His voice was quiet and clear.

Jihei whispered to Noboru, "She's his ex-wife. They divorced seventeen or eighteen years ago. Yes, Naka was her name."

Sahachi's eyes stopped on a point.

"You shouldn't have come," Sahachi plainly said. "I'll be going soon, very soon, so I won't make you wait much longer."

Smiling, he shut his eyes again and gently nodded like someone was there. Jihei looked at Noboru's face.

"He's babbling," said Noboru.

"They say a sick person who is dying speaks deliriously," whispered Jihei. "But I don't want him to die now. I want to act and bring him back to health. Sahachi is a reincarnation of a god or Buddha."

Jihei folded his arms and lowered his voice. "I found this out four or five days ago."

Earlier, he heard that Sahachi acted generously toward the people in the row house. He didn't wear what people wore, didn't drink, and of course, didn't smoke, and stocked up as much food as he could. Everything left over supported families in the neighborhood who ran into problems.

This fact went unknown for a long time. In a place where destitute people gathered, such as The Mujina Row House, people rarely lived in the same place for a long period. The lineup of faces changed completely over three years.

Perhaps no one knew what Sahachi did for a long time and Sahachi said nothing because the people he supported left one after another. When Sahachi fell ill five years ago, he told Jihei this for the first time.

Jihei said, "I told him to take it easy. I yelled at him. 'Isn't it stupid to do for people until you fall ill? What were you thinking?'"

Sahachi was sorry and apologized.

Pulmonary tuberculosis caused his collapse. Instead of seeing a doctor, he rested in bed for ten days and then went back to work. He was careful not to be a nuisance to Jihei in the future and promised to think about his body. However, in reality, he didn't keep this promise, even a little.

Jihei forced Sahachi to be examined by Kyojō because his condition was poor. Kyojō ordered him to follow a strict diet.

"But," said Jihei, unfolding his arms and thrusting both hands to his knees. "I found out four or five days ago that Nīde-sensei gave him money for various nutritional items to give to the people. Sahachi regularly made my wife deliver medicines but was dissatisfied after doing it once and had her make deliveries every day. If it were only that, it would have been fine. But when anyone asked, he also fed people. He gave people rice, fish, chicken, eggs, and even medicines, Sensei."

Jihei's whispering voice shook with anger.

"I wanted to say something and got so furious I lost my mind and stormed in here."

Noboru gazed at the sick man's face.

What could it possibly be? Noboru grumbled to himself while looking at Sahachi's emaciated, bony face. Sahachi's actions veered from the proper course. He wasn't so drained by people due to his deeply considerate nature. Jihei said, "He's like a reincarnation of a god or Buddha," but Noboru didn't think so. More realistically, he wondered if there was some all-too-human reason.

Sahachi took a deep breath and opened his eyes again. A smile rose on his bloodless, white lips, and he nodded to someone.

"You are beautiful. Yes," he said in a clear voice. "You are beautiful. Your dimples are indescribable. Naka, come here."

In a flash, terror appeared on Sahachi's face. His bony cheeks stiffened, his eyes opened wide; his white, dry lips trembled; and he bared his teeth.

He groaned in a hoarse voice, "That child ... That child can't. That child can't. Don't show this child. Please, send that child there … there …"

Sahachi firmly shut his eyes and panted.

They could hear a piercing scream and barks from what sounded like a mad dog going into the vacant lot out back. Meanwhile, the thunder went away, and the rain started. They distinctly heard a shout from the back.

"It's a skeleton."

Jihei slowly stood.

5

Yasumoto Noboru stayed by Sahachi's side until dusk.

The manager Jihei went out to see about the commotion out back.

"I'll be right back."

After a minute passed, he had not returned. The sick man was relaxed. He was sleeping peacefully with his mouth hanging half open.

Noboru was famished and quietly stood to go home.

Jihei returned. While wiping a towel across his forehead, Jihei said, "I'm sorry. As the workers were leveling the land out back, they dug up a horrible thing."

"I'm going home," Noboru quietly said. "The patient is asleep. I'm not worried about any sudden changes in his condition. If he wakes up, give him the medicine. Please make a thick rice gruel for him."

Jihei asked, "Will you have supper here? It's not so bad. Granny is making the meal now. If you like, please stay to eat."

Noboru thanked him but declined and left the row house.

The moment he returned to the clinic, the dining hall closed. Only Mori Handayū was there. Noboru sat beside him. The empty dining hall with a woodboard floor was tidy. Lit by only two lanterns, the surroundings were hushed and dark. The waitress on duty was a middle-aged woman named Hatsu. She heated the soup, but the baked fish and vegetable stew were cold.

Handayū finished his tea. As he stood, he said, "Can you come to my room later? Come when you've finished. There's something I wish to discuss with you."

"I'm worn out today. Will it take long?"

"While you were out, a young woman named Amano visited."

Noboru looked like he tripped, stopped eating, and looked at Handayū.

"Her name was Amano Masao-san," said Handayū and left the dining hall.

"There are leftovers," said Hatsu when she came to clear Handayū's tray. "If Yuki-chan is not the waitress, he's probably not interested. When I'm on duty, Mori-sensei never tries to eat everything."

Noboru ate in silence.

It wasn't the waitress's fault. Handayū's appetite had been waning since the beginning of spring. When Yuki was on duty, his expression, like an appeal to Yuki, was defeated, and he forced himself to eat. When she wasn't, he showed no interest in the side dishes. He seemed pained when picking up the chopsticks and was seen less and less.

It was an illness. He had no appetite because he was sick.

Perhaps, it's pulmonary tuberculosis. Noboru guessed that earlier. Was he unaware? Many sick people may be aware but avoid the truth. He wasn't sure which it was.

Kyojō loved Handayū, always accompanied him on treatments, and left him in charge when out on house calls. He seemed to view Handayū as his successor but said nothing about his health. Kyojō must have noticed the poor state of Handayū's body.

Sometimes doctors neglected their health and those close to them did not warn them. However, he couldn't believe Kyojō was that sort.

Maybe he knew.

That's it, thought Noboru. One time, Kyojō talked about this as a matter of life's vitality and medicine. One individual conquers an illness, but another succumbs. A doctor can confirm the patient's condition and progression but has no ability beyond the support he can give to an individual with strong vitality.

Also, as the medical field advances, there may be changes, but an individual's life force cannot be surpassed.

"They say nothing is more miserable than medicine," said Noboru, sipped his tea, and whispered, "The longer a doctor practices medicine, the more he understands the uselessness of the medical field."

While mumbling, Noboru quickly raised his eyes. At that moment, several thoughts about Sahachi, Handayū, and Masao's visit while he was out popped into his mind. Masao floated vividly into his consciousness. Feelings of gloom assaulted him.

Noboru left the dining hall and went to his room. Handayū soon appeared and called from outside the sliding door. With no enthusiasm, Noboru said, "Come in."

Handayū said, "It's a little humid. I'll open this."

He opened the shōji window and sat.

"Today, I'm worn out."

Handayū said, "There's no point in trying to avoid this. When you bump into reality, isn't it better to face it head-on?"

"I don't want to hear about Chigusa."

"Why won't you see Masao-san?"

"Won't see her, you say?"

Handayū said, "She came here to see you and waited for over an hour. You knew she was here, so why didn't you see her?" He coughed lightly and continued. "Today, I met with her and listened carefully. She said she wanted to tell you something and was obsessed with those thoughts, so we went to my room."

Shaking his head, Noboru said, "I don't want to hear. I don't want to hear about Chigusa. I feel sick."

"Then vomiting it all out is best. There's another problem."

Noboru eyed Handayū doubtfully.

"Amano-san is arranging for you to be a government doctor after you leave here."

Noboru's lips formed a tight line.

Amano Genpaku was a prominent physician with the title Hōin and worked as a government doctor for the shogunate. He and Noboru's father, Yasumoto Ryōan, were old friends. Their families often socialized. Amano had a son named Yūjirō and two daughters.

Noboru was Yasumoto's only child, but, for some reason, Genpaku favored him over his son Yūjirō. A smile lit up his face at the sight of Noboru. He often asked, "What kind of man will you become?

"Unfortunately, Yūjirō has set his sights on becoming an entertainer, a sorry fellow."

Amano clicked his tongue but said, "That was probably my fault. I was a heavy drinker when he was a boy."

Noboru was nineteen and could marry when Chigusa turned fourteen. Eventually, Noboru went to Nagasaki to study. When he finished, Chigusa was eighteen. Both her face and build were comforting.

She spoke at a leisurely pace. She said each word slowly and paused as she spoke. It seemed like her tongue was heavy. Sometimes, she sounded like a girl but occasionally gave the impression of a mature woman.

Handayū said, "Chigusa said she wanted to marry before you went to Nagasaki. Amano-san had the same wish, but you refused."

"Could I marry before going to study? The marriage would have been for four years after getting engaged. I studied for three years—"

Handayū quietly interrupted, "Your bride is eighteen. The only reason may have been a woman's desire for a wedding. Your priority was studying, but for a woman who turned eighteen …"

Noboru furiously shook his head and snapped, "Stop it! The woman had a secret affair and eloped with a destitute student. Hearing about it defiled my ears."

"That means, said Handayū, his voice tinged with sarcasm, "That means there's some regret."

Noboru's lips tensed into a line again.

Handayū said, "Please listen and don't get mad. If you have no regrets, shouldn't you pardon her? It seems a child will be born to the married couple disowned by Amano-san's family. This child would be Amano's first grandchild. Chigusa is seeking help from her mother. Now, if you calm your anger and make peace with Amano-san, the father and daughter will be as they were. Can't you do that?"

"Did Masao come to make that request?"

Handayū said, "One more thing. I've heard you're going to leave. Your benefactor who made it possible for you to come here was not Amano-san but your father. You can't misunderstand Chigusa-san. She promised to care for you until you felt better."

Handayū said, "From the beginning, however, Amano Genpaku objected. Rather than a long stay at a charity clinic that would not benefit you. He recommended you leave this place as soon as possible and take up the position of a government doctor for the shogunate he had arranged as promised.

"She said in the future, if you feel that way, you should speak directly to her," said Handayū, gently smiling. "She'll be seventeen, but Masao-san pays close attention to detail. Isn't she a pretty and clever young woman? She was worried about you and can't think of anything else."

6

That evening, Noboru could not sleep. Feelings closer to quiet reflection and regret and not agitation made him restless. For the first time, he revived Chigusa's face from their childhood friendship in his head and imagined she begged for his forgiveness.

Although she looked mature, Chigusa never voiced her thoughts. She could neither voice them nor show him through her actions. Noboru carelessly overlooked that. In addition to being a late bloomer, Chigusa was laid back by nature and still did not give the impression of being a woman. She thought marriage was far off in the future.

"We've been used to seeing each other since we were small, but our vision dimmed," he mumbled inside his bedding. "If I had known that I would have married before going to Nagasaki. The situation would certainly have changed."

He thought about her being a late bloomer, her laid-back nature, and her yearning for love, and concluded the serious wound of betrayal was huge.

"I was captivated only by me," he muttered. "I believed my coming here was the result of my father cajoling Amano-san. For a long time, my father was indebted to him. Even I relied on Amano-san for my future.

"I hated Chigusa, my father, Amano-san, and this charity clinic."

Noboru scowled while shaking his head from side to side on the pillow.

"Chigusa was hurt by my mistake. Amano-san and my father were hurt for different reasons. During it all, I was conceited and believed only I suffered a hard blow. What a selfish jerk," he said. His scowl deepened.

"I'm a selfish jerk. Think about what has happened since I came here. Oh, shouldn't I be embarrassed?"

Noboru shrunk his body inside his bedding.

The next morning, soon after Noboru, who slept little, finished a late breakfast, someone from The Mujina Row House came. They asked Kyojō to come right away because Sahachi's condition was strange.

Kyojō told him to go back immediately and handed him a packet of powdered medicine to give to Sahachi if his suffering intensifies.

Kyojō said, "If it's not needed, give it back to me. It's not a medicine that's usually used. Please take care not to forget."

Noboru got ready and went out.

When he reached the side of Dentsū-in, a middle-aged woman came running out of the alley, saw Noboru, and called to stop him. She asked, "Are you a doctor from the charity clinic?"

"Yes."

"Can you come and check on a very sick child?" she asked between panting breaths. She explained the child had been sick for six months, but she couldn't pay the medical fee and no doctor would make a house call. Now, the child seemed to be dying.

Thanks to this medical coat.

The medical coat indicates a doctor from the charity clinic. Other doctors won't come because the medical fee is past due. The woman came flying out of a house, recognized the coat, and called to stop him. Red Beard is a fine old fellow, thought Noboru.

He said to the woman, "Please go to the clinic. I'm on my way to see a seriously ill patient. Go there and ask or get someone else to run there."

The woman thanked him and trotted up the hill.

Jihei and the row house tenants were probably at Sahachi's house. Two women were caring for the ill man. A young wife was boiling water at the brazier, and an older woman was wiping off the old tatami.

At dawn, he threw up a little blood but, a little while ago, vomited a large quantity of blood. He missed the metal basin and half of the blood landed on the tatami. The old woman wrung hot water from a rag and was meticulously wiping off the tatami mesh.

Jihei whispered, "Last night, he ate a little rice gruel and only half of an egg yolk. "Granny planned to stay over and even brought a futon. Of course, he wouldn't agree. She came this morning while it was still dark. He tried to clean up the dirty articles himself."

Noboru moved closer to Sahachi's bedside.

Sahachi seemed to be asleep, but his eyes were slightly open. His lower jaw hung open, slack with no power. His skin color was dark and lacked vitality. The flesh on his cheeks was hollow like it was scraped off. His skin was wrinkled on his chin.

"He doesn't have much longer?"

"It seems so," said Noboru and moved away from the bed. "It's already out of our hands."

"Such a good man," said Jihei while sighing deeply. "Despite the hoards of useless good-for-nothings, a fine man like him is taken. I want to curse the gods and Buddha."

The young wife served Noboru tea.

"Today, it's quiet out back," said Noboru. Not touching the tea, he asked, "Have they finished leveling the ground?"

"No, town officials are coming to investigate. They can't work until that's done."

"Did something happen?"

Jihei screwed up his face and then spoke softly.

"When the remains of the landslide out back were being leveled, a corpse wrapped in a futon emerged. It was completely rotted and mostly bones.

"Probably because the cotton padding of the futon was bound tight, the head and the limbs were all there. They said it was a young woman. Remnants of a kimono and a full head of hair were found right away.

"The landslide moved the dirt seven years ago, so the original site is not known exactly. I think it was above the destroyed row house. Taking a guess based on what it looks like now, without a doubt, she was murdered and buried. Today, the town officials should come to investigate."

"It has become bones, so the corpse is fairly old."

"A gravedigger at Zennō-ji Temple was shown it. He said fifteen years have probably passed."

"How do you know she was killed and buried?"

Jihei said, "They didn't find a coffin. If she died from an illness, she wouldn't have been wrapped in a futon and buried.

"But if this happened fifteen years ago as the gravedigger said, there's probably no way to find out."

A man called at the door. A short, stout man who looked to be fifty stumbled in. He sloppily wore a long, plain, blue cotton *naga-banten* winter coat that hung unevenly in the front. A frayed, flat cloth belt closed the coat. White stubble stretched from his cheeks to his chin. His bald head glowed red as if painted with oil. He was probably quite drunk. Still staggering, he looked at them with blood-shot eyes.

"Hey, don't come in here," said Jihei, waving his hands. "The patient's condition is poor. Get out of here. Go home."

The man said, "Right now, you see, the town head is coming. He said to go get the manager. Ain't you the manager?"

7

"I'm not answering your unnecessary questions," said Jihei and then turned to Noboru. "Well, you heard, I'll be right back."

Noboru nodded.

Jihei left with the man. The elderly helper said she was going to the house to see and left from the back door. A little later, the man who went with Jihei returned alone and was giddy. Wearing an ingratiating smile, he sat with a thud on the raised floor.

"Stop it, Hei-san," said the young woman and came out of the kitchen. "The manager is mad because you're bothering a sick man. Please go home."

"You're a doctor from the charity clinic," the man said to Noboru. "I am Heikichi, an old acquaintance of Nīde-sensei. Sahachi and I are the tenants who've lived the longest at this Mujina Row House. They say Sahachi is pretty sick but won't let me see him.

"Matsu over there came from someplace else, so he tells me to go home because I'm bothering a sick man."

The young wife said, "He doesn't talk if he's not drunk, but the manager says when Hei-san's drunk he can't tell one thing from another."

"Oh, shut up," said the man called Heikichi, shaking his head and interrupting. "I've been drinking since I was nine. I had no desire to stop drinking for close to forty years. I have no idea what I look like sober. I've never tried to tell one thing from another when I'm drunk. If you think I'm lying, go ask Red Beard-sensei."

Heikichi laughed.

"One time Red Beard-sensei told me something when I drank too much, threw up some curious substance, and fell out. The sensei looked scared like this. He said if I had the money to drink until I got sick, I could think about my wife and child. I'm not joking. The sensei looked at me from the outside and said that. He looked into the human heart like mine.

"A wealthy or educated man probably can see the difference between what will benefit me, but either I can't do it or will be hurt if I do.

"But that guy has money or free time. The educated man can't play a smart trick on me. Right? A fellow like me works day and night. I don't eat rice until I can't eat one more grain. Every day my wife worries. What will we eat today? We made do today, but what about tomorrow? The kids were born. The rent piled up and eviction chased us. How could we improve our situation?

"We lived this way day and night for ten years. Yes, if seen from the outside, I may look dead drunk, but it was that way in my heart. I'm not joking. As soon as I think about my wife and kids, I have to drink."

Sahachi groaned and said something. Noboru slid closer to listen. His hoarse voice whispered, "I have to tell you something."

"Please, make Matsu-san and Hei-san go home."

Noboru nodded and asked the two to leave.

Heikichi did not stand. Matsu said he had work to do at home and left. Heikichi groused and complained but finally fell back there and dozed off.

Sahachi said, "Leave it alone. You're probably tired. I'm sorry, could I have a glass of water?"

Noboru adjusted Heikichi's sleeping position, took the patient's teacup, and poured hot water from the kettle on the brazier. Sahachi said he wanted water.

"Is it okay for me to drink something?" Sahachi weakly smiled. "Please."

Noboru went to the kitchen and returned with water.

"I'm happy you decided to wear that coat," said Sahachi and took a sip of water. "Now, you'll help dozens of poor people."

Noboru remembered that on his way here and answered in his heart, "It's as you said."

Again, Sahachi said, "What Heikichi said was simply a drunk's babbling. Please, don't laugh. Poor people mostly think that way.

"When only food is furiously chased down day after day, life is impossible if not drunk."

"I understand that, but men like Sahachi are among them, too."

"Me?" asked Sahachi vacantly, picked up the teacup, and skillfully took another sip while lying down.

"I know what I will say to the people living in this row house," said Sahachi and set down the teacup. "I heard everything the manager Jihei-san said to Nīde-sensei and you.

"It's ridiculous and a waste. Because nobody knows anything, I was praised. If they knew the truth or knew the sort of beast I am, none of them would sleep at all."

"Is this what you want to talk about?"

"Yes," said Sahachi and nodded. "I never told anyone until now and people never noticed. I was always anxious but not for a long time, today or all day tomorrow. No, please don't say anything. You may think what I'm saying means little, but she came for me yesterday."

Noboru was silent. Sahachi spoke with indifference, but his words brought on a chill. Noboru felt some sort of pressure.

Sahachi calmly said, "I want to tell you about my wife.

"Her name was Naka. We were three years apart and married one year after meeting each other."

Sahachi said, "It may sound like I'm bragging, but you may be uncomfortable because you can't understand if I don't tell you. I want you to be patient and listen to everything I have to say."

Originally, he lived in Kanasugi in Shitaya. While living in his parents' home, he was a tradesman who made wheel spokes. He only heard that his parents, who died young, had come from somewhere in Ōshū. He became an orphan at fifteen and was raised by the boss and his wife at the request of his parents and relatives.

Naka was a maid in a kimono fabric shop in a neighboring town and was twenty-one when they met.

The first time he heard her voice was early one spring morning. Sahachi was on his way home from the pleasure quarter in Shin-Yoshiwara.

Late the previous night, he went with a friend to a brothel in Kyōmachi. His friend decided to stay over, but Sahachi hesitated because of his boss's feelings and went home alone.

When he finally came to Daion-ji Temple at daybreak, rain showers began. He tucked up the hem of his trousers and scampered down the street.

8

He made light of the spring shower, but the rain poured down harder when he came to a street in Kanasugi, and then the downpour began.

I don't care, thought Sahachi. As he leisurely walked, water droplets falling from his head covered by a towel, a young woman called to him to lend him a plain, crude oil-paper umbrella.

"Why? I'm already sopping wet."

"But you'll get sick."

After this exchange, he borrowed the umbrella and went home. The woman was Naka.

After he went back and returned the umbrella, Sahachi could not forget about Naka. She flew out into the rain. When she said, "But you'll get sick," and lent him the umbrella, he was already attracted by her looks and voice.

After that, he felt compelled to invite her out. They met several times in a rice paddy in Iriya. He pressured her, but Naka didn't refuse. On days off during that time, the two rendezvoused at the Tennō-ji Temple in Iriya. Sahachi confessed his feelings.

"I'm so happy," said Naka, her face pale.

The simple phrase "I'm so happy" was straightforward but refreshed Sahachi like he was watching a morning glory bloom.

"I'm happy, but it's no good," said Naka.

Still pale, Naka gently shook her head and told her story. She had seven younger siblings and sent money home because their father was sickly. When she entered service as a maid, she borrowed against her wages for the next ten years. The money she sent home was much more than what the other servants sent. The reason was her father's previous job in a shop called Eichitoku. After leaving the shop, he peddled clothes bought from Eichitoku. At any rate, his body lost mobility.

"How many years are left on your service contract?"

"One more year, but I borrowed the money I sent home. So I can't leave even after my service term ends."

"The borrowed money should be returned."

"It is an obligation."

"It is not an obligation to restrict someone's life. Will you leave it to me?"

Naka shook her head.

"Even if I leave the shop, my father is ill and I have many brothers and sisters. If we were together, they would only be a burden to you."

Sahachi said, "Can we handle that?

"I don't have parents or siblings. Your father is my father. Your brothers and sisters are mine. I can support your father and siblings."

From then on, Sahachi worked hard to earn money. Once a month, he met Naka in the rice paddy in Iriya. Naka's home was in Sanya in Asakusa. Once a month, she took time off and went to visit her sick father. They met during that day on the road through the rice paddy that passed close to Sanya.

Sahachi used to drink sake but quit. He also stopped going out with friends. *Jōruri* recitations grew popular among his friends. Sahachi had been taking lessons for six months but quit to make money.

Naka saw his earnestness, decided to end her service by the end of the year, and promised they'd be together.

Sahachi said he wanted to meet her family, but Naka did not agree. She stubbornly refused to go near the neighborhood of her home.

"It's no good now. Please wait until we're together."

She said she was embarrassed because it was too miserable. Sahachi could not force her. However, he later understood. The other reason was a deeper dilemma.

A year later, the two married. Sahachi told everything to his boss who asked him to come to Eichitoku. Although he stumbled in Eichitoku, Sahachi paid back the entire loan instead of her father and eventually was given consent. The couple had a home in Yamazaki-chō in Shitaya. Sahachi worked at her father's shop. For about a year, the days passed peacefully and enjoyably.

Sahachi loved Naka from deep in his heart. They cherished each other so much their love was greater after they married than before.

He said, "Then the fire happened in the Year of the Horse." He quietly continued. "That was the daytime fire at the end of February. Everything burned from the Shitaya area to Asakusa Bridge, but I ran from the Kanasugi shop. One side of our house was on fire, and I couldn't get close."

Sahachi sipped the water again.

As his mind filled with wild thoughts, he searched on foot for Naka. The Kanasugi shop was also burned down by leaping flames, but he didn't know that. It was during the day, and the nimble body of a young woman would not burn to death. He believed she fled somewhere. One by one, he searched the places where the people who fled the fire would gather.

The next day, he went to Sanya, which had not burned down, but only heard "Naka didn't come here."

The monthly remittance had been sent. Sahachi visited that

house a second time because Naka hated that. The family's attitude was indifference.

"Their stance was our daughter has been stolen," said Sahachi and sighed deeply.

The Kanasugi shop burned down. The boss and his wife retreated to the countryside in Ebara. Sahachi slept at a friend's house.

In half a month, after he walked through the ruins of the fire and visited relief huts, he resigned himself to Naka's death. He immediately fell into a depression and slept in at his friend's house.

"I moved here to The Mujina Row House in July of that year," said Sahachi. His eyes seemed to chase something in the distance. "Of course, thanks to my friends, a workshop was added at the end of the row house. I took orders and delivered finished goods. I mostly ate meals at a simple restaurant. My life was without frills."

He was urged to find a wife but always avoided the issue by speaking vaguely and continued living alone.

Two years passed. In the summer when he was twenty-eight, Sahachi chanced upon Naka on the grounds of Sensō-ji Temple. On the auspicious day said to be a day worth 46,000 days, pilgrims filled the grounds. Inside the crowd beside Buddha's shrine, the two came face to face, recognized each other, and froze.

Naka carried a baby on her back. She was a little fatter and her hairstyle was different. She had changed a lot. Nevertheless, Sahachi recognized her at a glance. She recognized him instantly, too.

"It's been a while," said Sahachi.

"Yes, it has," answered Naka.

Jostled by the crowd, they walked to an inner temple.

9

After circling the grounds, they went out through the guard gate for noblemen. Sahachi found a soba noodle shop. He and Naka went to the second floor empty of other customers. Naka let down the baby and nursed it.

"Is that your child?"

"Yes, his name is Takichi."

"Has he had his first birthday?"

"He'll be one in September."

Sahachi felt like his heart had been gouged out.

"I felt like a chisel was plunged in and my heart scooped out." Sahachi frowned a little. "It wasn't hate or frustration. I felt pathetic and grief-stricken... It's a strange thing to talk about, but my wife gave birth to another man's child. There she was, right in front of me, breastfeeding her child. The truth is I tried my best to stay silent. I felt half dead. That alone was miserable, pathetic, but if I could, I wanted us to embrace tightly and cry."

Noboru took out a paper from his pocket and gently wiped the sweat from Sahachi's forehead.

They divorced at that moment.

Sahachi asked her nothing, and Naka explained nothing. The soba was served, but neither one reached for the chopsticks and eventually stood. Sahachi helped put the baby on her back.

"Are you happy?" he asked.

"Yes," she said, barely opening her mouth.

"We'll probably never meet again."

Naka did not respond and rocked the baby on her back.

They parted after leaving the soba shop but Sahachi's eyes followed Naka until she turned, bowed to him, and disappeared around a corner.

"Five or six days later, I hadn't worked but drank sake after a long time not drinking. All I did was drink and sleep." Sahachi gently shook his head. "Naka took away half of my body. I was pained while in Naka's presence. Why? I didn't feel the least bit of hatred or bitter disappointment. Seeing her leave when we parted and her figure turning and bowing was wretched. The pain seemed to stop my breath."

Then one evening, Naka visited The Mujina Row House.

Sahachi was drunk and asleep. Naka did not bring the baby. She closed the storm door at the entryway, stepped up, and sat beside Sahachi. Right away, he felt it was her. From the sound of the storm door closing, he thought, That's Naka. He realized that was not the least bit surprising but was surprised.

She whispered, "Risuke-san from Kuruma-zaka asked me to come."

"Oh, Risuke has been kind to me."

"I've heard. I'm sorry. Please forgive me."

Sahachi mustered the power in his entire body to keep from groaning. He quietly sat up and pulled the standing paper lantern closer. It was already late. The front door was closed, and the room was as dark as the night.

"Please, don't light the lantern," said Naka and cried.

"Can you forgive me?"

"I don't understand," said Sahachi, nearly moaning. He didn't understand but thought he was happy she was alive.

"Will you let me explain?"

"If it's not too hard on you."

Naka was silent, probably to quiet her sobbing. After a short time, she blew her nose and then spoke in an even tone that killed all emotion.

There was a man who was promised her. The child of her father's friend in Sanya ran away and came from his parents' home, lived in the same town, and worked odd jobs as a carpenter.

He was the same age as Naka. Ever since he was sixteen or seventeen, he said, "I will become a member of this family," and gave his earnings to Naka's family.

When he turned twenty, he told Naka he wanted her. Her parents were happy and gave their consent.

"I found out about that a little before you spoke to me."

Her feelings were still muddled. She didn't hate that man but felt obligated because of what he did for her family. However, she didn't have genuine feelings for him. Becoming his wife seemed like another person's affair. Around that time, she met Sahachi.

Naka was strongly attracted to him. While she thought she had to tell the truth and must reject him, she was hopeless. As though in a dream, she was drawn to Sahachi.

"There was nothing I could do," said the crying Naka. She restrained her voice and wept for a long time.

In time, Naka made her decision. She would be with Sahachi, and duty is duty, and there should be a way to give back somehow. With this resolve, she talked to the proprietor of Echitoku and her father in Sanya. Her powerful feelings scared her, too. She refused to cry. When Sahachi's boss went to talk, Echitoku's proprietor was hesitant. When Sahachi visited her family in Sanya, her family was distant and cold. That might have been the reason.

Then the two married. Naka's life for about a year was so happy and satisfying she would have no regrets for the rest of her life.

"That year with you, I thought was why I was born into this world. It shouldn't be good to feel this happy. Now I'm surely being punished. I often thought about that when I was alone."

During the fire, the thought "I'm being punished" flashed in Naka's mind. That was stupid. As she fled while chased by the fire, she rejected her stupid thoughts. But the more she rejected these thoughts, the stronger they became.

"The fire was proof I was living a happy life."

The fire was absolute proof. Those words sounded like someone whispered them so vividly in her head she could hear them. Sahachi probably thought she burned to death. The time came to bring this all to an end. While thinking, she realized she was standing in front of the Sanya house.

Naka thought, After that, I felt I was not the real me, I had become a different person. I'm true to myself when with Sahachi. The person here is a different person. In fact, so I'm not a coward in the future, I will marry this man like my father said, and we'll make a home in Honjo.

10

Two years later, when Naka believed her life had settled down after her marriage to that man and the birth of Takichi, she encountered Sahachi at Sensō-ji Temple.

Naka thought she woke up. She was sleeping for a long time,

and her feelings were awakened. She felt like a person who had been spirited away and abruptly returned home. Since the fire, nothing felt real to her.

"Talking to you now, I understand it's me, but I can't let myself think about that now that I have another husband and a child," said Naka, squirming. "Please understand I've come back to you. Darling, I've come home."

"Are those your true feelings?"

"Please, hold me."

"Don't you want to go back to them?"

"Please, hold me."

Sahachi gently embraced Naka. She straightened something with one hand and then hung both arms around Sahachi, hugging him with all her might. At the same time, she released a brief squeal.

"Don't let go," said Naka, clinging to him.

"Don't let go of me."

Then Naka died.

Sahachi said, "A dagger had plunged into her body below her left breast.

"I didn't call a doctor. She died instantly with one stab. Do you understand? She said, 'Don't let go of me,' and I didn't want to let go. I saw the dagger in her hand once, but Naka talked like she had to die. She resigned herself to dying and then ..."

Sahachi coughed furiously. His body strength drained away, he doubled over. He grabbed his pillow with both hands and coughed so painfully he thought he stopped breathing.

Noboru slid closer and stroked his exposed bony back. He waited for his coughing to subside and gently made him sip water.

"That's it," said Sahachi. After a short time, in a frail, hoarse voice, he said, "The woman dug out yesterday in the back was Naka. Before the landslide, that was my workshop. I buried her under my workshop. We've been together ever since."

He thought the neighbors wanted to hold a memorial service for Naka, but there was no reason to thank or praise her. He had no idea what happened to Naka's husband and child.

"I would only make them sad, like I had killed her. Someday the truth would come out, but until then, to memorialize Naka and atone for my sin, at the very least, I wanted to be useful to people.

"That's why I said, 'You've come to see me.'

"Yesterday, when I heard the excited voices out back, I thought, Is that it? Naka has come. We will now be together. Finally, I will have peace of mind."

Heikichi, who had fallen asleep in the doorway, moaned, brought water, and shouted in a ridiculously loud voice.

"The coldhearted old man of a manager and old grandma Ume are stingy.

"Sahachi's a dope. Red Beard is a coward. All you guys are ugly clowns. Hmph.

"This world is a small, square sake cup. Tomorrow will be difficult. The bottom is known. Outside of being charmed by sake and drinking… Hey, can't you hear? Bring water."

"Yasumoto-sensei," said Sahachi. "Can you go to the manager's home and tell him this story? Those bones are Naka's. I buried them. That way, we can avoid other problems."

CHAPTER 4
THE THIRD TIME'S A CHARM

1

HALF A MONTH after the rainy season ended, the madwoman Yumi tried to kill herself. She was the woman who lived with a young maid named Sugi in a separate house built by Yumi's parents. Thick lattices covered the windows of the building. The only door in or out of the house was locked with a key. The whole house was constructed to be a prison. Sugi used the key to unlock and lock the door to go in and out of the house.

One day, however, while Sugi was preparing supper in the kitchen, Yumi tied her obi undersash to the lattice of a window and tried to kill herself.

Yasumoto Noboru was not at the clinic. As always, he was accompanying Nīde Kyojō on house calls. They were examining a man called Ino at the home of a carpenter named Tōkichi in Sakuma-chō, Kanda.

Of course, Ino was also a carpenter and Tōkichi's twenty-five-year-old younger *brother*. It began when the older *brother* Tōkichi showed up at the clinic and determined to get help.

"All the other doctors said he's demented, but I didn't think so. We were raised together at the master carpenter's home. From the time we left his home until I married, we lived together in the same row house. We have known each other for over ten years. I knew all about his personality and his habits.

"So I can't believe he's crazy. If he's got some kind of illness, I think there's a way to cure it. Please, come and examine him this one time."

Kyojō agreed but had a backlog of urgent cases so he promised to visit in two or three days. Those several days turned into a week. On the day he came, they visited the home of a retired merchant named Ōmi in Gofukubashi and went around to Sakuma-chō on the way home.

Ino was a young man with a small frame and chiseled features and seemed skilled at his work. Probably because he felt ill, his eyes looked glazed and his movements were sluggish. He didn't close his lips. During Kyojō's examination, Ino didn't seem to realize he was being examined. Whatever he was asked, he answered half-heartedly but feebly grinned and laughed. When the examination ended, he quickly lay down and in a groaning voice asked Tōkichi's wife for tea.

"Chiyo-san," he slowly said, "Sorry to bother you, but could you bring tea, please?"

Tōkichi had not returned from work, and his wife Chiyo hosted them. As Ino requested, she cordially stood and quickly brought tea for the three men.

Using his arm as a pillow, Ino lazily watched Chiyo, unexpectedly signaled Kyojō with his eyes, frowned, and whispered, "Hey, women ain't worth a damn. Right?"

His face was filled with contempt and disgust. Kyojō said nothing but casually looked at Ino and Chiyo.

When they left Tōkichi's home, the streets were dim in the twilight. The row of houses in Yushima-dai were tall and appeared to be purple shadows.

As they followed the Kanda River, walking toward Hijirizaka, Kyojō, looking straight ahead, asked, "Yasumoto, what do you think?"

Takezō behind Noboru and carrying the medicine chest said,

"Huh?" like he'd been asked. Noboru waved his hand at him and answered Kyojō.

"I believe it's melancholy."

Kyojō said, "That's a fitting word. If his fever persists, it's malarial fever. If he starts coughing, it's pulmonary tuberculosis. If his organs become sluggish but do not fail, it's melancholy. You could start today as a town doctor."

Not seeming to care, Noboru answered, "Sensei, what is your diagnosis?"

"Melancholy," said Kyojō, calmly.

Noboru was silent.

"Tomorrow, you will make house calls alone," said Kyojō as they started up the hill. "Ask Tōkichi and his brother for details about their past. Since the patient doesn't speak, you only have Tōkichi to question."

"What should I ask?"

"Anything and everything. While you're asking specific questions, you'll probably hit on the cause. In that case, ask questions until you understand by centering on finding the cause to confirm your diagnosis."

Noboru wanted to ask if that was necessary. As he became accustomed to life at the clinic, he came to understand doctors must do something. Also, there were many patients who Kyojō originally examined at the clinic and were impatiently waiting for his treatment. That couldn't be said about patients like Ino who didn't think they needed to bother anyone for treatment.

Is it okay to leave him alone? Noboru wanted to ask, but Kyojō already seemed to know. He changed his mind because he had been given an order. He didn't say anything irrelevant.

Noboru returned to the clinic exactly at dinner time. While washing his face, Mori Handayū called to him and went to the dining hall. Noboru couldn't hear Handayū's reply from his room but went to the dining hall and found him beginning his meal.

Handayū waited for Noboru to be seated in front of his tray to ask him about Yumi. But he instantly realized something, acted awkwardly, and changed the subject. He still seemed to be worried about Yumi and Noboru.

The wound from that time remained deep in Noboru's heart. However, rather than feeling constrained, he felt a heavy responsibility.

"Why do you ask?" Noboru returned to the topic. "Because I couldn't help her?"

"No, you helped. It was a dangerous situation. The scar left by the strangulation by the undersash was awful. Her voice was left hoarse. The swelling of her face hasn't gone down. I don't understand how the suicide by hanging was not due to madness but an act of sanity."

Noboru stopped eating and looked at Handayū.

Handayū continued gloomily speaking. "I think I'll have her examined later by Nīde. When I examined her, the periods of the episodes of sanity were slowly getting longer. For the first time, she began to understand the facts of her insanity and confinement. I believe this led to hopelessness and the suicide attempt."

Noboru paused before saying, "Her mind is not insane. The origin is her constitution."

He laughed lightly and said, "Today, I examined a curious patient. If that young lady dies, this man may replace her in that home.

"On top of that, tomorrow, I will give my diagnosis for that man."

2

The next day, Noboru left the clinic while it was still dark.

By accompanying Kyojō, he became an expert walker. Tōkichi was still eating when they arrived at the house in Sakuma-chō. Chiyo called Tōkichi to the door. Noboru explained he had been sent by Kyojō.

"Ino is still sleeping," said Tōkichi, scratching his head. "I don't think this is a good place to tell the whole story."

"I can go with you to your workshop."

"I'll get someone to cover for me at work," said Tōkichi pitifully. "If the master carpenter refuses, I'll get someone else. Can you go to Horie?"

"You may not be able to get off work."

"I want us to talk and not be rushed. They can manage without me at my job. Please, wait a little longer while I finish eating."

Noboru went outside.

The Kanda River ran behind the house in 4-chōme, Sakuma-chō. The two-story house was snugly built with lattice doors. Many shuttered businesses were a common sight repeated in the surrounding neighborhoods. The low-lying towns formed a peaceful picture.

Tōkichi came out wearing a casual kimono tied by a flat obi sash and hemp-soled sandals. He looked like he intended to take time off from work.

"I'm sorry to keep you waiting," he said and started walking but stopped like he remembered something.

"I want you to see this," he said and walked around the side of the house to the back. On the other side in the back, a row of houses faced the Kanda River. A narrow vacant lot, nine feet wide, separated one house from the next. The kitchen doors of two houses faced each other. There was also a well. Miniature bonsai plants decorated handmade shelves. Trees and flowers grew around the bamboo fences.

"Please, look at this," Tōkichi said from his kitchen door, pointing to a line of flowerpots.

In each one of seven cheap, unglazed pots grew a small sapling. Noboru could not make out what was growing.

"Ino planted them," said Tōkichi while keeping an eye on the kitchen door. "Look closely. They're all reversed."

"What do you mean by reversed?"

"He buried the branches and the roots are coming out on top."

"Oh," said Noboru. "Of course, I see it now that I'm closer. The roots are coming out of the dirt in the pots. They were planted with the roots on top. I didn't know what type of trees they were."

"Why did he plant them like this?"

"I'll tell you later," said Tōkichi and started walking. "Shall we go?"

They crossed a new bridge. Tōkichi began talking as they turned toward Nihonbashi.

Ino was two years younger than Tōkichi. When he was twelve, he apprenticed in the home of a master carpenter called Daimasa in Horie, Nihonbashi.

Three years earlier, Tōkichi had entered Daimasa. He was the newest of the six apprentices, young, and naturally was nicer to Ino than the others.

"Ino was smart and skilled with his hands and mouth. Before six months passed, he was a popular fellow at Daimasa. Everyone loved Ino."

Not only at Daimasa, he was popular with the neighbors, too, and mysteriously adored by girls. The two Daimasa daughters, Shitsu and Sayo, were ten and seven years old. From the beginning, the sisters and their playmates liked Ino.

"When I grow up, I will become Ino's wife."

"No way Ino-san is going to marry an ugly bug like you. I'm going to be his one and only wife."

When four or five girls played, they often had this fight. Hearing their words made Ino turn red with anger.

"Hmph," Ino said. "What are women? Get married? Women ain't nothing."

Then he'd "Hmph" several times and stay away from the girls for a short time. He avoided playing with beanbags, marbles, and bouncing balls. Naturally, his open-hearted nature and pleasant looks attracted girls. On the other hand, Ino had no special interest in anyone. Shitsu and Sayo were no exceptions. If anyone acted too friendly, he severely rejected them to the point of heartlessness.

Tōkichi said, "He was like that until he turned twenty. It's a little thing to talk about, but I've heard it's related to what happened later."

Noboru silently nodded.

"As a skilled craftsman, when he reached marriageable age, he could get a local girl to marry him. The older apprentices persuaded him to go out and have fun.

"Honestly, they did that to me, too, but it was different with Ino. He never looked at the young women in town who looked flirtatious. Even when I invited him as close brothers do, he never joined me. The apprentices often said he might be deformed."

When Tōkichi was twenty-three and Ino was twenty-one, they left Daimasa and got a house. At Daimasa, Shitsu married and had a child; three new apprentices were taken in; and a nanny was hired. This made waking up and bedtime exasperating.

They lived in a row house on a back street in a farm town close to Daimasa. Their morning and evening meals were eaten at the master carpenter's house. Their laundry was done there, too. Because they only paid rent, the two lived a carefree life for close to a year, but Ino never approached a woman.

While they lived together, Tōkichi went out to have fun but Ino stayed at home.

Ino seemed to like sake and became a heavy drinker. He cheered up when he drank good sake. But no matter how drunk he was, when asked, "Wanna go out?" he shook his head no.

He always said, "You go. It's not for me." In February when he turned twenty-two, Ino excitedly said to Tōkichi, "There's a young woman I want to be my wife. Would you please arrange it?"

He made his request and bowed his head.

"This is the master carpenter's house," said Tōkichi, and stopped talking and walking. "Please wait here. I'll be right back if he refuses my request."

3

With a frontage of only thirty feet, the two-story building was large. Daimasa was written on the shōji-paper sliding double door. Tōkichi went in, came right back out, and walked south on the road along the canal.

"There's a sailors' inn this way. We'll have a drink and talk there."

"At this hour?"

"Morning drinks as we gaze at the water," said Tōkichi and forced a smile. "Am I a little too common?"

The sailors' inn was at Horibata at 3-chōme, Kobuna-chō. The small, weathered house had two rooms on the second floor. They passed through the shōji sliding door of the front six-tatami-mat room. The expansive residence of Makino Kawauchi stood on the opposite side of the canal. They looked out on the thick cluster of trees on the estate.

"Anyhow, we make this place look good," said Tōkichi and ordered the sake.

"The bride Ino wanted was the daughter of the owner of a sake bar also in Tadokoro-chō. She was seventeen. Her name was Kō. Both her face and body were round and plump, but she was a crass and rude woman.

"I told him to stop joking. Of all women out there, he wanted that woman. Was he stupid? Ino got mad and said, 'I'm not joking. These are my true feelings.'

"He said, 'You may not want that sort of woman, but I want her to be my wife. Please go and tell me when it's settled.'

"Ino was so serious even the color of his eyes seemed to change. He was sincere."

After Tōkichi was certain, he began the marriage talks. At first, the woman's father Daikichi thought it was a joke, too. His daughter Kō said, "He's teasing me. That's awful." However, her mother Raku believed Tōkichi and persuaded her husband and daughter.

Daikichi relented but under one condition. He would consent if her husband's family did not adopt his only daughter and his son-in-law joined his family.

It took only five days to reach that point. Tōkichi asked the groom. Ino thought carefully and immediately looked like he agreed.

"Yes, I'll become his son."

"Think carefully, Ino, this is your future. If you intend to become a first-class craftsman, you must hone your skills. If you become responsible for a bride with two parents, you'll have little hope of getting ahead your entire life."

"Who me?" said Ino and only shrugged. Tōkichi arranged the marriage.

To complete the arrangements, he asked, "When do you want the wedding to be held?" but Ino said, "There's no hurry. We made the deal, so there's no hurry."

Tōkichi said, "But they probably have plans. I have to give them a rough date. What should I do?"

"Let's see," said Ino, twisting his neck. "How about telling them in the fall? Say the fall. Yeah, because that's good for me."

"Ino persuaded me to not say anything to anyone for now," said Tōkichi and sipped the lukewarm tea. "It's been half a month since then."

The inn's proprietress brought the sake. Each of the two trays held a sake-warming bottle and three side dishes.

Tōkichi said, "Don't bother. We'll serve ourselves."

The proprietress left immediately.

"Would you like a drink?"

"Not for me."

"Well, I'll have one."

Tōkichi poured himself a drink and kept on talking as he drank although his drinking looked more like sipping."

One day about half a month later, Ino asked Tōkichi to break off the marriage proposal. Tōkichi felt like smacking him but stared at Ino's face and didn't speak for a moment.

"I'm sorry, Tōkichi, but she's no good. It has all gone bad—"

Tōkichi interrupted. "Wait a minute. What happened? What's no good? What about her is bad?"

"Last night, I went out for a drink."

"I know. I went with you."

"You went home before me," said Ino. "I went right home, but Kō followed and called to stop me.

"When I asked, 'Did something happen?' she came to my side and squeezed my hand. I asked again, and she acted strangely and sighed. Then she squeezed my hand hard and said, 'Don't throw away your life.'"

Ino rubbed his right palm over his kimono several times like something was clinging to it and frowned.

"That didn't happen, did it?"

"I felt like I would throw up. Tōkichi, you probably don't know this, but she squeezed me with a greasy, sweaty, warm hand. She said, 'Don't throw away your life,' in a strange, sugary voice. Like my spine was pulled out without warning, I felt awful and ran off."

"For someone about to be married, isn't it natural to say, 'Don't throw away your life'?"

"Was it said to you?"

"It's generally said in the world."

"Yes, people say that, but I understand the feeling of being dropped in a hole."

"People say different things."

"I felt like I was going to throw up like my spine was torn out without warning, and now like I was dropped into a hole. What about my spine being pulled out without warning? That's why, I'm breaking it off before my spine gets pulled out."

Tōkichi said, "I told him he was being selfish. I went to a lot of trouble to arrange this marriage. If he was going to break it off, he'd have to do it himself. I refused to do it."

Ino seemed to break it off. Tōkichi thought he did because he heard no more from the other side. It became hard for him to go to that sake bar. He had to switch to Kashi six blocks away in Sumiyoshi-machi.

"That was probably the trigger. After that, he showed interest in another woman," said Tōkichi, bowing with his hands. He took the sake-warming bottle on Noboru's tray. "Just like him, he doesn't notice the women who approach him. Like I told you, he's been a popular guy with girls for a long time. Why doesn't he ever show interest in those women? He's smug but falls hard for the woman who snubs him."

4

After winter that year, Ino again said, "There's a woman I want to make my wife," and asked Tōkichi to speak for him. Marriage talks for Tōkichi were beginning at the same time. His counterpart was the daughter of a carpenter who worked at Daimasa. The master carpenter from Daimasa approached him and asked for his consent to be the go-between. Tōkichi's intended was now his wife Chiyo. Tōkichi agreed although he found her childish when they first met.

She was sixteen and had delicate features. She didn't seem like a young woman ready to marry. He thought it would be pitiful for her to marry.

"Please let me think a little more about this," he said to the master carpenter, but Ino came with another story.

This woman also worked at a sake bar, a somewhat fashionable one called Umemoto. Her name was Yono; she looked around twenty years old. She had been working there for fewer than fifty days but was popular. She could hold her drinks and was friendly with the customers.

"I can't. I'm not doing that."

Tōkichi shook his head. He strongly opposed this marriage.

"How can I say this? She's not a total amateur. At least, she knows about men. It makes no sense to have a family when the woman's a heavy drinker. Giving up the idea of marrying her is for the best."

"But Tōkichi, I'm serious."

Ino sat properly and said, "She drinks because she's drinking with customers and probably won't drink any longer if she had her own family.

"Look at Jūhei-san's wife in Yokkaichi-machi."

Jūhei was a Daimasa carpenter who lived in Yokkaichi-machi. His wife Tsuna worked in a restaurant. While she was working, she drank so much she nearly bathed in sake. But when she married Jūhei, she never touched a cup of sake again, ran her home expertly, and was praised by her friends.

Ino continued, "You say she knows men, but you don't know a lot about the world because you're used to fooling around."

"What don't I know?"

"Women," said Ino. "I don't know about the old days, but these days women who are virgins become brides. Nobody wants one out a thousand, no, one in five thousand."

"You know this?"

Tōkichi fought back.

"I'll be getting married soon. You know her. Chiyo, a young lady from Kakigara-chō. Are you saying she's not a virgin?"

"This isn't a joke," said Ino, turning red. "Please stop. I'm not joking. I'm not talking about anybody in particular." Ino bowed his head.

"I'm saying it's common knowledge in the world."

"You're saying you've heard people say this."

"Tōkichi, when did I say that?"

"Stop repeating what I say."

Tōkichi went to the marriage talk at Umemoto. He was also engaged at the time. Ino was too serious and probably couldn't help it.

Yono consented. She said she was eighteen, naturally, she seemed to be twenty. She had a younger sister who was a live-in servant somewhere and didn't seem to be a problem.

"I will be a fine wife," said Yono and modestly shut her eyes.

Tōkichi also spoke with the couple who ran Umemoto and arranged the marriage. Later, when he notified Ino, he smiled like he was about to cry and said, "Thank you."

"Hey, what's wrong?"

"The talks are settled. Aren't you happy?" asked Tōkichi.

"Didn't I say thank you? Thank you. I mean it."

"Okay."

As Tōkichi watched Ino's face, for no special reason, he felt a shiver run down his spine.

"You said you'll get married at the beginning of next year.

"Right after the pine New Year's decorations are taken down, I'm going to Mito. The job is to build a retirement home for a marine products merchant called Sagami-ya in Mito. There'll only be twenty workers: carpenters, plasterers, and cabinetmakers. They left Edo three days ago to do preliminary work. Ino suddenly asked to bring him along."

The problem was the workers had already been chosen. Tōkichi explained the master carpenter had not given his permission.

Tōkichi said, "I watched him. He seemed strange. I asked him if something happened?"

"Um." Ino fidgeted, but eventually, his expression showed determination. He said, "There's a young woman I want to marry. I'm sorry, Tōkichi, but will you ask for me?"

Tōkichi quieted his breathing and asked again, "Didn't you get engaged not long ago?"

"No, I'm asking for the first time."

"Are you talking about Yono from Umemoto?"

"Of course not."

It took some time for Tōkichi to suppress his rage.

"What are you going to do about Yono from Umemoto?"

"Break it off with her. That nun," said Ino, curling his lips. "Looking at it now, I can't see how I fell in love with that woman. To be honest, even I think I'm odd."

"Hey, listen to me, Ino."

"I know. You're furious. I get it," said Ino impatiently. "I'll never ask you to do this again, but I'm asking knowing that you're angry. This third time's a charm because the young lady this time is not a mistake. She's the one."

Tōkichi stared into Ino's eyes.

"But if that young woman is here, why are you going to Mito?"

"To take a break."

"What do you mean by take a break?"

Ino scratched his head and then said, "I mean let things cool down."

"I screamed and yelled," said Tōkichi, realizing the sake was gone, he turned to Noboru and shook the sake bottle to show him. "I'd like a little more. Is that a problem?"

"It's fine," said Noboru and nodded.

Tōkichi clapped his hands and listened for a response from downstairs. They were probably figuring out the right moment. Soon, the wife came carrying two sake-warming bottles.

"But in the end, the shouter is the loser," said Tōkichi, pouring for himself and taking a swig. "In the end, I can only do what I can do. The story is a mess, but I fell into Ino's trap and started marriage talks again."

The intended this time was an eighteen-year-old named Matsu. She was a maid at Ōmiya, a wholesale business for tabi socks and *momohiki* pants.

5

Ōmiya was located in Fukui-chō outside the Asakusa Gate. Workmen had been coming from Daimasa once a month at the beginning of last winter to remodel the inner parlor. At that time, Ino explained Matsu extended various kindnesses to him. He fell in love but did not think about marrying her. When marriage to Yono of Umemoto was arranged, he remembered Matsu. If he were going to marry, his heart was set on marrying Matsu.

Tōkichi said, "Fortunately, Matsu seemed fond of him and the marriage talks were concluded. This time, I was cautious.

"Then the Mito work ended. He decided on marriage talks after returning home but kept everything a secret and made me agree."

Tōkichi went to Mito to begin the construction for Sagami-ya. He didn't talk about the job because it was not related. However, a retired man has rare fastidiousness. From the beginning, several times he revised the contracted plans, was constantly at the construction site complaining, and made them redo finished work. Tōkichi calmed the angry craftsmen and was exhausted although he could cajole the retired man. In this atmosphere, they made little progress on the job. Despite the frequent rains that year, they framed the house in close to forty days. March came, and cabinet-makers from Edo accompanied the craftsmen. Soon, however, Ino showed up without warning.

"I came because the master carpenter said, 'Go.'"

And like that, he left. There were already too many carpenters on the job. Tōkichi found his coming strange when half of the carpenters were about to return to Edo and pressed him for a reason.

"The truth is, I'm here because I asked," said Ino, looking uncomfortable.

"When I'm not around you, I feel like an old bachelor."

"Ino, be honest. What happened that made you leave Edo?"

"Tōkichi, you're a suspicious guy."

"Don't say that. What is it? Umemoto?"

"Stop kidding. Right after the proposal, they declined."

"Why?"

Tōkichi pressed for an answer, not letting up. Eventually, Ino couldn't hide it any longer and told the truth.

"Tōkichi, will you get mad?" he asked with a meek look in his eyes.

"I don't know," said Tōkichi. "Get mad? Don't get mad? Ask and we'll see."

"I was weak," said Ino in his mouth but grumbling loud enough for Tōkichi to hear. "I sound like I'm trying to put my head on the executioner's block."

Tōkichi was silent. Ino stuttered a confession like he was at a loss.

He said, "In short, Matsu from Ōmiya became horrible. I wanted her to reject the proposal."

Tōkichi closed his eyes for a long time and waited for his anger to subside.

With all his patience, Tōkichi said, "You said the third time's a charm. You were sure this time the bride was the perfect one."

"Don't get so mad. Please hear me out."

Waving his hands, Ino cut in.

"I did think that. Meanwhile, Matsu had time off. I invited her out, and we visited Sensō-ji Temple. On the way home, we ate at an eel restaurant in Komagata.

"We talked and drank sake while waiting for the baked eel to be served. I poured a cup of sake for Matsu. She said she hated sake and drank only three cups.

"Her face flushed. Her body movements and expression became sensuous. That's nice. That much is good. Finally, as Matsu poured a drink for me, she stared askance at me and told me not to cheat.

"She said, 'Do not cheat. I am yours, and you are mine.'

"My whole body trembled."

Tōkichi said, "If you've made your decision, you probably felt like something happened to your spine again."

"Tōkichi, did you feel something?"

"If someone's going to marry, it's no mystery to say something like that."

"You are mine. Yuck."

Ino shrugged his shoulders and shivered. He felt goosebumps erupt on his skin, exactly like someone who hates hairy caterpillars and a joker put a hairy caterpillar down his collar.

Tōkichi said, "It can't be helped. Driving someone away is piti-ful, so you'll stay in Mito.

"I must remind you. This time, you didn't fall in love with the woman. I'm not getting involved in another marriage proposal."

Ino smiled like he was relieved and said, "I'll never bother you again.

"Instead, I'll ask Ōmiya," said Ino, shrewdly imposing on them.

"That may be best," said Tōkichi. He thought if that happened, formal talks would be postponed. The rejection will not be a big problem.

The Sagami construction was extended. The master carpenter at Daimasa came from Edo a second time. Nevertheless, they were able to finish before the rainy season. However, during this time, Ino found another wife. Although he didn't mention it, in the half month since he arrived in Mito, he looked odd.

The craftsmen lodged in a small cabin built on the construction site. However, Sagami-ya gave Tōkichi, as the representative of the master carpenter, a house on the grounds and paid for his meals and other expenses.

"Ino also stayed with me. He said when he wasn't around me he felt like an old bachelor," said Tōkichi, who seemed to have started drinking.

"He's such a fool," Tōkichi said with a smile. "We ate dinner and served sake at Sagami-ya, but Ino never held out a cup for sake. From the beginning, he said he didn't want any. I thought, All right."

During that time, he noticed something odd.

After his bath, Tōkichi sat before his tray. Ino stayed seated and looked at his tray without picking up his cup.

Tōkichi asked, "Is something wrong? You're not drinking?"

Ino answered half-heartedly and kept staring at the tray. "No, I don't want any."

"Is your stomach upset?"

"There's nothing wrong with my stomach. I'm fine. You should drink. I'm fine."

It went on like that for four or five days. Then one day, while going through the same questions and answers, Tōkichi was frightened by a chill rushing down his spine.

This is the same as before, Tōkichi thought. From then on, he tried not to look at Ino.

6

Eventually, Tōkichi's patience ran out. Ino expertly probed Tōkichi's feelings and launched a slow attack. Like a termite eating into the foundation of a home, he ate into Tōkichi's heart.

"Aah," Ino sighed, still gazing at his tray, mumbled quietly to himself but loud enough for Tōkichi to hear.

"It's no good. I can't do that. Because I promised, because I promised as a man, there's no way I'm doing it again."

Ino let out a deep sigh again and lazily stared at the tray. One day, knowing a trap had been set, Tōkichi started the conversation.

"Who is the woman?"

Ino faked a clueless look.

"What?" he asked, sounding perplexed, and looked at Tōkichi.

"Stop playing dumb. Who is she?"

Ino dropped his head and was slow to reply.

"She's a crafty one. I'm not too bright. From the looks of it, I started it all. It's not what she says, not at all."

This twenty-year-old woman worked in a small restaurant in a place called Sentaku-chō. Her name was Sei. Tōkichi often drank at that restaurant and knew her by sight. The marriage was necessarily hard to arrange because the restaurant called Inaba was a simple establishment located in Sentaku-chō that resembled an Edo red-light district.

Tōkichi said, "Try to do it yourself."

"Okay," said a sad-looking Ino and only sighed.

"What's wrong? You can't do it?"

"Yeah, I can't. When I see her face, I can't talk. I can't even call out her name."

"You are going to break off with her," said Tōkichi. "Don't ask me this time. I'm through with all of this."

"I know. It's all right. Don't worry about me."

Then to himself, Ino said, "The third time's a charm."

Tōkichi found fault with his words.

"So the third time's a charm."

"It's nothing?" Ino quietly answered. He knew he had fallen in love with several women until now, but the one he loved the most and truly wanted to make his wife was this third one. Besides, this time he knew she was the real thing.

Tōkichi said, "Hey, think carefully. What about this third time? This time is already the fourth time."

"That's not true. All right? Matsu is two, after Yono."

"What about the first, Kō?"

"What? Kō?" said Ino and shrugged. "I don't include her in the count."

"For Matsu, didn't you say the third time's a charm?"

"That's because I was infatuated. This time is it. The third time's a charm. Really," said Ino with all the power he could muster.

"I will do my best to look the other way," said Tōkichi and gulped down a cup. "In the end, I lost, but there's no contest when it comes to patience. I went to Inaba for the talks."

That was a few days before the building was handed over. Sei agreed and said she wanted to talk to Ino alone.

She loved Ino and wanted to face hardship with a man like Ino-san. She said, "I thought my love was one-sided."

"You poor fellow," said Tōkichi to Ino. "It's like you're cursed in love. Your gullible nature drives people away."

"I'm sorry," said Ino and lowered his head.

"Now, there's the message."

"I'm terribly sorry."

Tōkichi looked at Ino's sad face and could not feel the tiniest bit of cheer. He said, "You go see her and come back."

Ino answered, "We're moving back to Edo in a few days, if you don't hurry, you'll have to leave this."

"Yeah, you're right. That's what I'll do. I'll go and talk to her."

Ino left but was back in half an hour. He said, "I'm leaving for Edo soon, before you plan to leave."

Tōkichi was shocked.

"She said we'll go together to Edo. I'm not joking," said Ino, fidgeting as he spoke. "It's not mating cats, but can I take on this burden just like that? I'm not joking. I'm so sorry."

"Calm down and tell me what's going on."

"I don't have time," Ino answered. "I'll tell you the reason once we're back in Edo. Sei's mad and may show up at any moment. If she comes, please send her away. Anyway, let me leave first."

While speaking, he rushed around packing to leave. He ran out without tying the straps of his straw sandals. Tōkichi was angry but not angry and sat groaning. Ino came back and peeked in from the door. He formed an ingratiating smile like he was about to cry.

Ino said, "Tōkichi, when you return to Edo, beat me up to your satisfaction."

Tōkichi said, "Sei never came. Uninvited visitors never came, but if the craftsmen came to drink, they got so drunk and seemed beaten down.

"That guy wasn't a man from the start. Everyone in Edo is covered in mud and crumbles into small pieces. This situation was like being trampled by mud-covered feet.

"That ends this story."

He picked up the second sake bottle and poured himself a drink as he continued speaking.

"Soon after I got back to Edo, my marriage talks moved forward quickly. At the end of May, I married Chiyo. We moved to our current home in Sakuma-chō."

Noboru asked, "So what happened to Sei in Mito?"

"Nothing," answered Tōkichi. "Ino went to talk to her. They met in a small inner parlor. Sei led him there and happily embraced him without warning. She said, 'You're going back to Edo soon, so let's go together. I will never forgive you if you trick me.'"

Noboru asked, "Did it go bad again?"

Tōkichi said, "It makes no sense.

"When he fell in love and obsessed over wanting a wife, she said, 'Excuse me? What?' Of course, she also talked of love, but her words changed completely and became so terrifying he trembled. He could not understand why she felt that way about him."

7

That night, Noboru told Nīde Kyojō what Tōkichi told him. Noboru thought he might not care, but the story seemed to spark Kyojō's interest. He encouraged Noboru to find out what happened next.

After Tōkichi and his wife moved to Sakuma-chō, Ino returned one time to the master carpenter's home and lived in the row house in Kyūemon-chō for six months. Although he visited Tōkichi's house, it was probably inconvenient being in Horie. Nevertheless, for three days, there wasn't a day when he didn't show up.

The newlywed Chiyo was astonished. After moving to Kyūemon-chō, Ino visited Tōkichi early in the morning, drank a lot of water, and cleaned around the house. Then the men left for work. They reappeared at dusk. Ino didn't go home until Tōkichi said he was going to bed.

Since Tōkichi got married, Ino no longer had problems with women. As usual, he didn't fool around before work or at bars.

Women often tempted him, but he played innocent and ignored them.

"The situation changed after the end of last year. Despite showing up at construction sites, he had no work and spent the day daydreaming and doing nothing. When asked why, he only answered, "Got nothing to do.""

Once in a while, he picked up a chisel or plane and did something stupid like make a hole in a finished pillar for the house framework or shave a thin board until it was paper thin.

"That guy is strange."

Tōkichi noticed and spoke with the master carpenter to make Ino take some time off. Next, the manager of the row house came to complain.

Ino wasn't rowdy, but his odd behavior disturbed the residents of the ordinary row house. The manager asked, "Can anything be done about him?"

Ino was the third son of a fisherman in Shinagawa. His father, older brother, and two younger sisters still lived in the family home. Was his connection with his father and siblings fragile?

Tōkichi said, "He hasn't visited them for some years, but because they are certainly father and son, could we make him go to Shinagawa?"

Chiyo heard that and opposed the idea.

"That is pitiful. For him to go to his father when their relationship is so flimsy, can't you be kinder to him?"

She gave a passionate plea.

"Ino-san depends so much on you and adores you more than his blood relatives. We still don't have children. Isn't it better to take him into our home?"

Around the middle of January, they took him in.

Tōkichi explained, "About six months later, we made him see a doctor and forced him to take various medications. We tried prayers and charms. He didn't get better, but he didn't get much worse.

"He walked around wearing his kimono inside out and closed the sash in the front. He was sound asleep during the day. But at night, he didn't lie down but talked to himself and hummed until I yelled at him."

"Maybe he didn't try to do any work because he was ill."

Kyojō said, "You said he planted plants upside down. You saw that?"

"Yes, they were planted with the roots on top."

Kyojō looked at Noboru and asked, "What do you think? Is the diagnosis an obvious case of insanity?"

"I don't know, but I believe the problems with women piled up and drove him crazy."

"No, it's not the women. It's Tōkichi."

Noboru looked doubtfully at Kyojō.

"Because Ino has a small stature, he is pampered by women. Even after becoming a man, women adored him. I saw this during his examination, but Ino was obsessed with Tōkichi," said Kyojō. "Women loved him. His love for women was pulled toward Tōkichi. Of course, this is not love. A man has feelings of love for another man, but in Ino's case, these feelings were powerful and became complicated."

"If that's so, he's living with Tōkichi now, so shouldn't the symptoms subside?"

"No. It's the opposite. He must be separated from Tōkichi," said Kyojō. "Up to this point, Ino has had various experiences. All of them caused trouble for Tōkichi. Of course, Ino did not think so and probably thought the events were natural. From the bottom of his heart, he was helping Tōkichi by bothering him and being connected to Tōkichi."

Noboru was silent, shut his eyes, hesitated, and then nodded.

"Tomorrow, you will admit Ino here," said Kyojō and faced his desk. He picked up a writing brush as he spoke.

"Speak with Tōkichi. It would be best if he left Ino alone for a short time.

"Aren't the mechanisms of the human brain marvelous and mysterious?"

The next day, Ino was admitted to the clinic.

Noboru relayed Kyojō's diagnosis to Tōkichi and stressed that he was not to visit Ino. Noboru was unsure about the diagnosis. He thought it was too logical somehow and a bit far-fetched. Noboru thought about clues for the diagnosis from his perspective.

Ino was placed alone in a room. The idea of being with another person, especially, a sick or elderly one, repulsed him. He also stressed his problem with women. Kyojō did not object and did as he wished.

For the whole summer, when Noboru found time, he went to Ino's room. While offering tea and sweets, he spoke casually and tried to draw out his story.

One day Ino said, "Nobody has visited me."

Noboru hinted, "Is there someone you want to see?"

Ino frowned and thought hard. Again, Noboru went on the attack.

"Perhaps someone from Sakuma-chō? I could send a messenger if there's someone you wish to see."

"No, forget about it," said Ino, sharply shaking his head. "Tōkichi is probably busy. Even if he came, it wouldn't matter."

Noboru ended that conversation.

The summer was over, but his condition did not change at all. He mostly stayed shut away in his room. Other than going out to the garden in the evening, he lazed away the hours doing nothing.

He no longer displayed his previous eccentric behavior, but little was seen in any recovery from his symptoms.

Noboru asked him, "Why do you hate women? Isn't it strange for a man to hate women?"

Ino answered, "I don't hate them. No, I don't hate women."

"When you were admitted, you said rooms with sick people, elderly people, and women were no good."

Ino thought for a moment and then nodded.

"Oh, I see. That is a bit strange."

"Strange, but those were your words."

"I have my reasons," said Ino. "This isn't the sort of thing you discuss with anybody, but it's probably okay to tell a medical doctor."

"Of course it is," said Noboru.

8

"I was eighteen," said Ino. "The head carpenter lived with his two daughters. The neighborhood girls often came over to play."

Noboru recalled what Tōkichi said. Of course, he didn't reveal he knew and listened, feigning apathy as much as he could.

"One of the friends, Tama, the daughter of the owner of a dye shop called Tamagawa-ya, was going on nine. Both her face and body were round. She was a well-behaved child. Oh, this is awful," said Ino, turning red. "Now it gets hard to talk about."

"I'm a doctor."

"Please, don't think badly of me," said Ino, rubbing the back of his neck. "She became attached to me. That's all right, I guess. I thought she was a cute kid but a couple of awkward things happened. One time she came over, hugged me, and kissed me on the lips. Please, don't get me wrong. There were no lewd feelings. I always thought she was cute. I felt nothing about being hugged out of nowhere. It was unexpected."

"That's not unusual," said Noboru. "Nearly everyone has a memory like that."

"But what came next was horrible," said Ino and continued talking fast, like he was trying to escape the rest. "The moment I kissed her, her tongue shot into my mouth. She was nine years old."

He swiped a hand over his lips and twisted his face like he was about to spit.

"I was eighteen but didn't know about that sort of thing. She was still nine. I thought she was simply a well-behaved, adorable child. But when her small, hot, soft tongue slipped in, I was so shocked I jumped up. Tama pushed herself away and ran off."

While Noboru gently smiled, he said, "That's not so unusual."

"What are you saying? Not unusual."

"I remember a similar incident happened to me."

Ino looked like he had just woken up and stared at Noboru.

"What? Something like that happened to you, too? Sensei, you felt nothing?"

"I might have been a little flustered."

"I wasn't too scared," said Ino. "A nine-year-old knows about this sort of thing. Women are scary, horrible creatures. It was horrifying."

Still smiling, Noboru said, "For a tradesman raised downtown, you were naïve."

"I guess you're right, huh," said Ino, tilting his head. "I really am."

"It looks that way," said Noboru.

Noboru thought this was a clue to his treatment.

One facet of reasoning was also in Kyojō's diagnosis, but that was not all. The Tama incident sunk deeper into his mind with each escape from falling in love with a woman. Noboru believed if that were removed, Ino would be on his way to recovery.

Whether Noboru's diagnosis was correct, fall would be here soon. Noboru made a rare discovery in the garden.

One evening, Ino was outside on a walk. When Noboru happened upon him, he was carrying a handbasket and walking with a woman.

"Oh," said Noboru without thinking and stared at them.

The woman was Sugi. She was probably on her way back from taking dinner to Yumi. The handbasket Ino held was for carrying the meals. Noboru had seen it many times before.

As Ino was saying something to Sugi, they left for Yumi's residence. Noboru went back to his room.

Noburu asked Mori Handayū to keep an eye on Ino because he was often on house calls with Kyojō. Although Handayū had little free time, he did a good job watching Ino and provided a detailed daily account of Ino's actions.

Ino began to change. He rarely shut himself off in his room and went outside. He went out to the medicinal garden, borrowed a saw or plane, fixed nicks in a fence, or hammered in the wood paneling in the dining hall.

Without fail, in the mornings and evenings, he carried Sugi's handbasket. Each time he entered the dining hall, he sharpened the knives, shaved the chopping boards, and sometimes helped by washing vegetables.

None of this was cause for concern.

Noboru thought perhaps Ino would soon be back to normal; naturally, he worried less and less about him.

Late one evening around the middle of September, Noboru returned from the house calls, changed his clothes, and went to the dining hall. When he was about to go in, Ino ran up from behind and called to him.

He whispered, "I have sake. Will you have a drink with me?"

"Sake? Why?"

"I got it from Ki-chan," said a smiling Ino. "Didn't you often make him buy sake for you in the past?"

Noboru looked away.

"But I'm hungry."

"I have sushi, too," said Ino. "Please come. The truth is I want to talk to you."

Noboru went to Ino's room. He hadn't been there in a long time. The room was tidy and swept clean. The cleanliness made him feel good.

In addition to the regular meal on the tray, sushi was packed in a wooden box, and the sake bottle was placed to the side.

Of course, the sake was not warm, but Ino seemed to want to start drinking it cold. The moment he sat, he drank the sake remaining in the teacup and poured for Noboru.

"None for me," said Noboru, waving his hand. "What do you want to talk about?"

"Please, drink a little first," said Ino. "If you're not a little drunk, it'll be a bit hard to say what I want to say."

Noboru quietly asked, "Is this about Sugi?"

"Yup," said Ino and looked at Noboru. "You know?"

"I don't know the details, but I guessed."

"I'm surprised. Okay. In that case, I don't have to be so formal," said Ino and poured sake into a teacup. He held the cup in both hands and looked at Noboru. "First of all, I want to stay here for now. What do you think?"

"That is not up to me."

"I have a purpose. I'll do anything I can. I could work here as a carpenter."

"It seems so," said Noboru. "What else?"

"It's nothing immediate," said Ino, quickly blushing red. He drank the cup of sake in a gulp. "I've said nothing to her yet.

"Would you like some sushi?"

Without thinking, Noboru blurted, "You want to marry Sugi?"

"It's pitiful," said Ino. "I will put up with serving such a crazy mistress not knowing when it will end, even helping with bedpans to keep from losing my family. My heart is gripped by pain only by watching."

Noboru asked, "So you would do it because it's miserable?"

"No way. I'm not joking," said Ino. He got serious and again said, "It's certainly miserable, but I love that woman and want her for my bride. I've seen various women until now, but a woman like Sugi is a first. If I'm with Sugi, I think I'd be fine with a lifetime of any sort of poverty."

Noboru was silent.

"It's true," said Ino, his eyes moistening. He stiffened his body and said, "After seeing Sugi, I thought I had to become reliable. Be dependable. I thought about how easygoing I had been. I could not pass through the world... This is the first time in my life I felt this way. I want to make Sugi happy and I'm sure I will."

"Should you be talking like that?"

"Please, ask Tōkichi. I'm saying this for the first time. If Sugi becomes mine, this feeling will never change."

Maybe so, thought Noboru. He was in love for the first time.

Until now, Tōkichi protected him, and women wooed him.

Noboru was starting to think he was always passive, but this time he felt compassion for Sugi and would make her happy. This would be proof that he could stand on his own as a man.

As he thought this, Noboru reminded himself to be cautious.

"Is the third time a charm?"

Ino doubtfully looked at him again. "What are you talking about, the third time's a charm?"

"Never mind," said Noboru and stood while smiling. "It's nothing. Don't worry. I'll discuss this with Nīde-sensei."

"Please and thank you," said Ino and bowed his head. Elated, he said, "If he refuses and says I can't, I'll run away with Sugi. That's not a threat. It's true. So please, somehow explain this to the sensei."

Noboru nodded with his eyes and went out to the hall.

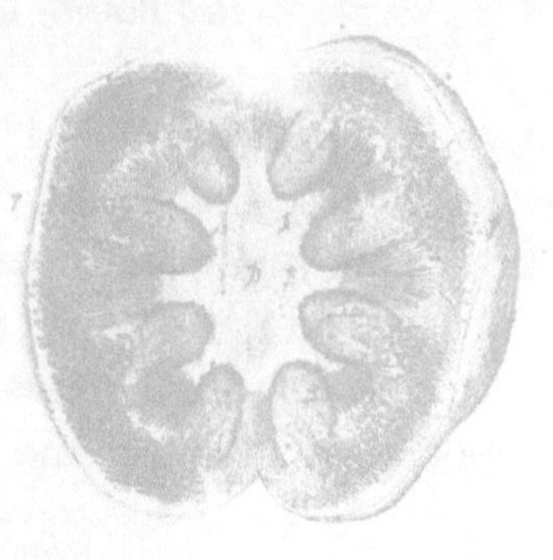

CHAPTER 5
THE HOPELESS GAMBLE

1

"I'm well aware of the patients' grievances," said Nīde Kyojō as he walked. "The clinic rooms have wooden floors. They sleep on bedding spread over rush matting. They wear the same uniform not closed by a belt but tied together by attached strings.

"It's not only the patients. The rooms for the medical staff are identical, and the patients say they feel like they've been sent to jail. The patients are not alone. Most of the medical staff appear to share this view. Yasumoto, what do you think?"

"I don't think anything about that," said Noboru but quickly added, "However, the hygiene is excellent."

"Stop sounding like a sycophant. I despise flatterers."

Noboru said nothing.

"The worst material for us is tatami. Long ago, that sort of material was not used. During the lifetime of the daimyo Mito no Mitsukuni, tatami was not laid throughout the palace. They say the simplicity and sturdiness of the ancient warrior were prized. However, that is not so. The truth is despite that pretense, how they lived was extremely sensible. Until the Genroku era when the tatami we use today came into general use, life was lived on wooden floors for more than two thousand years."

"But there were rooms with tatami floors."

"Those rooms were provided for aristocrats and only used for ceremonies or sleeping. The basic wooden floors did not change," said Kyojō. "If wooden floors weren't sensible, I'm certain tatami-floor rooms, which already existed, would have come into general use much earlier."

The road began to rise. At three in the afternoon in the middle of July, according to the calendar, it was already autumn, but the heat was worse than the height of summer.

No breeze blew that day. The sky was clear; it seemed out of spite. The sunbeams shining from behind pounded on them like a solid weight, a rock-hard body you could touch with your hands.

Noboru and, of course, Takezō carrying the medicine chest on his back were drenched in sweat on the backs and arms of their kimonos. They were busy wiping the sweat pouring down their faces from their foreheads and their collars. However, Kyojō was not sweating.

Noboru noticed this at the start of summer. Kyojō was not fat but had a solid build. The muscles in both arms and broad shoulders swelled. His hands were huge, even his fingers were thick like a farmer's. Only his waist was thin and tight like a young man's. A glance at his eyes gave the impression of an old bull.

Thus, his reaction to heat was exceptional. No matter what road he took at high noon, he walked with ease and never broke a sweat. Unsurprisingly, he never mentioned the heat, but Noboru could not understand why not one bead of sweat formed.

One time Noboru asked, "Sensei, aren't you hot?"

Kyojō promptly answered, "I'm hot."

Wondering why that's all he said, Noboru lost all interest in asking about sweating.

Kyojō continued, "The seasons in this country have high humidity. Tatami collects moisture and dust.

"Try this at any house anywhere. Dry the tatami right after sweeping it clean. There will always be dust. The matting woven from soft rush on a straw bedding absorbs and accumulates moisture and dust.

"Under the best circumstances, of course, people living an affluent life have the tatami replaced and frequently cleaned to lessen the filth to a great degree, but poor people can't do that. You probably know this because you've seen many backstreet row houses.

"In those places, the tatami are laid out and left on the floor for more than ten years. They aren't replaced or cleaned adequately. The core bedding becomes soft with moisture. The guts squeeze out between the worn-out tatami surface. Fleas and lice nest there.

"With each breath, straw dregs and dust are breathed in. The floors are low. The earth beneath the floor is always moist and has no time to dry. If you sleep and wake up in this sort of place, the mystery would be if you never fell ill.

"If the clinic is constructed with wooden floors, moisture from under the floor is prevented. Rush matting can easily be exposed to sunlight and wind.

"This comparison alone makes it clear which is the rational choice."

When they scaled the hill, they were where the path turned right in Hongō, 1-chōme.

As Noboru listened to Kyojō's explanation, rather than whether the theory was correct or not, he focused on his words and believed them to be correct. He admired Kyojō's passion and bravery to act immediately unconcerned with the opposition or dissatisfaction of others.

A man like the sensei is the ideal person for a special facility like this charity clinic. As Noboru pondered this and wiped away sweat with a hand towel, he observed a young man coming toward him.

He was wearing a faded, unlined kimono closed by a sash and straw zōri sandals. One sleeve was turned up. He staggered forward and as he passed, collided with Kyojō. Noboru behind him saw the young man deliberately run into him. Kyojō was surprised and stumbled slightly. The young man screamed.

"Hey, old man. What's wrong with you?"

Kyojō looked at his rival, quickly nodded, and said, "I'm so sorry. Excuse me."

"Excuse me?" said the young man as he rolled up his other sleeve. "You knock into people on this wide road. It's not over because you say, 'Excuse me.'"

Noboru instinctively moved forward, but Kyojō held him back. He politely lowered his head and said, "As you see, I'm an old man and rude because I'm lost in thought. I'm terribly sorry. Please forgive me."

"Dammit," said the young man, looking daggers at him. Kyojō looked up and down and left him no room to pick a fight.

The young man said to the side like he was spitting, "Dammit. This is bad luck. I'm feeling sick. You better watch out."

After walking about half a block, an annoyed Noboru said, "He's a hoodlum, a rotten fellow. I saw him intentionally bump into you."

"He probably wanted to do that," Kyojō simply said. "From time to time, people are inclined to act in such ways. I have some memories ... from my youth."

Noboru was about to say, "I thought I should punch him" but kept his mouth shut and walked with clenched fists.

2

A plot of hard earth in Mikumi-chō, home to the villa of Nikkō Monzeki, was an enclave of small brothels. This stretch of land was a red-light district of terraced row houses.

Two women were assigned to each building. Of course, they looked like brothels. Noboru wondered if they were going to stop somewhere around here. Permission had been given for visits at some time. The management of the district cycled between strictness and lenience. The number of brothels and the number of women varied over time.

About once every ten days, Kyojō went on house calls in this town of brothels. He gave the women compulsory medical examinations and treatments. This began about two years ago. According to

Mori Handayū, in the fall of the year before last, three prostitutes sought help at the charity clinic.

All three were infected with some disease and extremely malnourished, nearly starved to death. Kyojō provided emergency treatment and summoned their employer. However, he said he didn't know the women and never showed up. Therefore, Kyojō asked a town official to accompany him to Mikumi-chō.

"Bad people do not live in this world. People called bad people do not exist in this world," Kyojō seemed to mutter to himself when he returned to the clinic. His tone was not to agree with "bad people do not live," but suggested he was trying to persuade himself there should not be bad people.

Of the three women who sought help, one died; and the other two were treated for six months and nearly recovered to full health. One returned to her family home in Mito, but the other one ran away.

Because no one knew the identities of her parents and siblings, Nīde-sensei sought help from the local boarding houses. However, the woman who fled and where she went remained unknown.

He heard this story from Handayū. The two patients still in the clinic rooms were women Kyojō brought back and admitted for treatment.

Noboru assisted in their treatments but never went to Mikumi-chō on the house calls.

That day, when they turned onto a street in Hongō to Yushima Tenjin Shrine, at last, Noboru had a rough idea where Kyojō was heading.

"Yasumoto."

When they came to a place where they could see the Monzeki villa, while rubbing his leg, Kyojō asked Noboru, "Have you been to a red-light district?"

For a short time, Noboru kept his mouth shut and then said, "Yes, when I was in Nagasaki but only three times."

"As a doctor or a client?"

Noboru wiped his sweat and said, "I was coaxed by school

friends and went to have fun, of course" He gathered strength and added, "I didn't touch the women."

"Oh," said Kyojō.

"I was engaged to a young lady in Edo," said Noboru seriously. He said, "While I was away, she and another man ... no, she broke off the engagement. I believed she would wait for me, so I lost interest in touching other women even after being persuaded to go to the red-light district."

After walking for a while, Kyojō said, "I might have been wrong to ask and withdraw the question. Please forget about it."

Noboru wiped away sweat again.

A low fence of black boards encircled the lot in Mikumi-chō. A fire guardhouse stood beside the gate. Wood stripped off in places on the old, leaning black-board fence.

The oil-treated waterproof shōji door of the fire guardhouse was open. They could only see three men inside. Two were stripped naked to the waist. The other one was naked. They all noticed Kyojō passing by, and one whispered something. All three looked daggers at Kyojō and then at Noboru.

Noboru asked, "This time of year, is the fire watch on duty from noon?"

Kyojō answered, "They're officials. Here, dogs have the role of fire watchmen. Those men are the guards here."

Noboru didn't understand what he meant. Kyojō explained.

"Many of the clients here are servants in samurai families. Some of them are corrupt men who borrow the authority of the samurai and behave badly. At those times, these men go out, set things right, and prevent the women from running away. In other words, the brothels in this district employ them.

"The relationships are complicated and can't be explained in a word. Well, in time, you'll understand.

"I advise you to remember one thing. No matter what they say, never challenge them."

"What would they say?"

Kyojō said, "Maybe nothing. Perhaps they'll never say anything, but I'm telling you this as a warning."

"All right," answered Noboru.

Kyojō visited seventeen brothels and examined eight women. One was a thirteen-year-old girl who was said to be a maid. The madame said, "She's a maid entrusted to me by relatives."

The girl said she was fifteen, but her slight figure with a flat chest, narrow hips, and thin, childish face made her look no older than thirteen.

Kyojō seemed to have already focused on the girl. After he forced her to be examined, he sternly scolded the madame.

"Has this child been with your clients? If I report this, you will go to prison and eat meals of rotten food."

"What are you saying? That's ridiculous."

The madame became desperate and denied it.

"She is my relative. However long I've been in this business, I am not the sort of woman who would give a child entrusted to me by relatives to clients."

"This is syphilis," said Kyojō, pointing to swellings on the corners of the girl's mouth.

"I noticed them earlier. She also has eruptions on her body. She could not have contracted this disease if she hadn't been touched by a client carrying the disease."

"I don't understand," said the madame and looked at the girl. "Toyo-chan, are you hiding something naughty you did from me?"

The girl looked blank and said nothing.

"Toyo-chan, will you answer me?"

"Stop it," said Kyojō to the madame. "Your performance convinces no one. This child should be returned to her parents. Where are they?"

"I'm not sure."

Kyojō said nothing.

The madame said, "They were in Narihira in Honjo until the end of the year before last. Although they worked at the boat green-grocer, I took custody of this child when the family had difficulty making a living with so many children. Where did they go? I still have no idea where they are now."

Kyojō asked Toyo, "Please, be honest. Where is your home?"

"I don't know," said the girl, shaking her head. "My mother—" she started to sit. "It's what my auntie said, I came from Narihira."

"It's no good lying," Kyojō interrupted. "I will use my power to help you. Please, tell the truth.

"Don't worry. Don't hold back. I'll stand by you."

Toyo repeated what the madame said. She insisted she was fifteen. Kyojō insisted if that were the case, he suggested she be admitted to the clinic.

The madame said, "Please do."

She was grateful for being relieved of this burden.

"Please, take her with you," said the madame.

While Toyo broke out in tears, "No, I don't want to," she said, rocking her shoulders.

"I'm okay living here," said Toyo. She shouted, fretful like a child, "I won't go anywhere. I live here and won't go with you."

She seemed to be expressing her true feelings. Not out of fear of the madame, but she truly wanted to stay at this house. This was reflected in the tone of her voice and the expression in her eyes pouring out tears.

"Listen carefully," said Kyojō in an attempt to soothe her. "You have contracted a terrible disease. If you stay here, this disease will deform you or drive you crazy."

"No. No," said Toyo. Still crying, she screamed, "I live in this house. I'm not going with you. No, I'm staying here."

3

The madame calmly smoked tobacco from a metal-tipped *kiseru* pipe. Two women in the adjacent room were too quiet like they were trying not to breathe. They seemed to be listening to Toyo's crying and screaming.

Outside the door, a voice said, "What is this? What's going on?"

Two men stormed into the dirt-floor room.

"What's going on in here?" asked one man. "What happened?"

Both men were young, around twenty-one or -two. Their hair was styled into the popular top knots with the ends turned up. They wore fashionable, light *yukata* kimonos closed by unlined sashes and new geta sandals.

"It's nothing. Please don't make a fuss," said the madame and put down the pipe. "The clinic doctor said this child is ill and should go to the clinic with him for treatment. However, the child is misbehaving and crying. That's all."

"Why is she going with this man she dislikes so much she's crying?" said one young man. "Can't the disease be cured without going to the clinic? We have doctors around here. Right, Tetsu?"

"Yeah," said the raspy voice of the other young man. "The doctors from some random clinic aren't the only doctors. Those clinic doctors can't cure every disease. If they could, nobody in the world would ever die. A disease is a disease. A doctor is a doctor. A dead guy is a dead guy. We don't need some outsider butting in."

"I'm not going. I won't," said Toyo, crying and screaming while writhing in pain. "I don't want to go anywhere. I live here."

"Takezō," said Kyojō. "Bring the medicine chest."

Takezō at the riser stared at the two young men. He looked like he was about to leap up at any moment, and his fists were clenched. However, Kyojō called him, so he pushed the medicine chest toward Noboru.

"Settle down, Toyo-chan," said the first young man. "We're here. Nobody's gonna lay a finger on you. I'll protect you with my life."

"Yeah," said his partner. "Five guys will risk our lives for our turf because we don't live on this turf for nothing."

Kyojō passed medicine to the madame. He meticulously instructed her how to use an ointment in a seashell and an infusion, and showed her how to apply the ointment to Toyo."

Without warning, Toyo stopped crying. The sobbing was over like the crying and screaming until now had been a lie.

Kyojō said, "I've said it clearly, but from now on, do not let any client be with her. I will report you if any client is. Do you understand?"

"All right," she said and didn't pick up the pipe.

"I can't apply this every six hours to the child. She's mature for her age and can do it even while standing in the shadow of a shōji door."

"Do you think that makes it acceptable?"

"Even this child is human. There's no reason to shackle her with metal chains." She turned to the two young men and said, "Everything's fine. Tetsu-san. Kane-san. Good work."

"What a coward that doctor is. He was shaking."

The others could hear their comments as the men left. When about twenty feet away, they burst out laughing.

Noboru noticed Takezō's blushing face. Kyojō was unconcerned and said he'd come back in ten days, and the three left.

They went from Mikumi-chō around to Shitaya and visited the retired granary wholesaler asleep at a Negishi dormitory. The next house calls took them to a merchant in Kanda, Matsudaira Oki in the imperial residence in Kajibashi, and eight other places. They did not take rest breaks along the way in their walking sprints. Kyojō took this time to talk to Noboru.

Kyojō said, "As precious and beautiful as humans are, they are not pure or reliable.

"As vulgar and dirty people are, they are not stupid, evil, and greedy."

The brothel owners make the women work to eat. Something must atone for good and evil because the women feed them. However, the truth is often the opposite. They're only allowed to make money for the sole purpose of making money.

The town doctor, who works under a special contract, doesn't take proper care of their health even when they fall ill. The women will service clients until they collapse and are finally confined to bed. They take worthless medications and eat inadequate meals. The doctor is unconcerned about the cruelty like he's waiting for a quick end.

That example is probably uncommon, but that was the situation of the three women who fled to the clinic. Currently, several establishments in Mikumi-chō are like that.

Kyojō said, "I don't renounce prostitution. As long as people lust, the circumstances for satisfying that lust will naturally emerge.

"If prostitution were a vice, restaurants would also be unnecessary. No, even cooking must be renounced. It should be natural and the opposite of the way people eat because the appetite for food is stimulated unnecessarily by the created flavors.

"Of course, restaurants will prosper. Without a doubt, the existence of prostitution will expand. To satisfy human appetites, many undesirable conditions will multiply. Thus, it is futile to attack, censure, and destroy current vices. Rather, their existence is bravely acknowledged. We must make an effort to improve health by improving those conditions.

"I'm saying this because of my experiences. There may be no way to explain this. I also understand stealing, addiction to prostitutes, betrayal by a mentor, and selling out a friend. I am a man covered by mud and wounds, and well understand the feelings of thieves, whores, and cowards."

He quickly snapped his tongue.

"It's stupid," said Kyojō and stomped his foot. "Why am I worked up? What is going on with me today?"

Noboru was mostly shocked.

Thievery. Betrayal. Selling out a friend.

What on Earth does that mean? Did he have all those experiences? Is he speaking theoretically? In any case, why did he blurt this out?

Noboru wondered but said nothing as he walked beside Kyojō.

4

After finishing a late dinner that night, Noboru was summoned by Kyojō and went to his room. Kyojō picked up a package beside the desk, handed it to Noboru, and apologized.

"I'm sorry it's been so long."

"Since what?" asked Noboru.

"These are the notes and illustrations I borrowed from you."

Noboru nodded. The notes were from his time studying in Nagasaki. They recorded pathologies, autopsies, medical treatments, and prescriptions in various fields. When he became an intern at this clinic, he submitted them when Kyojō asked for them.

Kyojō said, "I copied the important parts.

"These were not for my benefit but useful for the patients. You may object, but please understand."

Perspiration oozed from Noboru's armpits.

The first time he was told to hand over his written notes and illustrations, he stubbornly refused.

"They are mine."

Noboru believed he had devised diagnostic techniques and treatments, particularly for internal medicine, that could bring him fame in the medical world. He even said, "Isn't one man called a renowned doctor in the world for his treatment of cataracts?"

While smirking, Kyojō said, "Today, I said I stole. This was probably one of those thefts."

"You're welcome to them, please," said Noboru and bowed low. "Back then, I lacked good sense. Thinking about it now, I'm ashamed. I have a request. Please don't mention this again."

Rubbing his beard, Kyojō said, "I'm embarrassed about my behavior today, too. I'm despicable when I think about the illogical nonsense I uttered and losing my temper so arrogantly."

Noboru said, "You seemed angry, Sensei. Those two hoodlums spoke abusively at the home of the young woman named Toyo. I got angry as I tried to control myself, but it came out on the way to Shitaya."

"That's a bit different. I sympathized with those two and was never angry at them."

"Sympathized?"

"For the past few years, young yakuza like that are growing in number." Kyojō sighed. "One cause is the shogunate's frugality. It would be best to forbid useless toys and luxuries. Because the administration goes too far, many men have emerged whose business transactions have stagnated, and who have gone bankrupt or have lost their businesses. The number of men with no place to work is high because large land reclamation projects, construction projects, and the construction of river canals were suspended.

"Families with elderly members and inventive men understand how to live. Young men with unsettled feelings easily go astray. A man with a yakuza personality by nature is different. An ordinary man probably wants to live an honest life. They're called yakuza or hoodlums but should not be hated by fortunate men.

"Not only the two men today, when I look at the young men wandering around town, I can't bear the sorrow I feel.

"The owners of brothels are the same. When I see the cold-hearted and cruel treatment of the women, I think I want to grab them and hang them by their heels. At first, I always felt that. Even now, this often torments me. But when I carefully look, they are not merely greedy.

"From the perspective of poverty, I know many examples of women no worse off than women with jobs."

Kyojō held his tongue, and then disapproval colored his tone.

"The people forced out of the world, shunned by the world, hated or despised are often people who are honest, timid, and virtuous but lack intelligence. However, they find themselves cornered, and most will self-destruct or lose their sense of right and wrong and do something awful. Most who become desperate self-destruct, but those who do something outrageous due to a lack of intelligence tend to be the exceptions. Yasumoto, you will probably see much more of that.

"Perhaps crime and corruption can never be eliminated from the world. However, if the majority of them are poor and ignorant, efforts must be put forth to devise ways to conquer, at least, poverty and ignorance.

"That would be futile. I've thought about what I've done to this point. Often it all ends in futility.

"The world is in constant motion. Agriculture, labor, business, and scholarship advance with no breaks. It doesn't care about those who can't keep up.

"However, the people who can't keep up are human beings, too. More than the wealthy, people bitter over poverty and ignorance, like me, feel the possibilities of humans and can think about the future with hope.

"The actions of humans have many facets. Some work looks like taking a break. While an action may look futile, work exhibits the accumulated effects of continuing that action.

"My thoughts and actions so far may have been futile, but I believe in throwing oneself into life."

Kyojō stopped talking and shook his head violently.

"What am I saying? It's stupid."

He rubbed his beard again and said, "Today, things went terribly wrong. Yasumoto, I didn't call you today to have this conversation. There's something else I want to say."

Noboru looked at Kyojō.

"It's about Amano's daughter," said Kyojō, looking askance. "I think you understand."

"Yes," answered Noboru.

"I don't know the details about this situation. Genpaku told me, but I didn't ask about the circumstances. Of course, I've made a general guess," said Kyojō and paused before continuing. "The main point is Amano will give his younger daughter to you, Yasumoto. She is eighteen. Now, what's her name?"

"You're probably talking about Masao."

"You know her."

"I remember her face."

"The older daughter broke off her engagement to you. If you married the younger one, various matters would be resolved. Your parents would probably be overjoyed. If you're interested, you should visit the house in Kōji-machi."

Noboru answered, "I'm concentrating on my studies. I didn't want to think about marriage."

Kyojō looked at Noboru and asked, "Are you worried about the older sister?"

"If I say no, it may be a lie, but now my priority is learning. Because I have rivals, I don't want to think about that now."

"But what if you only promise?"

Noboru's face contorted into sharp features.

"This is a big pain," he said and looked away. "I can't make that kind of promise."

Kyojō stared at Noboru's face but eventually turned back to his desk and quietly coughed. He said, "That's all I have to say."

Noboru bowed, picked up his package of notes, and left.

5

Noboru returned to his room, put the notes in the closet, and went to Mori Handayū's room. Handayū pulled the standing lantern closer to the side of his desk where he was writing in his diary. Every day he wrote notes about the admitted patients. This was one of the clerical tasks assigned to him.

"I'm almost finished," he said. "There's a straw mat over there. Please wait a little longer."

Noboru picked up the round mat beside him and sat.

Noboru visited Handayū because he wanted to learn about Kyojō.

He wondered about the meanings of what he said: "I stole," "I betrayed a teacher," "I sold out a friend," and the details on why a man with skills that earned greetings with bows from daimyos, lords, and wealthy men still did not have a wife and lived uncomfortably at a clinic.

Noboru thought Handayū served here for a long time, was closest to Kyojō, and should know his personal history, but Handayū barely knew anything about what he asked.

"Sensei never talks about himself," said Handayū. "I heard he was a pupil of Baba Kokuri. Also, the great scholar Udagawa Yōan of Kajibashi was a junior student to him."

"Baba-san was a scholar of the West?" Noboru asked abruptly. "So he was a senior student to Udagawa Yōan."

Handayū said, "I didn't hear this directly from him, so I don't know how true it is, but Baba-san was deeply devoted to Nīde-sensei.

"Baba-san intended for him to be his successor, but Sensei hated that, left his tutelage, and went to Nagasaki to study Western medicine."

Noboru was shocked. Once there was a patient who died of

pancreatic cancer. Kyojō spoke about the patient's condition in fluent Dutch. Noboru thought he probably learned that from his notes, but Kyojō had studied in Nagasaki and might have possessed more up-to-date knowledge than his own.

If he were a talented student of language, even being here, he could obtain Dutch medical texts and treat patients. Therefore, Kyojō probably hadn't learned anything from his notes.

Why had he copied the notes and illustrations?

Perhaps, Noboru thought, perhaps he had the humility to learn from any source.

Noboru was moved and cursed his shallowness.

Handayū said, "Why are you asking? Did something happen to the sensei?"

Noboru told him about the day.

Handayū said, "I don't know. The betrayal of a teacher may refer to leaving Baba's tutelage. Maybe it indicates going against the wishes of his teacher. Is there any truth in what he said about stealing and selling out a friend?"

"That's what I thought." Noboru nodded and said, "He sounded serious like he was confessing. However, it may not be as he said."

"Because he's too hard on himself," said Handayū.

A little while later, Noboru rose.

Next, he went to Mikumi-chō. The afternoons had been rainy for the past seven days until yesterday. While making six house calls on the hot and humid day, as if the rainy season had returned, an awful incident happened during the third visit.

At a money-exchange business called Isumiya Tokubei in Shirogane-chō in Nihonbashi, the forty-one-year-old lady of the house was suffering from paralysis and had been receiving treatments for the last six months. Kyojō charged a large medical fee for the case, but Tokubei thought that was unreasonable.

When his wife was examined and her medication prescriptions changed, Tokubei gazed to the side while offering tea, and, with a cynical look on his face, spoke to Kyojō.

"Sensei, excuse me for saying, but you don't appear to participate in matters of life and death."

"It seems so," said Kyojō.

"What do you do?" said Tokubei, playing dumb. "A doctor doesn't know which patient will be cured and which will die, does he?"

"That may be significant."

"Does it mean a country doctor is no different from a famous doctor, and expensive medications and nonprescription medications are the same?" Then he added pointedly, "Of course, a renowned man such as Nīde-sensei is different."

Kyojō answered, "I'm no different. As you said, the truth is no important differences exist between doctors and medications.

"People who listen to the judgment of a famous doctor, pay his high medical fee, and readily buy medicines with unknown effects are more foolish than those who throw good money after bad.

"Is there anything else you wish to ask?"

"That's it. I wouldn't want to upset you."

"No, never," said Kyojō, smiling as he stood. "Getting angry over this sort of thing, the doctor who flatters a wealthy man is not qualified. Your concerns are unnecessary."

Right after they went outside, Kyojō said, "What a miser," and spat. Then they went to the last three house calls, but the mood didn't improve.

Noboru went on with him on previous house calls but had never heard Kyojō say anything like that. Obviously in the homes of merchants, but also those of daimyos and lords, he was usually welcomed with more than adequate greetings.

That was a horrible man.

Noboru recalled Tokubei's sarcastic tone that feigned ignorance and a vulgar look that rose on his face marred by a bad complexion. He felt awful like he wanted to spit, too.

When they went outside after the sixth house call, Kyojō looked at the sky.

"Well now," he mumbled and stood for a moment. While jiggling the medicine chest on his back, Takezō gave a questioning look to Noboru who signaled with his eyes for him to be quiet.

"We're going home early," said Kyojō. He turned and said, "All right, let's go around to Mikumi-chō," and marched off.

He crossed the road in long, powerful strides, as if trying to drive off the ill humor in his body, and closed the distance from Matsushita-chō to the samurai mansions. They climbed a steep hill and continued at a rapid pace without a break to Mikumi-chō. Sweat poured from Takezō burdened by the medicine chest. He turned to Noboru to quietly complain.

"Getting our revenge on that miserly enemy will not be a dull story."

Noboru stopped talking and turned around. Takezō mopped his forehead with the soggy towel and tried to wring it out with both hands. The unbelievable amount of sweat wrung out looked as though the towel had been grabbed out of water.

Noboru gave a strained laugh and said, "Stop," and looked at a man passing in the other direction. He was coming from the brothel district and looked at them queerly as they passed.

The expression in his eyes was tinged with a kind of sharpness. When Noboru turned, the man turned to look at them but quickly spun his head back and hurried around a corner into an alley.

Takezō stuttered, "I know I've seen him before."

6

"When did you see him?"

"Earlier on the streets of Hongō, he bumped into the sensei on purpose and acted like it was his fault."

"Okay, I wasn't aware of that."

"I remembered his face," said Takezō. "Looks like the rotten sneak ran off."

"So it does," said Noboru.

That day, Kyojō called on all seventeen brothels. Although some houses objected, Kyojō refused to listen to what they said, forced his way in, and called to the women. Some were a little uncertain but submitted to the examination without hesitation. If affected by an illness, the proper medication was administered. Depending on the symptoms, the owners were cautioned.

"Give this woman a ten-day break."

"No clients should be with her until after my next visit."

The worst cases were given the order, "Return her to her family."

Mostly for appearances, he heard, "Yes. Yes, I will."

The medical examinations and treatments were free. Their gratitude was natural. However, some resisted.

"This woman works in our house," fired back the madame. "This woman will have too much free time. She hardly sees a customer every three days. If she's off for fifteen days, she'll earn nothing. Will you pay her room and board for fifteen days?"

Kyojō said, "She will be off work for fifteen days. If not, your problems will be far worse than simply not making money."

The madame's face twitched, and she glared at Kyojō as if looks could kill.

In the house where the young woman Toyo lived, they said, "She's not here anymore."

Worried she might be taken to the clinic, early in the morning three days ago, she fled unnoticed by everyone. They didn't look for her because they had no idea where she would go.

Noboru didn't know whether they were telling the truth or lying. Had she been sold?

On the previous call, Toyo called the madame "Mother" but when upset called her "Auntie." The claim that she was taking care of the child of relatives appeared to be a lie. So what she's saying now may not be the truth. He looked at Kyojō. With no further questions, Kyojō listened in silence and eventually stood.

After they left the seventeenth establishment, Noboru could hear Kyojō muttering to himself, "It's all right to be checked over by a doctor."

Dusk fell. Scattered solo or pairs of clients who looked drunk, although early, talked with women in front of brothels and laughed in jocular voices.

When Kyojō and his party were about to enter a gate, two men appeared and stood on the street like they were blocking the way. Both were young. One was stripped to the waist. The other only wore a bellyband of bleached white cotton cloth.

The half-naked man called to Kyojō. He replied sounding strangely humble and amiable. The dreadful look in his eyes said, "In the future, it'd be best for you not to come back to this place."

Kyojō stared back at the young men and calmly asked, "Why can't I come here?"

The young man answered, "This place is deserted now. You were with a town official the first time you came here. That was one time. Anyhow, the clinic is backed by the government, and you're a doctor from there. Of course, when a man, a doctor like you from that place, comes and goes here, the clients get nervous and stop coming."

Kyojō interrupted, "You shouldn't know that. Who told you to say that? Who?"

"This is our turf."

Kyojō pressed him. "Tell me the truth. I've been coming here for more than two years. If I'm interfering with your business, you should tell me. Be honest, who's giving you orders? Who's behind this?"

"You're a strong old geezer," said the young man and turned to his partner. "I think I should tell him or this may not end peacefully."

"He looks okay," said the half-naked man, raised his hand, and shouted. "Hey, guys, get over here."

Noboru turned to see three young men running toward them from behind. Two had argued earlier about Toyo. The other one was the man who brushed past them on their way here. Noboru recognized him as the man Takezō said bumped into Kyojō in Hongō, 1-chōme."

Kyojō said, "Yasumoto ... I'll go in with Takezō. Don't interfere."

"I can't let you, Sensei."

"No, don't." Kyojō cut off Noboru. "I'll be all right. Stay out of it."

Noboru and Takezō stepped aside. Noboru's legs wobbled. He

couldn't swallow. He looked at Takezō. His face was flush, probably from anger, but he didn't seem anxious.

The half-naked man said, "Old man, think about your age and back off. Skip us today. Be stubborn and be crippled for the rest of your life."

Kyojō said, "Do you fellows know this saying? A fellow who fights with a doctor and runs away says this, 'If you're ever treated by that doctor, your life is in danger.'

"You fellows better think carefully. I don't take lives but am liable to break an arm or leg or two."

The naked man seemed to be older. He smirked like he didn't take him seriously and walked closer to Kyojō.

"Hey, old man, are you sure you want to do that?"

"I advise you to stop," said Kyojō. "You may refuse, but you should stop."

The man leaped at Kyojō.

Noboru was shocked and stood dumbfounded with his mouth hanging open. He saw the half-naked man leap. Then six bodies got into a tangle where one couldn't be distinguished from another.

Meanwhile, they could hear the eerie sounds of bones breaking, the sounds of fists pounding flesh, and men shouting and screaming. However, after a brief time of fifteen or sixteen breaths, four of the men lay flat on the ground. Kyojō was pinning one to the ground. The flattened man moaned in pain. While crying, the man grabbed his leg and writhed in agony.

"Tell me," said Kyojō.

The pinned-down man was the half-naked youth who seemed to be the older one. Kyojō used one hand to torture his neck.

"Who's giving you orders? Who? Tell me. If you don't, I'll throttle you."

The man gasped while turning his head from side to side.

"It's Goan-sama."

"Tell me exactly who it is?"

"In Okachi-machi," said the man between gasps. "It's the young Ida-sensei."

7

Ida Goan? What is he talking about? wondered Noboru. Ida Goan is a doctor at the charity clinic. He runs a town practice in Okachimachi with his father Gentan. The two regularly treat patients at the clinic. This guy is making up a stupid excuse, he thought, but Kyojō let it go.

"That's probably true."

"There's someone else," said the man, sitting up. He massaged his neck that seemed to be hurting now. "He's a man called Aramaki from Yushima. Also, a sensei from Tenjinshita has been called here for a while."

"Is he a doctor, too?"

The man nodded and coughed.

"They're both doctors. This was being pushed by Ida-sensei. He, Aramaki-san, and Sekian-san from Tenjinshita make their livings on this turf—"

"I understand. I've heard enough," Kyojō interrupted. "Stand up and get a couple of scraps of lumber lying around here. About this size."

Kyojō showed the width and length with his hands. The man staggered to his feet.

Kyojō examined the four men sprawled on the ground. Two had broken arms. One was unconscious. The other had fractures in his shin bone. All four men had bruises around their eyes and cheekbones; blood flowed from split lips; and lumps covered their bodies.

First, Kyojō revived the unconscious man, told Takezō to open the medicine chest, and promptly treated each man.

Despite the disturbance, all the brothels kept their front doors shut. Not a soul was in the area. They were probably afraid to make a fuss.

Kyojō swiftly finished the treatments. The naked man returned with the lumber scraps. Kyojō had Noboru rip up bleached cotton strips and put splints on the broken arms of the two men.

"I guess I overdid it a bit," Kyojō constantly said to himself as he treated the men. "I should be a bit more restrained. Yes, this one is in bad shape. This sort of violence is horrible. A man who is also a doctor must not act in this way."

Noboru looked at Takezō.

"This isn't the first time," stuttered Takezō in a whisper. "It's a mystery how these guys didn't know. It has happened a few times before."

Noboru shook his head as he sighed.

"All right, come with me," said Kyojō to the naked man and stood. "This is a temporary treatment. Come with me to Ida's office and I'll fix it properly."

"But." The man held back. "After all of this, we're going to see Ida-sensei?"

"If you object, we'll go to the clinic," said Kyojō. "I'm not only going to treat the wound. If you want a job, we can discuss a possibility. You can't be a yakuza forever."

"Huh?" said the man, scratching his head.

Again Kyojō said, "I may be overdoing it a bit. Please forgive me."

Noboru turned and walked away.

"What sorry fellows," said Kyojō to Noboru as they walked down the darkening street at nightfall. "The conspiracy between those doctors and the brothels unfairly squeezes the women. They don't use decent medicines. Their treatments aren't treatments. They deceive the women and wrest high medical fees from them.

"I've known for a while that they did not provide the proper treatments. Squeezing money from those wretched women makes them no less immoral than thieves and murderers. Today, I could no longer suppress that anger. However, this situation is difficult."

"What is?" asked Noboru, nearly sounding like a challenge." Aren't Ida and his son doctors at the clinic? While running a practice as town doctors on the signboard listing them as clinic staff, they go as far as working with those yakuza."

Kyojō raised his hand to stop him.

"Ida is different. Ida and his son will be dealt with eventually. I've been thinking about the other two, Aramaki and Sekian."

"Those two will probably never change in their immorality."

Kyojō spoke like he was exhausted.

"However, they are also human beings. It's tragic. They must recognize that they are human. Perhaps they have families. Even knowing they have no talent as doctors, what alternatives do they have to make a living?

"To make a living and support a wife and children, even knowing it's immoral, they can do nothing other than the work they've learned to do."

"In theory, however, that is unreasonable."

"I don't understand. I don't understand at all," said Kyojō, shaking his head. "Any reasoning is fine with me. He's a man. I'm a man. He must live, too, and I also have the right to live. Simply, what and where is it wrong? Yes, my head seems to have gone completely senile."

Noboru laughed in his throat. Words similar to *completely senile* were flung out earlier by the six thugs (but with a different meaning) and brought back to mind a magnificent figure. He smiled. Kyojō looked at Noboru with doubt.

"No, it's nothing," said Noboru, shaking his head. "Nothing at all."

CHAPTER 6
THE BUSH WARBLER NUT

1

THE STRIP of land commonly called Izu-sama's Backside was sandwiched between the small Zen temple of Kane-ji and the expansive second residence of the daimyo Matsudaira Izu no Kami. This area stretched long distances to the north and south.

The small shops along the main street and the temple with a line of flowers and red barrels were joined by the humble retreats of merchants and the many quiet dwellings of former shops now inhabited by mistresses and clerks.

When Noboru and Kyojō turned down an alley having five offshoots, the eaves of the tenement row houses on one side of the alley rubbed against the eaves on the other. People unaccustomed to the area couldn't carelessly pass through the always-dim, narrow passages with the chaos of children running around.

There were forty-seven buildings, but no one lived in twelve of the most dilapidated ones. Seven or eight empty units were not rented. Twenty-eight or -nine families, totaling one-hundred seventy or eighty people, lived in the alley.

The two men entered a row house to examine a man dubbed The Bush Warbler Nut.

After they made five house calls on this windy day in the middle of September, dusk was falling. Smoke from cooking choked the alley. Of course, Kyojō was well-known in this place. Friendly voices constantly called out greetings brimming with respect on the left and right sides in the cooking smoke fanned by a strong wind. One shout came from the rooftop.

The manager Uhei was supervising and yelling at someone. He shouted, "Yasuke, what are you doing up there? You fool. So now we're calling to the sensei from the roof? Did a packhorse driver teach you manners? Get down here."

"So it's okay for the roof to fly away?"

"What about the roof?"

"The wind, Uhei," shouted back the man on the roof. "Don't get mad, Manager-san. Isn't Uhei your name? I'm real sorry for butting in, Uhei."

"Idiot."

"Come up, everyone, and see," shouted the man from the roof. "This roof has been cracking for about a half hour. It's okay now because I'm holding it down. I won't move because pieces will chip off and fly away."

Kyojō laughed and said, "Yasuke, what do you intend to do until the wind dies down?"

"The only thing I can do," said the man on the roof. "The rent is piling up. I've got nowhere to go if I'm forced out of this row house. Sensei, don't bother worrying about me."

"What an exasperating fellow," said Uhei. "He says all that but doesn't realize he put his foot through the roof."

The man on the roof said something, but only "Uhei" could be heard. Uhei snapped his tongue. While railing about the children playing in the narrow alley and the housewives baking fish under the eaves, he escorted Kyojō and his party to Jūbei's home.

Jūbei was forty-one. He had a wife, Miki, and a seven-year-old daughter, Tome. For a long time, he has worked as a peddler of assorted goods.

Moriguchi-ya is a shop in Bakuro-chō that sells tabi socks, work trousers, and miscellaneous goods. Jūbei used to work at that shop.

However, at the age of twenty-one, shortly before the completion of his free service after his apprenticeship, a woman embezzled a large amount of money from him.

He would never again part the noren curtain and walk in the shop. Close to ten years of service went down the drain. He was driven from the shop.

Through the compassion of the shop proprietor, he was not arrested. For the next five or six years, he hopped from job to job. When he was a delivery man for a soba noodle shop, he met and married Miki. He gathered the courage to set up a home, went to the shop in Bakuro-chō, and explained his situation. The proprietor of Moriguchi-ya understood and lent him goods for sixty days.

Over the next fifteen years, he carried and sold the goods in the city, of course, and beyond the city limits. He persevered at this work for fifteen years for another reason. The first two of the eldest three children died at five and four years old. Miki's condition deteriorated after their births, and she couldn't leave the row house to this day.

However, seven days ago, Jūbei went to a public bath with his daughter Tome and began behaving strangely. He made her undress and went into the shower room with her. Tome slipped and fell. Out of nowhere, Jūbei punched the man washing up beside him. After he hit the man, Jūbei hugged his daughter and said, "Tome," in a calm voice, "the strange man was worried because you fell. Be careful. Watch your step."

His behavior was so odd. The punched man forgot his anger and watched them in shock.

When they returned home from the public bath, he searched for a one-foot-square wooden board, brought a bamboo basket from the kitchen, and placed the wood board on the horizontal lintel above the door in a corner of the room, set the basket on it, and sat down. Miki didn't understand and asked what was he doing.

"Hush," he whispered.

"Quiet now. That's a bush warbler worth 1,000 ryō.

"What's a bush warbler?"

"At last, I caught one. Look. It's singing. That's the chirping of 1,000 ryō."

Jūbei looked up at the lintel in the corner and seemed happy. While listening in ecstasy to the "bush warbler's voice," he whispered to Miki, "Finally, this is our farewell to poverty."

From that time until today, Jūbei did not go out to work. Other than to sleep or eat, he sat staring at the bamboo basket. Once in a while, he woke during the night, listened like he was worried, nodded to himself, seemingly comforted, and sat there until morning.

When Miki asked him to go to work, he looked puzzled. That was no longer necessary. He only repeatedly said, "If I sell this bush warbler, our lives will be a breeze."

The manager Uhei told the doctors this story. At Jūbei's home, Kyojō examined him but found nothing he thought was a disease. He urged Noboru to examine him, too. Noboru made Takezō take out and light the candles for the lantern so he could examine Jūbei's eyes.

"All of you think I'm crazy," said Jūbei. He sounded pitiful. "I'm sorry, but you're wrong. I've never been so cared for by a doctor since the day I was born. This is useless."

"Aah, thief!" cried the children's voices outside. Three or four of them seemed to be jeering.

"Chōji's a thief."

"Beat up that punk Chō."

They could hear the children stomping on and rattling the boards covering the ditches.

"They're at it again," said Uhei at the window and snapping his tongue. "Why are they always bullying Chō? A bunch of hopeless brats."

He went out to the alley.

Noboru finished his examination and gently shook his head at Kyojō. He looked up at the top horizontal lintel of the frame. It was now dark. A sooty lantern dimly lit the interior of the house. Other than the Buddhist altar among the poor furnishings, three large angular packages, probably merchandise, were stacked in the room.

He lazily looked at the board resting on the lintel in a corner of the empty room and the basket set on it.

"Over there," Kyojō asked Jūbei, "What's in that basket?"

"Sh!" Jūbei stopped him. He lowered his voice and said, "Your silly voice is a problem. You asked, 'What's in there?' Can't you see?"

"I can't see anything."

"Oh, your eyesight is bad, so you can't see," said Jūbei. While pointing with the fingers of one hand and scratching his head with the other, he whispered to Kyojō. "Your eyes are bad but you can hear, so please listen to him."

Kyojō kept quiet.

"Those are the chirps of 1,000 ryō," Jūbei whispered to Kyojō. "There should be a buyer soon."

Kyojō stood and whispered to Miki, "I'll be back for a follow-up exam."

He stepped down to the dirt-floor room. Uhei returned and went out to the alley with them. It was already dark outside, and Takezō lit the paper lantern.

"Now, they're making a racket about the thief Chōji."

When they went out to the street, Kyojō asked, "Isn't that Gorō-kichi's child I once examined?"

"Yes," said Uhei. "A nasty woman moves into this row house and you hear uncalled-for comments. Gossiping wives and brats blindly follow that horse's ass and simply bully weaklings."

"Is Gorōkichi's wife healthy?"

"Healthy enough. It's probably because she can't sleep," said Uhei. "Anyway, what's wrong with Jūbei?"

"I can't say," said Kyojō, ducking his head to dodge a cloud of dust. "I'll send Yasumoto from time to time but won't know until I examine him further. There's probably no need to worry about him getting worse."

Kyojō's party started for home.

2

On the way back to the clinic, Kyojō asked Noboru why he examined Jūbei's eyes. Noboru said he learned that technique during his studies of Western medicine in Nagasaki. He explained, "Similar symptoms occur when a mass is growing in someone's head. Shining a light into the eyes produces noticeable irregular tremors of the pupils. I checked for them but saw nothing."

"Well, what do you think the illness is?"

"I have no idea," answered Noboru. "His body is free of abnormalities. I did not find any chronic diseases like syphilis. So I believe he may be unconsciously faking an illness."

"You cannot make the diagnosis that it's his imagination," said Kyojō.

Noboru continued.

"No, it's not imaginary. I believe his illness originated from his living conditions. He has worked for fifteen years and life is still hard. Two of his children died, and he has no clue when life will become easy.

"At the age of forty-one, he constantly makes wishes linked to escaping his current circumstances in life. However, an abnormality developed in his head but went unnoticed by him. I believe hallucinations like the 1,000-ryō bush warbler are manifestations of this."

Kyojō was quiet for a moment then quickly said, "If you have the time, go examine him."

He did not share his opinion of Noboru's diagnosis.

Five or six days later, Noboru mentioned he intended to visit that row house. Kyojō passed him the usual package of money and said, "Please, give this to Uhei."

As before, the day laborer Gorōkichi was beside the same water well of the row house.

He had changed and said, "Everyone is weak, so please go there and examine them."

From that time until the beginning of October, Noboru went five times to the row house at Izu-sama's Backside. Jūbei called The

Bush Warbler Nut by the other row house residents was always sitting before and staring at the basket on the lintel.

During this time, he got to know Gorōkichi's family. His second son Chōji was different from the others. Gorōkichi, his wife Fumi, and the other three children seemed withdrawn, timid, and never opened up to Noboru.

Gorōkichi was thirty-one, a year older than Fumi. The oldest son Torakichi was eight, the older daughter Miyo was six, and the younger daughter Ichi was four. Until Miyo, the children were born one year apart. Chōji was seven.

From the beginning, Chōji liked Noboru. He came running at the sight of Noboru and never left his side until Noboru went home. On his second visit, Chōji brought a basket filled with ginkgo nuts he picked, showed them to Noboru, and told him a secret.

"I'm gonna give them to you the next time you come."

"Why so many?"

"They're from Izu-sama's land," said Chōji. "Izu-sama has a huge ginkgo tree. When the wind blows, the nuts drop outside the wall."

"A whole lot, it seems."

"I'm the best," said Chōji, while digging up the ground beside the kitchen door and burying the least ripe nuts. "They're hard to pick up, and nobody comes close to beating me. I'm going again tomorrow," and added with stress, "I sell them at a good price."

Noboru looked puzzled and gently changed the subject.

"Why are you burying them?"

"In six or seven days, the smelly skin on top rots and peels off. Then I wash and dry the nuts that come out."

A woman passed by and gave a curt bow to Noboru as she gazed at him with a lewd look in her eyes. She was around twenty-eight, fat, and broad-shouldered. Her waist wasn't bound. Her wide shoulders had the same width as her hips.

The thick makeup covering her large, flat face with protruding cheekbones was almost grotesque. A knotted bun of a few reddish-brown hairs glistened from cheap oil.

"You are Yasumoto-sensei," said the woman, whose voice was shockingly deep and hoarse.

"I am Kinu. I live at the end of the row house across the way. Lately, I've had a headache that never stops. Nothing helps. While you're here, could you please come over and examine me?"

Noboru said nothing but nodded and immediately went inside Gorōkichi's home. When he stopped to see the manager after leaving Gorōkichi's, Uhei's wife Tatsu shook her head and said, "That woman is no good."

"She's an appalling she-devil," said Uhei from the side. "She's an old fox who completed years of indentured servitude in Kotsu, the red-light district in Senjū. Because I'm a clueless fool, I rented her a shop. Thanks to her, there has been nothing but trouble since April in the row house that has become impossible to manage."

"She says her name is Kinu."

"Yes, indeed," said Uhei. "She looks like a big drinker. Kinu is dreadful. No incidents have involved knives in that house yet, but I'm scared."

Kinu's situation was complicated.

While she worked in Senjū, she became deeply involved with three clients. She was engaged to marry one of them. Although her indentured service ended, that man didn't have the power to set up a household. She cleverly deceived a client named Tomekichi and got her a space in the row house as his mistress.

Tomekichi ran a tatami shop in Shinken-chō, Ikenohata. He was fifty-two or -three and an unbelievably nice man. She trapped him in this row house.

His business was not doing well. However, he could not resist the woman's selfishness and devised various schemes to earn money and bring in money and goods.

The woman supported another man engaged to marry her. Tomekichi never knew about that man who appeared to be a playboy. He was about five or six years younger than she and seemed ready to move on.

Kinu was too proud of him and spoke fondly of "my man" to the other row house residents. She never mentioned where he lived, his job, or even his name. "My man" usually visited during the day. When she saw him, Kinu instantly became flustered and ran around preparing food and drinks. Even during the dog days of summer while glistening with sweat, she closed the rain shutters. Although being quiet would have been best, she let loose and was rowdy.

The nearby neighbors accustomed to her shamelessness lost their nerve when faced with the horrible popping sounds reminiscent of a soft boil breaking, howling, and crying. The innocent children often fretted and asked, "Is he killing the lady?"

After it was all over, Kinu looked refreshed and dispersed the group of wives by saying, "I'm so mad at my man and going through a rough time," or "Could you hear me crying?"

That wasn't all. She flirted with the men in the row house. It didn't matter if they were young or old, whether she liked or hated them, if a chance came, she seduced and probably tricked the weak ones. She was also a vicious gossip around the row house. Her gossip was malicious.

"Who is that wife sleeping with?"

"Who is eating that smelly meal?"

Most often, she targeted the poorest or weakest families in the row house and said, "So-and-so is a thief."

"These days, she bad-mouths Gorōkichi's family," said Uhei with a sigh. "Despite the men coming and going, right now, I don't feel right making a fuss. I'm a wimp."

Noboru asked, "Why don't you drive her out?"

Hearing that, his wife moved away. Uhei turned around but didn't look like he was going to say anything.

"She's not a woman you can push around."

Like he was throwing up, Uhei said, "If I could, I would."

Noboru recalled the woman. Kinu had a sturdy physique, like a millstone; a bun of short red hair shiny from oil; a flat face with bony cheekbones painted white; and lascivious eyes. He felt a chill race down his spine.

She is that sort of woman.

As Noboru listened to the harsh story and was overwhelmed by hatred, he thought this to soothe himself.

Any row house anywhere has one or two people with strange brains like Jūbei's and loose, shameless women who start trouble with neighbors like Kinu.

"That's not her crime" sounds like something Kyojō would say.

He didn't know her age, but while indentured as a prostitute, she probably experienced unimaginable acts.

Her innate personality turned Kinu into the worst sort of bad woman in a life of affluence or selfishness.

"The crime is not Kinu's alone. An unnatural environment of poverty and ignorance creates that personality."

Noboru felt as if he heard these words Kyojō might have said and smiled a weak, bitter smile.

One day near the end of October, Noboru obtained Kyojō's permission to visit his parents in Sanban-chō, Kōji-machi. Around ten days earlier, he was notified that his mother was having trouble with her leg and sleeping.

His mother Yae was forty-six. She had suffered chronic gout in her right leg since she was around thirty. The change of seasons brought on pain. She had been sleeping a lot for the last half a month to a month.

For about a year after joining the clinic when he returned home from Nagasaki last year, Noboru stubbornly refused to go home and was reluctant to visit Sanban-chō. However, he had no reason to hold back and was resolved to talk to Amano.

He arrived home at noon. His father Ryōan had gone out of the sick house and an unfamiliar student met him at the entryway.

"Your mother is asleep."

Noboru went to her bedroom. A young woman at her bedside was reading to her. Noboru realized who she was. Amano Masao. He was surprised to see her. Masao probably did not expect to see him either and stared at his face with widened eyes.

She opened her mouth and released a lone "Oh." She put down the picture book, turned red, and ran out.

3

Nearly an hour later, Noboru left his Sanban-chō home without waiting for his father to return.

His mother suffered from gout, a chronic disease. The gout had only been in the kneecap of her right leg, but now the pain spread from her thigh to her waist. Moving around had become difficult.

Hearing this, Amano suggested Masao go to Noboru and urge him to see his mother's condition for himself.

When Masao visited the charity clinic, Noboru did not see her but only recalled her younger days. Her physique and facial features were nothing like those of her older sister Chigusa. She was thin and petite but looked healthy. She moved nimbly like a young doe. Her face was charming despite a slightly protruding chin. The expressions on her face never stopped appearing and disappearing and responded sensitively, like the surface of a clear mountain stream.

The sisters were so different.

The beauty of Chigusa's face was striking. Her manner was gentle and graceful. He was reminded of a flower rich in color and fragrance. She was quite different. Mysteriously, Noboru liked Masao much more than Chigusa now. His strong attraction to her surprised and seemed to embarrass him.

When his mother obliquely touched on marriage, after a brief pause, he gave a curt reply and immediately returned to talking about the clinic.

"At last, your situation is stable," said his mother when he left. Noboru spoke with enthusiasm and realized he was no longer angry about joining the clinic. Reassured, his mother weakly smiled and said, "Given what happened while you were away studying, I worried about your temper. I thought you'd be angry because Nide-sensei discussed this with me."

"That's already over."

A smiling Noboru said, "Instead, my joining the clinic was fortunate."

He advised her to keep the parts afflicted with gout warm and to watch her diet to regulate her urination, in particular, and her bowel movements. Then Noboru announced he was leaving.

Masao saw him off at the entryway. He said, "Please take care of Mother."

"Of course. Please visit again," she said and stared into his eyes.

Noboru went outside and felt embraced by happiness as he walked. When he placed both hands on the entryway and looked up, Masao saw his eyes twinkle a few times. She sensed her face blossom with new vitality, like some exotic flower wiped of dew.

"Those eyes," he mumbled as he walked. "Such thoughtfulness, wisdom, and sensitivity appear in her eyes."

What does Chigusa think? He thought and shook his head with resolve. His impressions of Chigusa had faded. He had no lingering affection for her left in him now and, of course, felt disgust.

"I've probably matured," said Noboru to himself. "Yes, what I experienced at the clinic has helped me to grow up. Yes, this is better for me."

He thought about having seen all sides of human life in every sense. Especially from the perspectives of unhappiness, poverty, and the pain of illness, my eyes saw the naked figure of a human being revealed. From these experiences, I gained the judgment to see the difference between Chigusa and Masao.

"But I'm not upset." Noboru paused and then spoke mimicking Kyojō. "Now, I have seen Masao. I am not quick to anger. That would be disgraceful."

These thoughts made him blush. To revive his spirit, he decided to put his remaining time to good use. It was a little before two in the afternoon. Noboru did not return to the clinic but went to Izu-sama's Backside.

He thought about first checking on Jūhei's condition. He passed in front of the manager's house and Uhei came flying out while calling to him.

Uhei said, "I was about to send a message to the clinic. It's awful. Please come. There's been a murder-suicide of a whole family. Kōan-san tended to them moments ago. Oh, it's horrible. It's not Jūhei. He's staring at the bush warbler. They're at Gorōkichi's home."

"How was it done? With a knife?"

"Poison," said Uhei in a hoarse voice while running into the alley. "According to Kōan-san, they probably used rat poison. The vomit stinks of it. The whole house smells horrible."

4

Gorōkichi's family drank rat poison. The rat traps of Iwami and other silver mines seemed to have helped the married couple. The youngest child Ichi was dead. Noboru went to check on the other three children. They were in grave condition. The room was filled with the stench of sulfur and the acidification of matter. The desire to vomit swept over him.

"I'm sorry."

Chōji recognized Noboru right away. His gravelly voice spoke intermittently.

"I'm sorry, Sensei, please forgive me."

"What did you do wrong?" Noboru smiled and said, "You wouldn't do anything bad?"

Chōji's throat choked up. "The ginkgo nuts," he said meekly. His voice barely came out. Noboru leaned in closer to hear the boy.

Chōji explained, "I promised to give you ginkgo nuts. I lied."

He said, "I didn't forget. Mama bought barley meal but there wasn't enough, so I sold all the nuts."

"Chō, stop," said Noboru, shaking his head. As forcefully as he could, Noboru said, "I don't like ginkgo nuts. I forgot all about them. Worrying about something like that is not manly."

Chōji said, "I'll give them to you the next time. If not this year, then next year. Pinky promise."

"All right, pinky promise."

The two hooked the pinkies of their right hands and shook. Chōji's finger was hot like fire, but Noboru felt its weakness.

It'll be next year, Noboru declared in his heart. Chō, you must live and never give up. Dying over something like this is no good."

Noboru wrote the name of the prescribed medication and had the messenger take it to the clinic. He explained the situation to the messenger and gave him this message: "I may spend the night here."

Around four in the afternoon, the six-year-old Miyo died. After dusk, the oldest son Torakichi died. Right after his death, Noboru was careful to keep this from the others and moved the bodies to the manager's home.

The only child left was Chōji. Gorōkichi and his wife Fumi seemed to know this, so he said nothing to them.

Noboru prepared the medications delivered from the clinic and made Chōji drink them in an infusion. Chōji couldn't drink it. His parents quietly refused it.

Noboru said, "Do you understand how worried everyone is?" With all his heart, he yelled at them, "After causing all this trouble, shouldn't you keep everyone from worrying even more?"

Eventually, Gorōkichi and Fumi drank the offered medication.

Soon after dusk, a doctor named Yahara Kōan visited the patients. He was a plump man, around forty. Indifferent to the presence of Noboru, he briefly examined Chōji and his parents and then went home with a somber look on his face.

A little later, the manager Uhei came and said to Noboru, "Please come, dinner is ready."

Noboru was hungry. After he invited the neighborhood wives who came to help, they all went to Uhei's home. The meal was fish simmered in soy sauce on boiled barley, miso soup, and pickles. While they ate with Uhei, they discussed what happened that day.

Around seven in the morning, Gorōkichi announced, "We're going to visit Sensō-ji Temple." He gathered his wife and children and went out, shutting the door behind them. That was not out of the ordinary. Even if it were a little strange, the neighbors didn't notice.

It was not normal for him to gather his family and go to Asakusa. Uhei said, "He lied when he said they were going to Asakusa and came right back.

"None of the neighbors on both sides saw them return and go back inside their house. I was busy at the well, and few people were inside. It would have been easy if they wanted to go back inside unnoticed."

After noon, Kei, a neighbor's wife, heard strange groans and noisy tantrums of children coming from Gorōkichi's home. Then a big commotion broke out.

"But why?" asked Noboru, while putting down his chopsticks. "Did you soon realize something was happening in that house?"

"I don't know," Uhei simply answered. "People who live like this are weighed down by a mountain of reasons why they want to die. It's awful. Even some insignificant trigger leads many people to want to die right away."

Noboru thanked him for dinner and stood but remembered something.

"Did that Doctor Kōan come?"

"He came," said a frowning Uhei. "He asked who was going to pay his medical fee. He certainly came but said nothing about the sick people. He always asked about who would pay him. I called him because it was an emergency.

"The prescriptions are awful. He's a doctor who's good at making decisions only about counting his money."

"That's not true. The treatment was good," said Noboru. "Treatment that swift is amazing. To say it was awful is a mistake."

Noboru went outside. The skies were cloudy, and a chilly wind blew. The doors to most of the row houses were shut. The light leaking out was sparse. He was startled by the echoes of loud squeaks as people walked over the boards covering the ditches.

Just before he reached Gorōkichi's house, Noboru stood still shivering. Coming from somewhere before him, he heard eerie muffled voices he couldn't believe were real. The gloomy echoes sounded like someone calling from underground.

"What's wrong?" asked a voice from behind him.

Noboru was on edge. Before realizing it was Uhei, he nearly jumped, and goosebumps spread over his entire body.

"Oh, that."

Uhei noticed the voices coming to them. He smiled and said,

"You probably don't know what's going on. Let's go see. It's a group of wives from the row house."

Uhei walked out first, followed by Noboru. Six or seven women carrying paper lanterns were beside the well. Two women at a time took turns calling into the well.

"Hey, Chō. Chōji-saaan!"

They drew out each word.

"Heeey, Chōōō!"

Their voices were different than usual, they were sad, mournful, and pleading. Their echoes filled the well. The eerie sight could chill your spine.

"They keep on calling back Chōji," whispered Uhei. "The well continues to the bottom of the ground. It's said if a dead person is called like that, he will return to life."

Not one star was visible in the sky. The wind blew through the narrow alley. Although it wasn't strong, the wind was cold enough to penetrate as a sign winter was coming.

For a short time, Noboru was quiet and listened to the calls of the grieving voices of the women echoing inside the well.

He thought Kyojō would come when asked in the message, but he never appeared. Noboru stayed at Gorōkichi's house until around eleven. When told he should nap, he returned to the manager's house and was given a bedroom.

He thought he'd have trouble falling asleep in a strange bed, but his mind drew the figure of Masao. He wondered if he should agree to marriage talks if given the opportunity. Feeling happy, his entire body was enveloped by warmth. In time, he dozed off.

At three in the morning, Noboru was awakened by someone calling.

Uhei said, "Sensei, I'm sorry to bother you, but please get up. Chōji is demanding to see you."

Noboru sat up. "Has his condition changed?"

"I don't know. I didn't ask, but he said he wanted to see the sensei. You don't seem to understand."

"What time is it?"

"Eight-thirty," said Uhei, adjusting the collar of his nightclothes.

"Yahei's wife is here to see him. Are you coming?"

"Okay, I'll get dressed," said Noboru and stood.

The wife of a temple stall tradesman called Yahei was waiting. Her name was Kei. She was around forty-two or -three and a neighbor and friend of Gorōkichi's family. Kei discovered them and has been providing constant care since then.

She's strong-minded and willful. While quickly instructing several wives, she cared for Gorōkichi, his wife, and Chōji after the children's bodies were removed and carefully threw out everything including hot water and tea.

However, Noboru was at a loss when faced with the women's outspoken nature. He heard abusive language he had never heard before.

"Dammit, what's with his posture?"

When he got closer to the side of Gorōkichi's bed, Kei shouted like a man to one of the wives facing her on the other side.

"That position can't be comfortable. Raise his ass more, the ass ..."

That time, Noboru felt his cheeks redden. As lantern light illuminated their footsteps, Kei guided Noboru, but she was quiet and dejected.

She asked, "Sensei, can that child be saved? Can you save Chō?"

He said, "If he makes it to morning, I think he'll be all right."

"Good," said Kei with a deep sigh. "Your few words are a relief. Fumi-san doesn't say much. What was she thinking?"

5

Kei stopped. As she pressed her apron against her face, she made a bitter appeal to Noboru.

"Fumi-san and I have come to be like sisters. Sensei, I'm helping not because I want to brag but because this is my daily life, too. We've confided in each other and talked over every detail. We would share a plate of salt and a spoon of soy sauce."

Kei stifled her crying and was quiet for a moment.

"We were closer than sisters, but why couldn't we talk about an important matter like life and death? If she had reason to die and take the children, wouldn't it have been better if she had said something to me?"

Noboru said nothing. He carefully observed these people and had these thoughts.

Poor people rely on each other. The government, of course, and wealthy people in the world do nothing for them. Poor people feel they can only rely on poor people, fellow residents in the row house, and neighbors.

On the other hand, strong people differ from weak people. Differences exist between envy and jealousy and between showing off and arrogance. Also, they have little control in a life that always grinds you down. They were often exposed.

Even among friends who always easily lent a spoonful of salt, on rare occasions for an extremely trivial reason, a friend could hate the other like a bitter enemy, for example, spit at her, speak an indifferent morning greeting, or act stuck-up.

People who do not live in poverty may not understand the mutual warm feelings and willingness of the poor to sacrifice themselves to help another. There is no difference between the inability of people with a good life to understand and, at the same time, the inability to understand the naïve and open display of their vanity and arrogance, and pride and hatred.

Although they borrowed spoonfuls of salt from each other and were closer than sisters, she never talked about a reason for the need to die.

Noboru wondered whether her holding back from a companion beyond what was necessary happened because of great poverty or pigheaded and unreasonable self-importance. Gorōkichi and his wife had a reason for saying nothing to others. Kei blamed no one and was certain no one was to blame.

"Hey, Sensei," said Kei as they walked. "I have a favor to ask. Please save Chōji. All three dying would be awful, but at least, save the boy Chōji."

"I'll try," answered Noboru. "I'll do my best."

At Gorōkichi's home, two neighborhood wives who joined Kei

kept vigil all night. Chōji's eyes were wide open. Short, quick breaths came from his open mouth. He was sleeping on his back and, from time to time, turned his head to the left or right, and weakly groaned.

Noboru sat at his bedside.

"Chōji ..."

He asked for the lantern to be brought closer and examined Chōji's face.

"It's me. What happened?"

In a soft, hoarse voice, Chōji said, "Sensei, I was a thief. I wanted to tell you that."

"You can tell me later."

"No, I have to tell you now. Right now. That's why you had to come." He sounded serious. "Sensei, did you hear about Shimaya-san's back fence?"

"I'm listening, Chōji."

"I ripped boards out of Shimaya-san's back fence and brought them home. I was bad. I was a thief. Papa and Mama got mad. She said, 'I've had enough' and 'Our child is a thief.' If you're called a thief in the neighborhood, it's over, and we all have to die. Water, please."

Noboru looked at the women. Kei was about to pick up a teacup when Noboru said, "Bring me a clean bleached cotton cloth."

Chōji's throat was inflamed from throwing up the poison. Noboru thought he didn't have the strength to drink. Kei washed a hand towel, soaked one end in water, and brought it to him.

Noboru took one end, twisted it tighter, and put it in Chōji's mouth.

"Suck on this," said Noboru. "Gently suck in the water with your tongue. Gently, yes, gently."

However, Chōji choked violently and vomited a foul-smelling substance with the small amount of water he had taken in. His exhausted body twisted.

"It's because I'm bad, Sensei," said Chōji, a little depressed. "Forgive me, Mama and Papa. Forgive me, Sensei. Okay?"

"Okay," said Noboru and grasped Chōji's hand. "I understand, so now you can sleep a little. Talking is too hard on you."

"I want water," said Chōji. "But it's no good. Later, right?"

"Soon. Soon, you'll be able to drink."

Chōji closed his eyes, but his eyelids didn't meet. The white parts of his eyes were visible. Purple blotches appeared on the sides of his nostrils. His breathing had quickened and was choppy.

"Sensei," said Kei and then whispered like she was startled, "Isn't that how someone breathes when he's about to die? I know that breathing, Sensei. These may be his last breaths. Please do something, Sensei. Can't you do something?"

"Please, let him die like this," said Fumi from across the room.

Everyone seemed to jump up and turn. Gorōkichi and Fumi had not said a word until now. They had been lying on their sides, barely moving. However, she called out despite her voice being dry, hoarse, and not sounding human.

When they turned, Fumi was lying face up, her eyes shut.

Fumi said, "I knew that child was stealing." She spoke sluggishly and slowly.

"Even if Kinu-san never said a thing, I knew. I had no choice. Chō's not a bad boy. What else could we do?"

Kei said, "Kinu!" and got closer. "What did that woman say?"

Fumi said, "Let the child die. Please, let him quietly die like this. That would be best for the boy."

"Fumi-san," said Kei. She peeked in and carefully asked, "Tell me plainly. What did that bitch say about Chōji? What did she say, Fumi-san?"

Fumi frowned.

"Shimaya-san summoned my husband. Kinu-san was at the store and said she saw what Chō was doing and was a witness."

"That slut!"

"Forget about it. I was wrong. Don't blame Kinu-san."

"Dammit," said Kei, sat up, and stared into space. "That damn bitch acted fancy but always looked like an excited bitch in heat."

"For crying out loud, Kei-san," said Fumi, like she was pleading. "I'm sorry for causing trouble for you, but please leave me alone. Please let Chō die."

Chōji died at dawn.

Gorōkichi and Fumi were asleep.

The women's faces and eyes told the story. Kei embraced Chōji's corpse and carried him to the manager's house. The bodies of the four dead siblings were washed for burial. After they were dressed in burial clothes, they were moved to the empty shop next to Uhei's home.

Noboru learned about this later. When Chōji was carried out, he softy said in his heart, The brothers and sisters are together. Hold hands and take care of each other.

The stained shōji sliding door at the entrance was faintly brighter. The temperature dropped. The cold chilled the kneecaps and toes of the seated Noboru. He extinguished the lantern light and lit the coal in the brazier.

Fumi said, "Sensei, ... Did the child suffer?"

"No," said Noboru and pulled his hand away from the brazier. "No, he did not suffer. He peacefully took his last breath."

"It wasn't painful?"

"He was no longer suffering when he died. His brain died from the actions of the poison. It might have looked painful to others, but he no longer felt anything. Chōji showed no signs of anguish."

Fumi looked at her husband for a short time and then lay down on her back again. She timidly said, "I'm sorry, but may I please have some water?"

Noboru picked up the earthenware teapot for infusions but changed his mind. The kettle was cold. He poured a little water into a small empty teapot and took it over to her.

"Drink carefully. Sip the water," Noboru warned. "It's better to drink directly from the mouth of the teapot. If you're not careful, it will sting."

Fumi grimaced but didn't gag.

The breathing of the sleeping Gorōkichi became lighter. More than being exhausted, his sleeping breaths were those of a man whose mind and flesh were set free and was comfortably and peacefully asleep. Fumi looked kindly at him, staring at the sleeping face of her long-time husband.

"This is the first time he has slept like this," she whispered in a hoarse voice. "Although we've been together for ten years, this is the first time I've seen him sleep so peacefully."

6

After a short time, Fumi said, "Why didn't we die, too?"

"Why, Sensei?" she asked.

Staring at the ceiling, she said, "After thinking a long time, we could do nothing else. The parents and children were going to die together. We had no options. Why didn't they leave us alone?"

"This ..." said Noboru and then paused, "Dying this way is no good. It's a crime to throw away the life you waited to be born into, especially, if you take along small children. Naturally, everyone couldn't stand by and watch them die."

Fumi shut her mouth. She didn't move and said nothing for a long time. The condition of her throat made her cough lightly. She spoke in short bursts and softly like she was talking to herself.

Gorōkichi was born in Fukagawa and Fumi in Itabashi. Both came from poor families. From the time Gorōkichi was seven and Fumi was five, they were experienced in watching younger children.

Their parents had similar upbringings. Gorōkichi's father was a hefty fishmonger. Fumi's father changed jobs and worked as a junkman, day laborer, and a helper.

From the age of twelve, Gorōkichi was a live-in apprentice for a medicine wholesaler. At seventeen, a load was dropped at a warehouse, broke apart, and struck him hard in the head.

For some time, nothing happened. About six months later, he suffered an unexpected seizure. He lost consciousness and could no longer make decisions.

When putting away a box of medications, he stood in front of the shelves but had no idea what to do, why he was there, or what he was supposed to be doing.

One time, he was pulling a cart to receive goods and had a seizure. He pulled the cart and wandered the city for two days without drinking or eating.

Fumi was a live-in apprentice at a modest restaurant in Namiki-chō in Asakusa when she met Gorōkichi. He had been given time off from the medicine wholesaler and was working as a stevedore in Kuramae. Gorōkichi was twenty-one, and Fumi was twenty.

Soon after they met, they ran away from Edo and went to Mito. Fumi had been sold to the red-light district. She told him, and he said, "We'll run away."

"I agreed," said Fumi.

"During the three years we were in Mito, Torakichi and Chōji were born," said Fumi. "My husband had a weak spirit and was sickly. We couldn't make a living in that strange place and finally returned to Edo."

Fumi smiled as she remembered.

"Before leaving Mito, we took the children to visit the shrine for Ōarai-sama. We brought bento lunches. For half a day, as a family, we spent a lazy day looking at the sea. Before and after that day, I never had such a relaxed fun time. From the day I was born until today, that enjoyable time happened only once."

Nothing good happened after they returned to Edo. For the last three years, Gorōkichi had no seizures but gradually lost interest in everything. From the beginning, he was not sensible and couldn't stick with a job. Whatever he did was not for long.

Meanwhile, the number of mouths to feed grew with the births of Miyo and Ichi. Even if Fumi was kept busy with piecework, they couldn't get enough clothes or food.

Torakichi was a dreamy child and not much help. The girl was still small. Of the children, only Chōji was smart. From the age of three or four, he racked his brains to protect his mother.

Fumi said, "It was truly from three or four years old. Sensei, you probably wouldn't understand.

"There wasn't enough to eat for dinner. I always ate after everyone else was done. When he thought there wasn't enough food, Chōji didn't eat, too. He'd say he wasn't hungry or his stomach hurt and be watchful. He'd leave food so I could have a little to eat."

"Three or four years old," Fumi said again. Then she vaguely said, "He was a cute little guy."

We barely made a living. When Gorōkichi earned nothing for three days in a row, they sipped thin porridge. Even in the winter, they always bought coal dust and had trouble getting firewood for cooking.

Chōji was aware of this and picked up and brought home anything that could be used as firewood. He'd bring home wood chips, wood scraps, dried branches, rice sacks, and straw mats. Often, they looked like wooden boards swiped from construction sites and cut tree branches. However, on days when Fumi had trouble getting wood, she could not bring herself to scold him or say, "You can't do this."

Then the Shimaya incident occurred. Shimaya was a general store on the main street. Once in a while, Gorōkichi was asked to help and earned several *sen* coins.

Jobs like spring cleaning or washing grime off the wood panels of houses only added up to several times a year but were greatly anticipated earnings.

Shimaya had a cottage on the shop grounds. It was surrounded by a small garden enclosed by a wooden fence. A tree grew old and sagged where crosspieces ran sideways in the lower half of the fence. The rusty nails were loose.

Chōji removed and brought home the crosspiece boards. The boards were a little over two inches wide and four to six inches long. They weighed about the same as a small bundle of firewood.

The next day, Gorōkichi was called to Shimaya. Thinking it was a job, he went. There was no job. Kinu was in the store. Chōji was holding wood detached from the fence.

"I saw him do it," she said. "That child has been a little thief for some time."

The proprietor of Shimaya said nothing severe but cautioned him to be prudent in the future.

When Gorōkichi returned from Shimaya, he didn't go out to find work but sat idly. Finally, using his arm as a pillow, he fell asleep.

"That happened five days ago. It's already day six."

Fumi's face showed concern.

"After the children went to bed that evening, he talked about what happened for the first time."

Gorōkichi cried as he talked. Fumi had lost hope.

The neighborhood children had called Chōji a thief many times. But it was different this time. Kinu was a witness who saw him do it. He brought home the boards ripped off a fence. For some time, people openly said he was a compulsive, born thief.

In a cold, lifeless tone, Fumi said, "That night and the next day, we talked about many things. We made the decision and talked to and asked the children. They told us that way was good."

Fumi spoke in a hollow, almost indifferent tone.

"Please don't misunderstand, but we didn't resent what Kinu-san said and didn't want to die. But we knew there was no point in living and understood that living only brings hardships.

"From our parents' generation, life is so poor there's no time to breathe. We can't read or write or raise children properly. Were we raising the children or teaching Chōji to steal?

"From our parents to us as a married couple, the children will suffer the same burdens if we go on like this. There are too many, already too many more than this."

Her voice weakly trailed off.

Sounding uncertain, Fumi said, "The children kindly died for us. My husband and I can die anywhere at any time and not be a nuisance. So the children died for us. We were relieved from our hearts.

"I may be terrible for saying this, but why wasn't everyone happy for us? If they let us go, the parents and children would have died together. Why did they try to save us? Why, Sensei?"

Noboru barely had an answer. "Anyone, if he's a human being, had to try."

Fumi laughed. Noboru felt like she laughed. He probably misheard. The sound might have been her breaths scratching her throat. To Noboru, however, he thought she was laughing.

Fumi said, "Seeing the anguish of living, wouldn't dying be a release?"

She swung the cover over the pillow.

"Now that we were saved, what should we do? Will we suffer less? Should I have even that little bit of hope?"

Noboru was silent and lowered his head. In his heart, he wondered, Can anyone answer this question?

She is not the only person with this question. All people, like her family, are exhausted from always being chased by senseless poverty. Are there answers that do not deceive? Is there a way to give them lives that are a little more humane?

Noboru made fists that dug his fingernails into the palms of his hands.

"Sensei ..." said Fumi, and then paused a short time. "What are those people doing?"

Noboru raised his head.

Boisterous, loud noises outside and women's shouting voices were heard filling the quiet alley in the morning.

Fumi said, "They're doing something to Kinu-san. Please, tell them to stop."

Noboru didn't stand.

Fumi kept pestering him.

"Please, go and tell them to stop.

"It's not Kinu-san's crime. We were wrong. Sensei, please do something."

7

The night ended. A dense fog fell. Visibility was less than twenty feet.

On both sides of the alley, many people were cooking outside. Only the figures of the men and the old women near the fire could be seen.

From beside the fire blurred by the red fog, the men called to Noboru. While smiling, he jerked his shoulder in the direction of the commotion heard.

One man said, "The wives' group is having fun. Everyone has been waiting for this. That woman looks like the enemy of those wives. Better stay out of it, Sensei. If you mess up trying to stop them, you'll get scratched up."

"It seems so," said Noboru and stopped.

It was hard to tell in the fog, but they seemed to be throwing articles, even household goods, out of Kinu's home. The sounds of breaking vessels and women scuffling and yelling at each other. Kei's and Kinu's voices rose above the racket.

Kinu said, "I didn't hit you. My hand didn't hit anyone's head. This woman ... hmph."

"Is this a human head? This here," said Kei. "Yours is probably only hips. Those hips steal men. Your mouth kills. You're a murdering slut."

"What do you mean kill people?" yelled back Kinu, accompanied by punching sounds. Then a strained, bold voice said, "I said he's a thief because he is a thief. Why are you going on about killing?"

"If Chō is a thief, you're a man-stealing bitch. Hey! Watch it!"

As blows were exchanged, Kei screamed, "Get out! Nobody needs you around here. You shame the entire row house. Get lost! Get out!"

Another woman's voice could be heard.

"Get out, you bitch! You even set your slutty eyes on my hubby. Dammit! Somebody, kill her."

"Oh, I'll do it."

"Kill this crazy bitch. Die."

Noboru turned and walked to the manager's house.

After half a month passed, Gorōkichi and his wife left the row house. They carried the remains of their four children but did not say where they were going. They went around to thank all those who helped and left, nestled close together like a married couple.

The town officials placed blame on no one after considering the notification affixed with the clinic's stamp and the written witness statements of the manager and residents of the row house. However, some form of compensation had to be paid.

One day, Noboru hurried past Izu-sama's Backside on his way to the manager's house to visit Jūhei.

He was told, "Uhei is working his side job and went to Jūhei's home."

When Noboru entered the alley, a woman coming from the other direction called to him. He was surprised to see Kinu. She was wearing her usual thick makeup and a small bun of red hair. She had the overwhelming scent of cheap oil. Her whole face projected a flirtatious smile.

"Oh, Sensei, I haven't seen you in a while," said Kinu, and then in a seductive tone said, "You're working very hard. I am still bothered by headaches. Would you please come again to my home this time? Please come."

Noboru paid no attention to her as he walked. He was so disgusted his body tingled as if touched by a poisonous, hairy caterpillar.

He went to Jūhei's house, found Uhei, and said, "I just saw Kinu. Does she still live here?"

"I raised my hand to her," said Uhei, sounding fed up. "If I chased her from the row house, she would inform the town about the murders and attempted suicides in Gorōkichi's family and the deaths of the four children.

"I'm not surprised because she's that sort. If that happened, the row house would be in an uproar. Fate is in everything. Finally, this came to be. It's horrible. She's a vile woman."

Noboru felt disgusted. To escape those feelings, he said, "I'm going to examine Jūhei, now."

Miki stood and prepared tea. Jūhei, seated in his usual spot, looked up and stared at the lintel. He seemed plumper than the first time they met. His shoulders were round, and cheeks, fleshy.

Noboru went to his side and sat. He was about to ask, "How are you feeling?" but Jūhei immediately silenced him with "Sh!"

Jūhei turned an ear toward the lintel. While gently pointing at it, he nodded at Noboru.

"Please listen. What a pretty voice," said Jūhei with delight. "I wouldn't sell this bush warbler for 1,000 ryō. What a wonderful chirping voice. Doesn't the warbling sound like it comes from deep in its heart?"

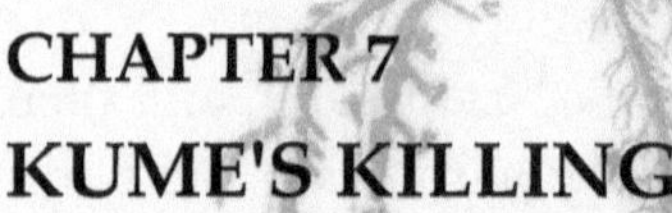

CHAPTER 7
KUME'S KILLING

1

A LITTLE PAST eight one evening soon after December began, Nīde Kyojō was speaking to Yasumoto Noboru as they walked along the gently sloping road past Dentsū-in Temple to the clinic.

Takezō walked in front of Kyojō to light their way with a lantern. Noboru carried the medicine chest.

Kyojō always said, "I don't make one servant do two jobs at the same time."

The medical staff were exceptions, but this private rule was strictly observed for all servants and the guards. Until now, Noboru loading the medicine chest onto his back was not unusual. Kyojō did not exempt him.

He's exhausted, thought Noboru, gently shaking his head while listening to Kyojō, who became angry when he got tired.

They had seen many sick people that day. After Kyojō examined patients at fifteen places, he returned home an hour later than usual. Fatigue and hunger further aggravated him. Nevertheless, he condemned the inhumanity of the call by government officials to end house calls.

During the summer, they cut the charity clinic's expenses and

168

issued a directive to suspend house calls. Kyojō vigorously objected but, in the end, could do nothing. Under the condition that he would be responsible for the expense, he had tacit consent to continue the house calls.

Therefore, Kyojō relied more than ever on daimyos, wealthy men, and prosperous merchants to cover the reduced funding and the costs of the medications for house calls. However, several days ago, he was summoned by a police officer attached to the clinic and told "House calls will be eliminated," and the admitted patients whose relatives had earnings, no matter the amount, would "pay for their meals."

"One lantern given by a poor man is worth far more than ten thousand lanterns given by a rich man," said Kyojō as they walked. "This means a poor man's piety fulfills Buddha's will, but that is deceptive."

There are limits to a rich man's donation of ten thousand lanterns. He can't always donate ten thousand lanterns. However, many poor men can donate one lantern. Also, the donation of one lantern could be satisfied at any time.

A memorial service to Buddha for the dead is connected to the afterlife and is said to be the path to a peaceful death. Tormented by the hardships of poverty in this world, the people who go nowhere their entire lives want to trust in, at least, dying peacefully and attaining Buddhahood in the afterlife.

A sly wisdom seizes on this weakness and deceptively donates only one lantern and passes unchanged into politics.

"Needless to say, the shogunate's finances consist of annual land and business taxes," said Kyojō. "However, their support always comes from the much larger number of small businessmen, small farmers, and tradesmen. There's probably no need for me to list examples.

"Of course, you can't generalize, but I cannot stand the inhumanity of imposing taxes even on the smallest wages of day laborers and the costs of meals being paid for by the patients being treated."

Kyojō stamped his feet as he walked.

He said, "Naturally, I've tried hard but cannot budge the officials.

"For example, I was able to move several officials but unable to move the shogunate's politics. My screaming and hollering were mere silly complaints.

"If I were Genji or Heike, once I gained power, I would lay down laws and govern to protect my power. This is the way in any age.

"Yasumoto, how many times have you heard me say this? You're surely bored by now and may be thinking, Oh no, not again."

Kyojō raised his voice and rudely interrupted when Noboru seemed about to say something.

"No, don't say a word. It doesn't matter what you think. It doesn't matter what anyone thinks.

"This is me voicing my foolish complaint and will scream and holler for as long as I live. Oh—"

Kyojō stopped walking. They had come to the end of the earthen wall at Dentsū-in. Takezō yelped and directed the paper lantern to a ditch along the earthen wall.

Kyojō asked, "What is it?"

Peeking into the ditch, Takezō said, "A man has fallen in."

"Hey," Takezō called to him. "What happened? Hey, are you okay?" He got a little closer and yelled, "Ah, there's blood. Sensei, the wound looks bad."

"Don't touch it," said Kyojō. He moved closer and saw a young man collapsed in the ditch lined with stones and not even three feet wide or deep. There was no water inside. The man had fallen onto his side and seemed unable to move.

Kyojō had Takezō bring the light closer to examine the man's condition. He seemed to be twenty-seven or -eight and wore a long winter coat made from plain blue cotton and closed by a flat belt. His shapeless clothes were loose.

His chest and legs were nude. His crudely cut hair was tied by a paper cord. Half of his face to his chest was bloodstained. He struggled to breathe and was softly groaning.

When Kyojō spoke to him, his entire body twitched. He turned to face up and placed his right hand on his chest. That hand clutched a dagger that gleamed like a shard of ice in the lantern light.

Kyojō said, "Relax. I'm a doctor from the charity clinic in Koishikawa. You're seriously injured. What happened? Was it a fight?"

The man raised his head and said, "Is anyone over there? Over there?"

"Nobody's there."

"He did it. Dammit!" he groaned. "I almost—"

"It was a fight."

He answered, "I was gonna kill the bastard, but a guard was across the way. What a shame. I'm sorry, please help me up?"

Kyojō said, "Takezō," and took the lantern. Takezō got into the ditch, put his hands under the man's arms, and grabbed hold of him. The man could barely stand, and then his right leg gave way. He howled and sat like he would topple over.

Kyojō passed the lantern to Noboru, went to the side of the man, and applied a tourniquet to his right leg.

Kyojō said, "It's the shin bone. It doesn't seem to be broken but may be fractured. Takezō, carry him on your back."

"What will you do?" the man asked doubtfully.

"What will I do?" said Kyojō, sounding angry. "I said I'm a doctor."

"But I ..."

"Takezō," said Kyojō, "Carry him."

Takezō got the man on his back. Kyojō walked off in long strides.

2

The man was a twenty-five-year-old named Kakuzō. He lived at 5-chōme, Otowa in Koishikawa at an establishment called Yabushita.

When they took him to the clinic and examined him, they found two knife wounds on his head, and five or six more wounds on his back from his shoulders, his waist, and legs. All the other wounds came from being hit by something like a pole. His shin bone was fractured, too.

Kyojō was familiar with the row house Yabushita. He went there once in a while but knew nothing about this man Kakuzō.

"I left home at twelve," said Kakuzō. "My old man's name was Kakichi. He died two years ago."

"Kakichi," said Kyojō again, narrowing his eyes. "In those three eight-unit row houses set up over there, I believe Kakichi was a tatami craftsman who lived in the row house at the end."

"That's right. My old man couldn't move around because of gout in his leg, but he was headstrong," said Kakuzō, frowning as he tried to turn over. He clenched his teeth to bear the pain.

"Sensei ..." he deliberately tried to sound calm to distract himself from the pain. "Sensei, do you know Tasuke?"

"The elderly man who runs the Yotaka Soba Shop."

"Yes. I'm sorry but I have a favor to ask. Could you get a message to him?

"I'd like to see a young lady named Tane. I have something important to tell her. Please tell her to come right away."

"I'll call on them tomorrow. Tonight, you need to sleep."

"Can I go tonight?"

"Someone tried to kill you," said Kyojō. "What will you do if you're noticed and questioned at the town gate? I'll send a messenger in the morning. You need to calm down and sleep tonight. If you don't, you'll further injure yourself."

Kakuzō shut his eyes and said, "I understand. Please don't forget in the morning."

Kyojō looked up at Noboru who wondered if Kyojō would go with him but sensed from his expression that would not be necessary. He stood and left the clinic room.

Kyojō was going to go to his room, but when he saw Noboru leave, he asked, "Would you please bring me a rice ball?"

His words instantly reminded Noboru he was hungry, too. The dining hall closed at eight, so he rushed down the corridor to the canteen, the only choice after eight.

At the canteen, only one lantern remained lit. In the dim

light, a man was on the wide earthen floor making what looked like a box. Yuki stood beside him watching. As Noboru asked Yuki for two rice ball meals, he realized the man was Ino.

"Is that you, Ino?" Noboru yelled. "What are you working so hard at making?"

"Yeah, wait a little bit. I'm almost done," said Ino evasively. "It's probably hard on you doctors, too. It's cold outside."

"Don't change the subject. What are you making?"

Ino blushed as he said, "Well, it's a seat for a bedpan."

"A seat for a bedpan."

"You probably know about the young lady who's a little strange in the head, Yumi-san," said Ino. "She has gotten feeble. Her body is unsteady when she uses the bedpan. If I make a seat, it'll be easier for her, so I'm trying to make one."

"I see," said Noboru. "Sugi asked you."

"Because it's my job," said Ino enthusiastically in a loud voice. "I'm helping by promising to do this work. It's not about who asked me. Please, don't say such queer things."

"Did my question upset you?" asked Noboru with a smile. "I'm sorry. Forgive me."

"That's ridiculous," said Ino, blushed again, and scratched his head in confusion. "If the sensei apologizes, I'll be ashamed. Forgive me for boasting. Please forgive me."

"Mutual courtesy is proper," said Noboru and smiled again. "Give my regards to Sugi."

Ino made an awful racket with a hammer. Noboru took the handbasket from Yuki. As he left the canteen, he heard her say, "I'll bring tea later."

Kyojō waited for dawn to send the message to Yabushita. He returned with the young woman Tane. She seemed older than nineteen and levelheaded. She saw Kakuzō, his head wrapped in bleached cotton cloth but didn't get upset at all and calmly listened to Kyojō.

"He'll probably be able to be up and around in ten days," said Kyojō and explained the injuries. "You'll have to see his leg to understand its condition. I believe it will heal in a month. Until then, he shouldn't stand or walk."

"He probably shouldn't come home with me, should he?"

"He can stay here for five or six days," said Kyojō. "That would be best for treatment. If something goes wrong, it wouldn't be good to take him home."

"Yes, but what is going on?"

Kakuzō said, "Tane, what happened? Have you heard from the people at Takadaya?"

"Yes," answered Tane. "Late last night, Izō came with three men. He said a man tried to kill the young master at Mito-sama's residence. He knew that man lived in our row house and ordered him to come out."

"Really?"

"They went house by house. I—" said Tane then closed her mouth.

Sounding concerned for Kakuzō, she said, "I told them you went to visit relatives in Toshima. There was the death of a relative who lived deep in Toshima. I said you would spend the night there."

"Thank you, but they probably didn't believe you."

"I thought so, too. If you return home, it will get worse."

"Did they threaten you?"

"If you didn't return, that would be proof of what you did. They said the entire row house was in on a conspiracy," said Tane and swallowed. "They said they would sue all the residents of the row house."

"All right, I'll go back to the row house."

"Wait," interrupted Kyojō. "We probably need to discuss this. What's going on?"

Kakuzō said, "Please don't ask anything. I don't want to cause any more trouble for you."

"I'll decide whether it'll be trouble or not. We, at least, have to talk this over."

Tane said, "You ..."

Kakuzō turned on his side. "Ow," he said, contorting his entire face, and bit his lower lip to bear the pain.

Mori Handayū came in and announced it was time to examine the clinic patients.

"All right," said Kyojō and nodded. He stood and said to Noboru, "You'll listen to their story."

3

The row house called Yabushita at 5-chōme, Otowa consisted of three buildings with a total of twenty-four units. Twenty-one families lived there.

The landlord was Takadaya Matsujirō who lived in Kagurazaka in Ushigome. His late father Yoshichi ran a small pawn shop at 5-chōme, Otowa for a long time. The humble shop that went by the name of Todanajichi didn't have a storehouse. He was good at business and bought cheap houses and land.

Yoshichi was probably lucky, too. In line with his personality, he hoarded land and houses but didn't expand the pawn shop. He gradually accumulated property. Fifteen years ago, he quit the pawn shop and moved to Kagurazaka to specialize in land sales and building homes.

The three row houses of Yabushita were where Yoshichi ran the pawn shop at 5-chōme. More accurately, he leased the units to tenants for free for the last nineteen years. In addition to not paying rent, if repairs were needed, Takadaya did them. The tenants were not responsible for one *mon*.

Kakuzō said, "The manager Gensuke was the witness to the agreement in effect not only for the master Yoshichi but continuing through his son Matsujirō's generation."

"Was there some reason for this?"

"There may be," said Kakuzō. "Without a reason, that sort of agreement never would have been made."

Noboru asked, "Do you know the reason?"

"No, I don't," answered Kakuzō. "The manager also changed the rent. Only Tane's father knew about that, but he's gone senile."

However, everyone knew about the agreement. The current manager, Sukesaburō, managed the Takadaya lots and rental houses in the neighborhood. He heard that from his late father Gensuke. In addition to hearing this from his father, a ledger of the shop rents written in Yoshichi's hand also remains.

Naturally, the landlord often changes at a row house. The line-up will change every five or six years. With the rare condition of no rent, most of the residents probably had jobs related to Gokoku-ji Temple. Other than three vacant units, the tenants changed in only seven units.

Close to twenty years have passed since that time. The only other older person was Tasuke. Unfortunately, he was also senile. However, everyone knew about the agreement with Takadaya.

"But that changed without warning."

In May of that year, Yoshichi died at Takadaya. His only son Matsujirō succeeded him. He was twenty-three, married last fall, and a son was born.

"Last month, Matsujirō came at the end of October and said to vacate the row house," said Kakuzō. "He came with three men, who looked like hoodlums, and said the row house will be torn down and all twenty-one households had to go."

"Did he know about the agreement?"

"He said he knew about the agreement, but there was no written proof. He said, 'I don't know about my father's generation when you came and lived here free for nineteen years, so I can't protect an agreement like this scrap of paper.' And he rejected it."

Noboru looked glum.

"I think this conversation will be difficult."

Kakujō said, "There's probably some reason he's saying this. Matsujirō may be evicting us because he has money problems. He has some ulterior motive.

"It could be to buy a house in Yabushita, make an empty lot there, and build a cluster of restaurants or whorehouses. The priest at Gokoku-ji Temple seems to agree with me."

Noboru thought that was likely true. Religion and red-light districts are mysteriously linked. Sensō-ji Temple, Nezu-Gongen, Hikawa Shrine in Akasaka, Shiba no Shinmei may be few, but their neighbors are red-light districts.

Gokoku-ji Temple was built during the Genroku era and attached to a temple estate worth 1,300 *koku* from the shogunate. The story is at one time, the widow of some shogun was a zealous, devout believer. The temple was not prosperous given its isolated location and brief history. Naturally, among the monks were certainly people who thought nearby lots could be created. Noboru thought this was a possibility.

He said, "Even so, this will be difficult. Of course, I'll talk to Nīde-sensei. Having come to live here for free nineteen years ago, wouldn't it be better to move somewhere nearby?"

"Yes, I guess you're right."

"More than getting caught up in a mess, I think it's better to move and start fresh in a new place."

Kakuzō feebly said, "That may be best, but that bastard is too shameless."

Tane said, "If you're going home, you better go now. I've been out, and if it gets too late, they'll suspect a conspiracy."

"Wait a minute," said Noboru and stood. "Well, I'll go speak to the sensei to get his opinion. Please, wait a little longer."

Noboru left the two. He had to wait a short time for Kyojō to finish an examination. While waiting, he went to the dining hall, had tea, and then went to Kyojō's room.

As Kyojō changed his jacket, he listened to Noboru's story without saying a word. Next, Kyojō faced his desk and wrote out the day's prescriptions.

A register listed the condition and drug prescription for each hospitalized patient. Each time, he wrote the prescription mixture and the change in dosage depending on the condition.

"Please continue," said Kyojō as he wrote. "Then what happened?"

When Noboru finished the story, Kyojō said nothing and kept moving his writing brush. Eventually, he wrote the last entry. As he put away the brush, he sighed deeply, nearly groaning.

Kyojō said, "I know about Takadaya," looked at Noboru, and continued, "But what is Kakuzō's situation?"

Noboru said, "Well …" and shut his mouth.

"It's not unusual to brood about killing one's rival. There may be some reason."

"I didn't hear that."

"Isn't that important?" Kyojō quickly asked. Displeased, he said, "Well, all right. It's probably not too late to go there."

4

Kyojō decided to send Kakuzō home to the row house. Otherwise, Takadaya might accuse the residents of the row house of being in a conspiracy. He doubted whether the town would accept that complaint. Perhaps Takadaya had spread money around. Either way was a problem.

The story would be Kakuzō went to relatives in Toshima-gun. Kyojō found where he fell from a cliff on his way back home. He told Kakuzō he'd take him back to the charity clinic for treatment.

Kyojō instantly devised a plan. After much discussion, he made Tane return home first, made a stretcher from a sliding door, and had Kakuzō lay on it. Kyojō left the clinic a little later than usual.

Kyojō, Noboru, and Takezō carrying the medicine chest on his back left the back of Dentsū-in for Otsuka and headed to Otowa, a town of many temples and small mansions of military families.

On the way, from inside the covered stretcher, Kakuzō said, "I forgot something."

Kyojō snapped, "Forget about that object."

Noboru had no idea what it was but realized it was probably the dagger he was holding last night.

Kakuzō said nothing more.

When they came to the back streets of 5-chōme, Otowa, and turned down an alley, Kakuzō said "It's on the corner on the left."

The house on the corner was a row house that looked recently renovated. The entrance and latticework window faced the back alley. The storm door and shutter box were new. Upon examination, the box was built like a sake bar. Planks only five inches wide were hammered into an X over the storm door at that entrance.

"Where do we go in?"

"The kitchen's in the back," said Kakuzō. "We can go in there."

They went around back.

People quickly gathered around because someone was being carried in on a door. Kyojō urged Noboru to open the kitchen door to move Kakuzō. Two men brushed aside the gathered residents and stepped out in front.

One was around thirty and looked like a fireman. The other was much younger, still twenty-two or -three. He wore a striped kimono closed low by an obi sash and hemp-soled sandals on bare feet. He had thick eyebrows and a thin, pale body. Noboru thought his lousy mood would burst from his entire body like a smart dog about to bark.

"That's Kakuzō," said the older man. "He looks hurt. Let me see."

"Show you, for what?" asked Kyojō.

"Last night, someone made a big mistake," said the man. "Some punk tried to kill the landlord of this row house, and we're looking for that criminal."

"Who are you? A town official?"

"No, my name is Izō. I do business with Takadaya-san."

"The search for criminals is an official's job," said Kyojō. "Is a guard with a short, hooked truncheon holding him at Takadaya?"

Izō was silent.

As the younger man stuck his right hand into his pocket and was about to say something, Kyojō was faster and introduced himself.

"I'm Nīde Kyojō, a doctor at the charity clinic."

He thought hearing that name would startle his companion. He expected some surprise, but the young man's expression showed no change.

An instant of truth was revealed in Kyojō's eyes. Noboru was amused but had no reason to laugh. Of course, Kyojō quickly stood.

"Listen carefully," said Kyojō. "I don't know what mistake happened and where. However, this man collapsed last night at Nezumiyama in Nakamaru-mura in Toshima-gun. I discovered the bloodstained places where he tried to take a shortcut and fell off a cliff. I carried him to the clinic and treated him. When and where did that mistake happen?"

The young man said, "Yesterday at sunset around six, I was with Mito-sama."

His voice was gentle like a woman's but echoed unpleasantly.

"Didn't you already agree?" The young man smiled. "Because I know, I'll make the first move. Nezumiyama in Toshima is probably in another direction. Right? Old man, that's probably it."

"Izō … I told you," said Kyojō, looking at him. "Was the landlord of Takadaya killed or injured?"

"No, fortunately, three workmen were with him."

"He wasn't wounded, was he?"

"No, because the three immediately came running."

"Why were they violent?"

"Well, he had a dagger. They beat him down because he was dangerous."

"That's when that man was injured," said Kyojō, like he was making sure. "Takadaya is safe. Those roughnecks received some injuries and suspect Kakuzō."

The young man said, "Hey, old man ..."

"Silence," shouted Kyojō. His voice wasn't loud, but the shout was piercing. His eyes glared at the young man.

"You, shut up," said Kyojō. Almost instantly, he softened his voice. "Listen to me carefully, Izō.

"The clinic belongs to the town magistrate. The police are always packed in there. I found Kakuzō in Nezumiyama and returned to the clinic with him.

"The police were also notified of that fact. Even if this weren't so, nothing happened to Takadaya. The three thugs did what they did and were injured. If this were made public, consider how this would be viewed in court?"

"But that bastard tried to kill the landlord."

"What is your proof?"

"That bastard said so, and the landlord—"

"Enough," interrupted Kyojō. "Who said what? Who heard what? Do you think the government accepts this sort of incident resembling a fight at a well? Four people versus one. With no clear proof one person set out to kill and that person being seriously injured, Takadaya will be blamed."

Kyojō glanced at the young man.

"If this sort of ruffian is used, even for a good reason, there is no solution. It'd be best to return home and discuss this thoroughly. At some time, I will become a witness."

The young man looked at Izō. His right hand was still in his pocket. His expression seemed to be saying, "Should I do it?" But Izō shook his head.

Kyojō signaled Noboru with his eyes. They lifted Kakuzō off the door stretcher and carried him inside the house through the kitchen door.

In front of them, Tane flew out from the crowd, entered the house before them, and spread out the bedding.

"I have a question," said Izō from the door, "Kakuzō won't be leaving, will he?"

"This man broke his leg when he fell off the cliff," answered Kyojō in the house. "Don't worry. He won't be going anywhere for twenty or thirty days."

5

When Izō and the young man left, the row house residents came to visit the patient. The wives brought live coals. Tane prepared tea. Kyojō left Noboru there and went to get answers to some questions at the manager's house.

"Kakuzō must sleep," said Kyojō as he went out. "The visits are over. Please go home."

A short time later, everyone left.

"He's a sensei with power," said Kakuzō, smiling from his pillow. "I never would have taken him to be much of a doctor. I thought, Has some damn fool come out?"

"Maybe I could do it," said Noboru, forcing a smile. "With three or five yakuza if needed."

Noboru shut his mouth. He thought this was dangerous, like

talking about the fight in Mikumi-chō in Hongō.

From the side, Tane said, "A little while ago, Gen-san was chased from the brush shop."

"What happened to Gen-san?"

"It's like what happened to Kichisaburō-san," said Tane. "Three strange men, probably laborers, came. This time, they said they rented this house, chased out Gen-san and his family, and threw out his belongings. Those three men are staying there now and drinking sake."

"What happened to Gen-san?"

"A rival is a rival, but what will he do? He's staying with his wife and children at Yohei-san's home."

"Why?" asked Noboru.

In a low groan, Kakuzō said, "It's Takadaya's doing.

"He probably thought the negotiations weren't working out. Five days ago, two men who looked like laborers were sent to force out the old man Kichisaburō and his wife."

Feeling pressured, Noboru asked, "So aren't there senior town administrators or a five-man council here?"

"If I could depend on them, I wouldn't do anything stupid," said Kakuzō. "I tried so hard to strike a bargain, I even thought about killing them."

However, all the conditions were unfavorable to him. Even if the priest responsible for clerical duties at Gokoku-ji Temple in this area became the shield to protect them from the rear, the reasoning would not win. Besides, if Takadaya could use money and create an empty lot here, the five-man council and the group of town administrators would be like wolves pouncing on food. Kakuzō went out with four representatives of the row house residents to seek help but were no match for their opponents.

They said, "You have lived there free for close to twenty years and still have that deep desire."

Of course, it would no longer be free.

Their decision was "From now on, you will pay appropriate rents."

"They didn't listen to us and said it would be best for us to leave immediately."

As he listened, Noboru had no idea who was right.

Wouldn't it be best to move somewhere else?

If he intended to pay rent from now on, this mess would be cleaned up. Noboru didn't ask the questions he had for Kakuzō. Isn't moving away the simple solution? Why is he being so persistent? Is he stubborn? Is he so attached to the home he's used to living in?

Kyojō returned in half an hour but without going inside told Noboru and Takezō to prepare to go home.

He said to Tane, "There's nothing to worry about. I've spoken to the manager, and Izō will not attack. Someone will come again tomorrow. Please tell Kakuzō and the row house residents so they don't get angry."

As they walked, Kyojō shared the details about his house calls from Otowa with Noboru. Since Kyojō only spoke, Noboru listened until the end but grasped the details.

Kakuzō and Tane should be congratulated for getting married in the middle of next month although they took four years to reach this point.

Kakuzō was going to be twenty-five. His father, Kakichi, was a tatami craftsman but unable to run a shop of his own.

When Kakuzō was twelve, he became a live-in apprentice as a cook in a restaurant called Nadamon in Shitaya and gained the skills needed to become a chef. He chose a job he liked but probably didn't have the talent. He realized this before he turned twenty.

"I don't have the skill to work at a first-class restaurant."

Since then, he felt he should open an eatery serving simple foods. He didn't drink or play around and saved his money.

Many restaurant chefs live fast lives. Probably the environment and the job make sake and women unavoidable. However, Kakuzō knew the limits of his skills and was determined to run an eatery. Although scorned by friends, he saved as much money as he could.

During this time, Kakuzō got to know Tane and eventually

planned to propose marriage. She was young when her parents died and was raised by her grandfather Tasuke.

Tasuke ran The Yotaka Soba Shop. From the age of twelve or thirteen, Tane was trained and helped out. At night, she went out to work with her grandfather. In the winter of the year before last, however, her grandfather Tasuke suffered a mild stroke. Immediately, his legs were impaired; and his brain became foggy. He could no longer work. Tane searched for a job at a teahouse she could commute to and worked there for two years.

Kakuzō's father died before Tasuke collapsed. His mother fell ill and died five years earlier. He was alone. Spurred by this, he stopped the live-in work arrangement and commuted from his home in Yabushita to Nadamon.

The two met once every day and talked about running an eatery. Given Tane's long experience in helping her grandfather, she would benefit any future eatery.

"Through hell or high water, I'll be reliable," said Tane many times. Being from a poor family, she worked hard to amass a little money.

In August of this year, this house had a vacancy, so she spoke to the manager and later moved in. The house was on a back alley but close to the pilgrims' road to Gokoku-ji Temple. Many samurai estates were in the area. They thought the servants in the samurai homes would become exceptionally good customers, and business would be good.

A carpenter named Yohei and a plasterer named Sasuke lived in the same row house. Both were heavy drinkers and only skilled at odd jobs. He asked them for advice on rough estimates for buying the necessary materials and performing the renovations.

Odd-job men could do this work. Of course, allowing for their spare time, the job couldn't be done quickly and easily but was finally completed at the end of September.

Meanwhile, Kakuzō and Tane bought knives, pots, kettles, and tableware for the restaurant. Kakuzō quit Nadamon at the end of September.

They made various preparations, opened the eatery on October

15, and began their business as a couple. After the busy period of New Year's, they would marry. Because the row house has eyes, they promised to be faithful to each other.

Kyojō said, "Then they were told they were going to be evicted from Takadaya in six months. Their business was off to a good start. They were beginning to attract regular customers."

Kakuzō had invested the money saved for more than ten years (including Tane's contribution) in the eatery and borrowed money from the sake shop and other merchants.

6

If driven out now, Kakuzō would be broke and burdened by debt. Tane would have to work again at a teahouse. He talked with everyone in the row house and negotiated with Takadaya.

Kyojō continued, "But as Yasumoto heard, Takadaya did not agree. Whether or not support came from Gokoku-ji Temple, the town officials were allies of Takadaya who could attract support through the prosperity of the land.

"The biggest handicap for the row house residents is twenty families living rent-free for close to twenty years. Unless their situation becomes a public matter, society will take Takadaya's side on this point alone."

"Now what?" answered Noboru. "Why was the promise of no rent exchanged for such a long time?"

"There was no exchange. In the previous generation of Takadaya Yoshichi, the promise was made spontaneously. I looked at the register of rents at the manager's. Yoshichi's name was clearly listed. The free rent until Matsujirō's generation was noted. The signatures and thumbprints of Yoshichi and the five row house representatives were registered."

"That many could write?"

While walking, Kyojō turned to look at Noboru and said, "A patient with a bad liver not knowing his liver is bad makes no difference to the bad liver."

"That's true," said Noboru vaguely.

"There's no problem with how the five representatives wrote characters. Is there any proof of no rent? The man speaks foolishness."

He seemed to say those last words to himself but immediately returned to the main topic.

"What I want to know is why this promise was made in the first place. Did Yoshichi make that promise? As long as that remains a mystery, the row house residents can't win."

After they walked for a short time, Noboru asked, "Is there anyone who knows the reason?"

"Like what Kakuzō said." Kyojō cleared his irritated throat. "Two of the five representatives moved. Two died; Kakuzō's father was one of them. The last one is Tasuke."

"And he's senile ..."

"I visited him earlier. He may be senile because of a stroke. I gave him a few tests. The elderly man tried hard to remember, but his only memory was Kume's killing."

Noboru looked at Kyojō's face.

Kyojō said, "Kume's killing. He said, 'Look at my face. I don't know anything.'"

Kyojō waved his hand for no reason.

"Nobody knows what he meant. The row house residents also tried their best to ask all possible questions. The elderly man only remembered that one phrase. I have no idea what it means."

"There may be no connection at all," said Noboru, somewhat agitated, and then changed the subject. "So I almost understood."

"What did you almost understand?"

"The feelings of Kakuzō who brooded to the point of thinking about killing Takadaya," Noboru answered as he thought, Today, I'm so stupid, it's absurd.

"His toil over a dozen years turns to foam. His approaching marriage also goes bad. Moreover, his rival has the aim of making money. That makes me think his threats were not surprising."

Sounding indignant, Kyojō asked, "Does that make him admirable? To kill someone for any reason can't be forgiven. On that point, Kakuzō is a fool.

"There are many examples of poor people who enjoy what's right before them and destroy themselves through despair. With no fixed job or property, they are unsteady and live lives with shallow roots. When circumstances fall outside of their expectations, they immediately run from one extreme to the other. In the end, only powerful people enrich themselves."

Kyojō said, "If we knew the reason for the promise, we could certainly do something.

"By having the priests and greedy parties create a questionable empty lot, we may be able to protect the eatery. But no one knows why the promise was made to Yoshichi. The loss of the reason is a stumbling block."

After walking a short while, Kyojō looked up to the sky as if to ask if this was real. His fevered voice whispered, "What did Yoshichi get in return for making that promise?"

Noboru repeated in his heart, When a patient with a bad liver is examined, the doctor who does not know what is wrong or where the problem lies will seek help from the gods and Buddha.

The next day, Kyojō ordered Noboru to check on Kakuzō. With Tane's help, he washed the wound, replaced the salve, and rewrapped the cotton.

An old man poking a cane forward staggered through the kitchen door. Tane was surprised and raised her voice.

"Oh, Grandpa, what's wrong?"

She went over to him. "It's dangerous for you to go out alone."

That's probably Tasuke, thought Noboru as he pulled the metal basin closer to wash his hands. He glanced over.

With help from his granddaughter, Tasuke whose jerky movements resembled a broken wooden doll, sat where the kitchen floorboards were removable for storage under the floor. His cane fell over with a loud bang. The old man was thin. His skin was pale like candle wax. His expressionless face was like a mask, and his lip drooped.

"I don't know," said Tane and asked again, "What happened?"

Kakuzō looked with curiosity at Noboru, who said nothing and shook his head.

"What's wrong?" shouted Kakuzō. "What did Grandpa do?"

"Wait a moment," answered Tane.

Noboru said to Kakuzō, "I'll come again the day after tomorrow," and stood.

Kakuzō's fever was gone. Noboru was not worried about the wound festering. He instructed them to change the salve on the leg one time tomorrow and left.

As he passed by Tane and Tasuke, tears streamed from Tasuke. Noboru noticed he was struggling to speak but was tongue-tied. He was drooling from his lip and pressed his throat with one hand as if trying to squeeze out the words he couldn't speak. He looked so pitiful Noboru could barely look at him and was affected by the grim sight. From behind, Noboru heard Tane say, "It's all right, we'll go home. Kaku-san is fine. Don't say the altar brings bad luck. Grandfather, we'll work hard, so there's nothing to worry about."

Noboru stepped into the street from the alley.

7

Noboru went around to Koishikawa Bridge. He planned to join Kyojō at Matsuhei Wakasa's home but finished early at Otowa. He waited a half hour for Kyojō to arrive.

After that, they made eight more house calls and returned to the clinic at five in the evening.

Back earlier than usual, Noboru entered a fresh bath for the first time in a long time. He set his tray beside Mori Handayū's and leisurely ate his dinner.

During tea after the meal, Handayū casually said, "Tsugawa's back."

Noboru had no idea what he meant.

"Yasumoto, he's the man you replaced," said Handayū. "Tsugawa Genzō. Don't you remember him?"

Noboru remembered and said, "He was a jerk." He looked doubtfully at Handayū and said, "That guy's returned ... here?"

"Yes, here."

"Didn't he intend to become a court physician?"

"It looks like he didn't," said Handayū. "He was given a seat once but blundered and was kicked out."

"So he came back here?"

"It seems so," said Handayū and sipped tea. "And we need people here."

"We need people here?"

"Yes," said Handayū and changed the subject. "Did you know Ino and Sugi are engaged?"

Noboru shook his head. Handayū stayed on this subject. Noboru was intrigued and listened. He had never thought about the meaning of "we need people here."

According to Handayū, the madwoman Yumi doesn't have long to live. Given her condition, she may or may not live to the new year. If she dies, Sugi will return to her parents' home. She probably does not want to go back to her family and will marry Ino. The two have decided to set up a home together.

"This is my first time hearing a promising story at this clinic," said Handayū. "Perhaps since the start of this clinic, I noticed that and it weighed heavy on my heart.

"I think when you live in this world, seeing people who are truly happy is rare."

That's it. Seeing joyful people is extremely rare, Noboru felt this and nodded in his heart. Ino and Sugi don't know their future. Happiness as husband and wife will be short, but their lives will be long. As he had these thoughts, Noboru shook his head and smiled.

He said, "I'm in this situation. I can't become an old fogey. No, this is me."

The next day, Noboru accompanied Kyojō. They called on a man he didn't know at a place with a gate. A guard came out to meet them. As he approached, he said, "Yasumoto-sensei?"

The guard wore a livery coat, work pants, and zōri sandals. He was a short, powerfully-built man around twenty-six or -seven. The stubble on his unshaven face stretched from around his mouth to both cheeks.

"I'm from Otowa," he said in a gravelly voice. "I live in the same row house as Kakuzō. I'm a carpenter. My name is Yohei."

Noboru thought, This is the man who took in the brush seller Genji and his family.

"Has Kakuzō's condition changed?"

"No, I'm not here about that," said Yohei and scratched his head. While scratching his head like he discovered something bad, he said, "The truth is. A little thing happened. I'd like you to visit today around four this afternoon. I'm asking for this reason."

"Was there trouble?" asked Kyojō from the side. Did Takadaya do something?"

"No, that's not it," said Yohei, scratching and turning his head. "There's no trouble. Takadaya is not the reason. But there might be trouble. You'll understand if you come. So, will you come?"

"At four," said Kyojō. "Very well. Tell them I'll arrive by that time."

Yohei looked at Noboru who nodded and said, "I'll be there."

After the pair made five house calls, Kyojō told Noboru to go to Otowa. During the cloudy afternoon, darkness fell a little before four. The air was so chilly, weak north winds penetrated the skin.

When he called out at the kitchen door of Kakuzō's house, Tane came out. She noticed Noboru looking doubtfully at the footwear in a jumble at the door and said, "Those belong to the residents."

Noboru entered, was greeted by four men beside Kakuzō's bed, and offered a seat.

Yohei was one of the men and introduced the others: Kosuke, a plasterer; Chōjo, a fishmonger; and Masakichi, a rickshaw driver. Kosuke was about the same age as Yohei. Chōji and Masakichi looked to be around thirty.

"I'm sorry for taking you from your work," said the reclining Kakuzō. "It's about Takadaya. I know what happened nineteen years ago."

"You know," said Noboru, narrowing his eyes.

"Grandpa Tasuke came. Oh, you were there," said Kakuzō. "His speech was garbled, and his mind was muddled, so no one understood what he was saying.

"After you went home, I listened carefully because he calmed down a little. He said there should be something in writing about what happened nineteen years ago.

"First of all, Tasuke repeatedly mentioned the Buddhist altar. He said the agreement with Takadaya was written down. In addition to his signature and thumbprint, those of the four representatives were added. He said the agreement had been entrusted to the late Kakichi.

Kakuzō said, "This was my first time hearing this."

He explained that Tasuke said, "Kakuzō, you never heard about this from your father. That may be so. Back then, you were a live-in apprentice. You rushed back but didn't make it in time to speak to Kakichi-san before he died, so Kakichi-san told me.

"None of it may be true, but he said if trouble broke out at the row house to look behind the mortuary tablet at the altar because something was written there back then.

"Tasuke heard that but had forgotten. The uproar here reminded him of 'Kume's killing.' He had been trying to recall that incident and finally remembered yesterday."

8

"Was it there?" asked Noboru.

"It was," said Kakuzō, taking out a flattened rolled-up paper from under the desk. "It's what Grandpa said. This was hidden behind the mortuary tablet."

"The reason is written here."

"The details are right here. The thumbprints of the five representatives are pressed. Please wait a moment," said Kakuzō as he passed the paper to Chōji. "Later, we'll talk about what's written here. First, I have to talk about something terrible. I think you may want to stop what we will do from here on."

Noboru stared at Kakuzō's face and said, "In that case, why was I called here?"

"I wanted a witness."

"A witness to what?"

Yohei said, "You'll understand later. We'll start right after our rival comes. He should be here soon."

"Who's coming?"

"Takadaya," said Yohei, who looked at Kakuzō and asked, "Is he coming?"

Kakuzō said to Noboru, "I sent word to Matsujirō that I found proof of the promise of free rent at the row house and would show him the proof when he came. He said he would come."

"But why do you need a witness?"

"This guy is bossy—," said the plasterer Kosuke.

Kakuzō interrupted, "Keep your comments to yourself. You need to worry about what you're supposed to do. Chō-san is probably okay."

Chōji turned to Yohei and said, "Please bring a lantern. It's getting dark early today. We'll need light to read."

The rickshaw driver Masakichi said, "I'll get it later. I'll get one right after he comes. That should work."

Noboru said nothing but wondered, What are they planning to do? What am I supposed to witness? I have no idea. They don't seem to want to talk about it. Whatever it is will begin soon. I can do nothing more than keep my mouth shut and wait.

Tane brought tea to Noboru. Masakichi stood and left after he said, "I'll go home and get the lantern ready. Everybody, go through to the field below and hide."

Takadaya Matsujirō arrived a little after four. Izō and another young man came with him. Only Matsujirō and Izō went inside.

While Kakuzō was speaking, Noboru often stared at Matsujirō from the side. Noboru heard he was twenty-three but looked three or four years older. He had an average build and height, and no distinguishing features. He felt the haughtiness and fearlessness of a man spoiled in his upbringing were glaringly obvious in the expression in his eyes and his way of speaking.

"This is certain?" asked Matsujirō again. "It may be a fabrication."

Kakuzō answered, "If you look at it, you'll see. A bunch of

dopes like us don't have any reason to trick a man as smart as Taka-daya-san. We're not that brainless.

"This gentleman is Yasumoto-sensei from the Koishikawa Charity Clinic. He is here as a witness. Would you like to see the proof?"

Matsujirō turned to look at Noboru.

"Yasumoto Noboru. Pleased to meet you."

"Takadaya Matsujirō. The pleasure is mine," said Matsujirō and stared at Noboru's clothes. "I recognize your attire. You're surely dressed in the uniform of a clinic doctor."

He said the words "in the uniform of" in a peculiar tone. His contempt was unmistakable. Noboru just smiled.

Kakuzō said, "Chōji and Kosuke will escort you. Yasumoto-sensei, please go and have a look, too."

"Where is it?"

Kakuzō said, "In the vacant lot at the foot of the cliff. However, Sir, please leave your companions here and go alone."

"Why can't they come?"

Kakuzō gently said, "You may be embarrassed.

"The late landlord shared that concern, so he kept others from knowing. That's why we did not know anything until today. There-fore, please go alone."

Matsujirō hesitated for a moment. Izō whispered, "Young Master."

That seemed to stimulate Matsujirō's pride, and he shook his head at Izō.

"It's fine," said Matsujirō and coolly nodded. "Will you see my embarrassment? Yasuda-sensei will be present, too."

Noboru said nothing, but Matsuzō corrected him.

"Sir, it's Yasumoto-sensei."

"Oh, I beg your pardon," said Matsuzō to Noboru with a pompous bow and then said to Izō, "Call Tatsu and Gin and wait here. All right. I'll be fine alone. Aren't I Takadaya Matsujirō?"

Noboru stood and went out ahead of him through the kitchen door.

"Aren't I Takadaya Matsujirō?" muttered Noboru after going out to the alley. "He should be sure. I am Takadaya Matsujirō."

Soon Yohei came out, followed by Matsujirō, Chōji, and Kosuke. Chōji said, "This way," and walked deeper into the alley. Noboru and the other three men followed.

Dark twilight already engulfed the area. Cooking fires could be seen around the row house. In the smoke spirals, children noisily jumped around and made the boards covering the muddy ditches ring.

When far from the row house, the vacant lot was more elevated. On top of the cliff on the opposite side was a samurai estate not visible from below.

That lot was about half an acre and covered by withered grass as high as a man's chest. On one side, two old, miserable-looking pine trees stood.

Chōji was closer to the pine trees and, while looking around, said to Matsujirō, "It's in this area."

"This area, you say," said Matsujirō and asked, "What is in this area?"

"This place holds the proof," said Chōji. "Please, look here."

Matsujirō looked at Noboru who politely gestured with one hand, "You first." Matsujirō was anxious but bluffed boldness and approached Chōji.

"It's a little further back," said Chōji. While looking back and forth between the pine trees and the cliff, he said, "I'm sorry, but please go a little further in."

Matsujirō kept moving forward.

Chōji said, "Just a little more," and squatted down to the ground. "That's it. A little more."

Matsujirō took two steps in. He lost his footing and wildly waved both hands around in space. He plopped down into the withered grass and disappeared.

9

What was the meaning of this incident in the light of the dark twilight? It happened so quickly. Noboru didn't understand, even a little. When his figure disappeared in the withered grass with his arms flailing, Matsujirō screamed. The shocked Noboru heard Matsujirō's voice go below the earth as he dropped, being pulled down by his buttocks.

Yohei said, "That's Kume's killing Grandpa talked about. The truth is it's not someone's name. He's talking about an *old unused well.* It's an empty well with no water that is thirty feet deep.

"I investigated yesterday and found out it's not poisoned. It was so long ago, so I don't know when. A girl named Kume fell in and died here. The old man knew that. They called it Kume's well. A stone lid was placed on it, and a fence built around the well. Children never went near it."

Chōji said, "Shut up, Yohei. Hey, is Sei here?"

Masakichi returned with a lantern."

"Is everything okay?"

"Yes, it's all good," said Chōji.

"There's shouting inside. Are you sure? That asshole is probably stunned."

"Give me the light," said Chōji. Noboru was silent and watched what they were doing.

"You're the witness," said Chōji to Noboru. "Come here. From now on, please listen to what I say to this bastard."

Noboru nodded. The sky was still bright, but that vacant lot at the foot of the cliff was pitch black. Shaken by strong winds, the withered grasses swayed. The lantern light illuminated the figures of the five men from one side.

Chōji advanced slowly to the side of the water well. It was only a hole covered by withered grass, the place where Matsujirō fell in. He could only see the crumbled remains of dirt. Nothing remained of the shape that would reveal a well.

Chōji shouted, "Hey, Takadaya, are you hurt?"

The scream echoing from the bottom of the hole was impossible to make out.

"Well, you sound fine. I guess you're okay. Listen carefully," said Chōji. He took out a paper from his pocket. "Now, I will tell you the reason for this. Hey, can you hear me, Takadaya?"

"Clean out your ear holes and listen," said Yohei.

"You'll change your tune and say something new," jeered Kosuke.

"Quiet," said Chōji to check him. He faced the inside of the well and read the paper. "Okay? Listen closely, Takadaya. This is the empty water well of a samurai estate that was here long ago."

Chōji explained in more detail what Yohei told Noboru. The girl was six years old. The well had been capped by a wooden lid.

Chōji said, "On October 15 nineteen years ago, you were four years old and fell into this well. Right?

"You were an only child, to your parents, an irreplaceable, important child. Your disappearance caused an uproar in the neighborhood. People were hired to search for you. Of course, they probably came to look into this well. Whatever. I don't know. Were you spirited away or kidnapped?

"They also tried fortunetellers, incantations, and prayers. Despite all those efforts, nobody knew where you were.

"Your mother lost her mind and fell ill. Your father gave up all hope. Had you been taken to a foreign country or were you dead?

"But on the fourth day, a resident of this row house found you. If you don't believe me, look at what is woven into the cord you're wearing. It is you at the bottom of this well.

"Right now, you are at the bottom where you fell. They would rescue you and a doctor would examine you, but the doctor probably said there was no hope."

Inside the well was quiet. Nothing could be heard. Chōji's voice echoed and stood out in the surrounding silence.

Chōji continued, "But you were saved. You probably understand how happy your parents were. They said this debt of gratitude would not be forgotten by their descendants.

"They promised the rent for the twenty-four units in the three row houses would be free for your lifetime. However, the master said to keep this a secret.

"You were four years old and would forget about the incident in a short time. I didn't want this horrible thing to happen to you a second time. It wasn't for the rent but for you to keep the promise.

"It's your parents' compassion. Don't you think so, Takadaya? The residents of the row houses kept their promise but until today did not know why they paid no rent."

Chōji described the paper with the joint signatures taken from the altar in Kakuzō's home.

"Now you understand," said Chōji. "You turned an agreement of the previous generation into trash. You didn't hear us when we said we'll pay rent from now on. If so, that's it. You nearly died here nineteen years ago. You are actually in that place. Do you understand this place is the proof you asked to be shown?"

They heard a shout from the bottom of the well. Amid the horrible echoes, a frightened voice sounded so shrill, his words could not be heard.

"Hey, don't shout," said Chōji. "When you shout wildly, the power quickly fades. This is a forgotten place. Even we knew nothing about it before the writing appeared.

"No matter how much you scream and shout, the consideration of others will never come. More than clumsily raging, calm down and think carefully ... about when you were four in that place and dying…. So long."

When Chōji gestured, Yohei and two others came carrying the stone cover and capped the mouth of the well.

Chōji said to Noboru, "You probably understand why we didn't tell you this. If you heard we were going to do this, you would have fiercely objected."

"I wonder," said Noboru, smiling.

"Even men like us wanted to settle this matter. So this ass will give some answers," said Chōji. "Kakuzō is probably waiting impatiently. Let's go back home and read the paper to him."

"But what about him?" asked Noboru. "You don't intend to leave Takadaya down there."

"We'll see," said Chōji cryptically.

The five men returned to the row house. Kakuzō told Izō, "Your master has already gone home to Ushigome." Then he went inside Kakuzō's house and told the whole story.

Noboru read the paper that verified in written detail what Chōji said."

Noboru said, "I'm not meddling but am the witness to an unexpected event happening to Takadaya—"

Kakuzō interrupted, "Yes, I know. We won't cause problems for you, Sensei. If anything happens, you will be notified. Please, don't concern yourself."

Not long after, Noboru said his goodbyes. After that, he visited every other day to treat Kakuzō, but Kakuzō said nothing more. For the first time on the fifth visit, Kakuzō said, "The matter has ended well."

"Last night, they raised him from the well," said Tane. "We're all here as we were before."

"You're not worried about revenge?"

"He responded from his core," said Kakuzō. "The names written and the thumbprints pressed on the paper convinced him. He responded from his heart."

"From the bottom of that well ..."

"We intend to pay rent. Ow, ouch."

The peeling off of the salve appeared to hurt. Kakuzō frowned and moaned.

"Sensei, I beg you to be gentle."

CHAPTER 8
A SPROUT UNDER THE ICE

1

On December 20, medicines from Ōkaku-dō were delivered. From the morning of the twenty-first, the clinic was busy with inventory. Kyojō had taken the day off from house calls and was busy barking orders.

Yasumoto Noboru promised to visit his parents in Kōji-machi as Kyojō had advised him three times. When he left, Kyojō and Mori Handayū gave half-hearted goodbyes and continued with the inventory.

At two o'clock tea, Noboru went with Handayū to the dining hall where they enjoyed tea and cakes. Handayū told him the madwoman Yumi was in critical condition.

"It hasn't been ten days."

For a time, the episodes of madness were shorter, but recently, that reversed. She was sane less and less. They thought she lost her appetite, which exacerbated the disorder. She continued to have insomnia and rampaged when she suffered a seizure. The pain never stopped coursing through her body. Once, she tried to hang herself. Her weakening condition was obvious. Now, she refuses meals. Her conscious state is gradually becoming chaotic.

Handayū said, "Her father came yesterday.

"He's a thin man, fifty years old, and mild-mannered. Where he lives is kept a secret. Yasumoto, has Sensei said anything to you?"

Noboru shook his head no.

"Even now, only Sensei knows," said Handayū. "I believe I met him. He has the demeanor of a retired successful merchant. From start to finish, he told his daughter's story and shed many tears."

The cause of Yumi's madness was the misbehavior of a sales clerk. It might have also stemmed from her constitution. However, this sales clerk, a thirty-year-old man, harmed the young nine-year-old Yumi and threatened her.

"If you tell anyone, I'll kill you."

Because her father didn't know what happened and made other mistakes, the sales clerk was fired. After a long time passed, a husband was arranged for Yumi. But when her future husband broke the engagement, Yumi's strange behavior began. Only then her father discovered the truth.

"Her father said, 'Even now, I think I want to kill that sales clerk.'"

Handayū shook his head while pouring the tea.

"Even if he were that sort of man, if that clerk had not committed those despicable acts and made those threats, his daughter probably wouldn't have gone mad.

"But if he found that man, he said through tears, 'I will kill him and die myself.'"

Noboru thought to himself, That would be a mistake. He heard Yumi's story from her and confirmed most of the facts. He thought, The sales clerk appeared to have a mental illness and could be said to hold some responsibility. However, many men and women have similar experiences when young. In Yumi's case, in particular, the sudden death of her mother and the broken engagement took their toll.

Most people would endure even the repetition of these sordid acts, but Yumi could not bear it.

Yumi must have had extreme sensitivity to sexual passion. Thus, when she suppressed those feelings, the harmony of her entire body went haywire. The cause lay there. Saying he "hated enough to kill" the sales clerk was probably a father's bias.

When he returned to inventorying the medications, Noboru didn't see Kyojō. While working with Handayū, Noburu asked, "Can anything be touched in that building?"

Handayū answered, "It'll be donated as promised. If it's okay, they said the annex will be donated. It was funny. No, not funny, it's probably bad."

Handayū chuckled.

"I probably heard it from Sugi. Ino came to negotiate."

"Negotiate?"

"If the young lady dies, he seems worried Sugi will be taken with her. I'll barge into the place where they're still talking because I'll want to see her. It will be a critical event in the ups and downs of life."

"Indeed."

"No, I was frightened by that," said Handayū with a smile. "I'm saying I want Sugi to be my wife. A man called Tōkichi, a carpenter in Sakuma-chō in Kanda, knows me well. If she asked Tōkichi, she would know about me. I would show Sugi happiness for her entire life. And I'd swear to something like an obscure god."

"What did she say?"

"She was overwhelmed. Sugi's parents live in Ebaragōri. She went to speak with them and said they didn't object to me."

Handayū shut his mouth and looked over his shoulder. He heard noisy footsteps in the hall and a woman's crying voice.

"It's no good. Stop it," she said while running down the hall toward them, weeping. "Don't touch me. Let me go. Stop it."

Noboru went out to the hall. The young woman ran in alone, clung to, and hid behind him.

Coming from the opposite side in pursuit, Kyojō followed, saying, "Calm down." A fortyish woman followed close behind Kyojō and tried to push him aside.

"Help," said the young woman, still clinging to Noboru. "Help me. Make them leave me alone."

The woman who came from the side said, "Her name is Ei." Kyojō interrupted and said to Noboru, "Take her to my room."

"Relax. Everything's all right," Noboru said to the young woman, "Many people are here. No one is going to do anything to you. Please, come here."

"Calm down, Ei," said the woman. "Aren't we doing this for your sake? Nothing bad is going to happen to you."

"Do that later," said Kyojō. "You, wait out here."

"Can't I be with my daughter?"

"I have to talk to the young lady. Please wait."

While Kyojō stopped the mother, Noboru took the young woman to Kyojō's room. The medicine cabinet was open. The drawers were pulled halfway out. Medications in pouches were stacked on the floor on one side. He was confused about where to place the round straw mat for the young woman to sit on.

The young woman was eighteen or nineteen. A brown belt closed her short padded garment with coarse stripes. Only one comb held her hair. Her hands and feet were rough from working in water. Cracks already formed on her reddened cheeks showing no traces of makeup. Her features were pleasant but expressionless like a mask.

When she sat, she immediately started grinning like she forgot to cry.

She seemed to be a fool.

Noboru wanted to snap his tongue in exasperation.

2

Kyojō came in, sat, and began questioning the young woman. Her name was Ei and she was nineteen. The first woman was her mother Kane. Her father disappeared three years ago.

Ei had an older brother, older sister, younger brother, and younger sister.

From the time Ei was ten, she was a live-in maid at a candle shop called Chikaroku in Ikenohata Naka-chō in Shitaya. She got pregnant, was fired, and returned to her parent's home in Funakawara-chō in Ichigaya.

Ei only said this much but slurred her words and was often silent or repeated the same thing three times. It seemed painful for her to answer the questions. She wiped the palm of her hand over her forehead and around her mouth like wiping away drool.

Of course, she's an idiot, thought Noboru again.

Ei got pregnant while a live-in maid at Chikaroku. No one knows who the man was. The family she returned to after being fired lived a sparse daily existence. Her mother didn't want this foolish young woman to have a baby and came to the clinic because she wanted her to have an abortion. Until now, depending on the situation, Kyojō performed abortions.

Kyojō said, "*Mabiku*, the killing of a newborn because of financial problems, happens everywhere. Examples in the north country are reflected in the proclamations declared by feudal clans.

"Given the extreme poverty of people with many children and the food supply in the countryside, people can't have as many children as they want and raise them. In this situation, mabiku gets tacit consent. However, killing a person born into this world is tragic and the opposite of humanity.

"If the need is recognized, it should be disposed of before becoming a human being, that is, while still in the womb. With this as the favorite theory, Ei's child should be aborted, too."

However, Ei heard this and paled. "No," she said. She dodged Kyojō and other medical staff and escaped down the hall.

"I am having this baby," said Ei, slowly and emphatically. "This child in me is my child. Whatever happens? It will be born and grow up. I don't need anybody to help me."

Kyojō said, "It would be fine for you to become a mother. However, that is unreasonable. Your head is not normal. If you're alone, you'll probably find it hard to have a satisfying long life."

Ei grinned, turned to Kyojō, and whispered like it was a secret, "Sensei, I am only acting like a fool."

"Okay. I've heard that three times."

"It's true, Sensei, it's true," said Ei. "When I was twelve and a live-in maid, I was helping put baggage in the storehouse, fell off the ladder, and hit my head and back. Then I thought, I'll act like I'm stupid. Really. I'm really not stupid. I can raise my baby right."

"Yasumoto ..." said Kyojō and turned to say, "Tell the mother in the waiting room we will look after her daughter for a few days and persuade her to return in three days."

Noboru went to the waiting room, and Kane came running to him from the other side of the room. She didn't wait for Noboru to finish but launched her complaint, sounding annoyed.

"Why will it take so much time?" Kane pursed her lips and said, "At first, she was stupid and stubborn. I tried to persuade her, but that was pointless."

Noboru answered, "She doesn't agree so there's no hope. Whether stupid or foolish, the feelings of a woman who wants to carry a child do not lie."

"So, will he make my stupid daughter have a stupid baby?"

"He said to come in three days."

"She's coming home with me," said Kane. Showing her anger, she added, "I came here because I heard the medical fee is nothing if a doctor here gets rid of the child of a troubled woman. In that case, I'll spend a little money and quickly end this problem. Please call my daughter."

Noboru thought about doing it himself. However, Kyojō stubbornly refused to consent. Kane repeated the deadline of "three days" and finally went home. In contrast to her initial forlorn pleas, she sounded overbearing and demanding gratitude from them. Her face with fleshy cheeks seemed filled with disdain for others.

"What is she going to do?" asked Noboru, unable to suppress his indignation. "Right after the money is spent, the child will be taken care of. She probably has some reason?"

"I'll be going soon, if that's all right," said Kyojō. "Later, I'll be working with Mori. I have to prepare and then will go to Kōji-machi. It's already past three."

Noboru stood.

Amano Genpaku, his wife, and Masao went and were waiting at his home in Kōji-machi. It looked like rain all day. Dense gray clouds were stacked low in the sky. Although it was nearly four, lights were already on inside the houses.

Noboru first called at his father's room. His mother was also sitting in there. They said they were about to drink sake in a private ceremony.

Noboru said that was an awful idea. The idea of drinking sake in a private ceremony brought to mind thoughts of his relationship with Chigusa. His mother noticed this and was about to say something as she scooted forward on her knees. However, his father Ryōan shook his head and opened his mouth to speak but said nothing.

"This is Amano-san's wish. I also consented," said his father in his usual gentle tone. "Because we will have the wedding ceremony in March, it probably won't be a problem to have celebratory sake now."

"Because we'll celebrate in March, I don't believe we need to do it now."

"But this is the custom."

Noboru didn't answer and looked at the alcove. Imitation pine and apricots were arranged in a bronze flower vase. Far from the paper lantern light, they looked sick and tired, bored, and in despair, as though a familiar sight for one hundred years.

His mother practiced flower arranging and did not understand how insensitive and bored his father was by its repetitiveness.

It's always fake pine and apricots.

Noboru grumbled to himself, If that's the case, wouldn't it be better to not do this sort of flower arranging?

His silence was taken to be consent. Looking relieved, his father said to his mother, "Please, prepare."

"Everything is fine now," said his father after his mother left. "I was worried because of what happened before. Now, I'm relieved. Amano-san should have a positive response."

Noboru looked at his father's face. A satisfied smile rose.

3

After changing clothes, they drank the sake for the private ceremony in the parlor. An old folding screen with gold leaf was set up, a scarlet rug spread out, and two candle stands set out.

Noboru wore *kamishimo* ceremonial dress. Masao wore a long, pure white bridal robe. Her hair was in the traditional *bunkin takashimada* style. Her face caked with makeup looked so mature she looked like another woman.

Of course, Ryōan and his wife and Amano and his wife wore formal dress. An unfamiliar woman carried in the nuptial sake cups and decanter.

No friends are here, Noboru lazily thought.

After the customary exchange of sake cups with Masao, the woman who brought in the sake cups and decanter thrust out her hands toward the sliding screen a slight distance away. With her arms still out, her quavering voice said, "Congratulations."

Noboru's face tightened when she dropped her head and saw her sob.

Chigusa. That's Chigusa.

He felt like his eyes had been rinsed and looked at her condition. Noboru observed how ancient she looked. Almost no traces remained of the striking charm and brilliant, dazzling beauty she had when they met before he went to Nagasaki. She probably had her eyebrows shaved and her teeth blackened. Living with a man, being hidden from the world, and giving birth to a child surely changed a woman.

When he gazed at the figure of an ordinary dedicated wife, familiar anywhere, Noboru was relieved, like he dropped a heavy load. He told himself that was good despite no clear meaning for the word good.

"Oh, Chigusa-san," Noboru quietly said. "I heard you had a child. Is the child in good health?"

"I did," answered Chigusa softly in her throat. "But the baby recently recovered from the measles."

"Really?" said Noboru. "I haven't had the pleasure of meeting him, but please give my regards to your husband."

"All right," said Amano Genpaku to Chigusa. "You can go now."

Chigusa bowed and left.

"Please be patient, Noboru-san," said Genpaku and bowed to Noboru. "You probably think I'm a silly parent, but more than anything, I hoped for your acceptance. I'm also grateful to be able to visit them and hug my grandchild."

Noboru returned a slight bow and looked at Masao. Smiling, Masao stared at him with eyes filled with appreciation.

Thank you, said her eyes.

Noboru thought, Her intelligent eyes exhibit subtle emotions. I'm a lucky man. Masao's beauty is not conspicuous. However, as time passes, her beauty will gradually emerge.

Chigusa's beauty is the beauty of a flower in full bloom. Stems and leaves only play the role of making the flowers bloom. The flowers are recently past their peak and scatter petals. The fruits of the stem and leaves appear to cling noticeably.

Masao is a modest flower, but as the stem and the leaves quickly grow longer and mature, the true beauty is polished. If one side is a flowering tree, that side should be compared to a form that doesn't change the color of the pine. She's a woman suited to be a wife for a lifetime, thought Noboru.

The two couples, the Yasumotos and the Amanos, exchanged cups of sake in friendship. When done, Genpaku sat properly and looked at Noboru.

"Noboru-san, you have worked a year at this clinic. After speaking with Nīde-sensei, when the season changes in March of next year, you'll be promoted to a government doctor."

Noboru looked doubtful.

Genpaku continued, "When you returned from your studies in Nagasaki, the promise was that the position would be immediately arranged for you.

"I discussed the situation with Nīde-sensei who said you should temporarily join the charity clinic.

"I told him that the betrayal by your fiancee Chigusa while you were away studying was devastating to a young man like you. You may have felt desperate about your place in the world. Of course, a different life in a busy charity clinic was best. Also, the clinic needed fresh medical knowledge. Regardless of what you wished for, Noboru, you would return home and join the clinic."

"I often met with Nīde-sensei to discuss your situation," said Genpaku. "At the beginning, he smiled, saying you were a hard worker even when training. You quickly got your footing and treated the horrible patients he recommended. Now, the sensei is delighted. Our plan made sense. The result was the opposite, and we knew it was good. We were also not very pleasant, and you showed great patience. Again I thank you."

Noboru said nothing and returned the bow.

They moved to the tatami room for the meal. Noboru listened quietly to Genpaku and understood.

Thanks to Kyojō, I regained my footing. Even thinking now about the mistake with Yumi, that foolish mistake that makes me shrink from embarrassment threw me into despair. I got drunk from sake, which I hate, and found fault in everyone around me. I tried to hold Yumi's hand. Kyojō didn't reprimand me and left me alone. After being rescued from the mistake with Yumi, he buried that humiliating incident with no soul other than Mori Handayū knowing.

Noboru thought, That was my opportunity to right myself.

That humiliation forced me to change. Until then, he said nothing. Kyojō's magnanimity became my support. He always said he stole from friends, sold out friends, and betrayed teachers. I have no idea how much of what he said was true. Kyojō was patient, and I regained my footing. I felt when I saw his nearly unlimited love for poor people, I atoned for my criminal behavior. Only those who don't know crime judge others.

Noboru heard a voice say in his heart, "Those who don't know crime judge others."

Noboru thought, I don't know what happened, but the sensei knew the darkness and severity of the crime.

After the meal ended, Noboru said he wanted to speak with Masao alone and invited her to his parlor. Masao came after she changed. A belt woven with fine fall colors closed her short-sleeved kimono with a fine Edo pattern and a delicate design along the hem. She had removed all her makeup. The same as when she was young, long before wearing the wedding kimono, the downy hair around her healthy but tense cheeks absorbed the lantern light. A fuzzy halo enveloped her skin resembling a ripe peach.

Noboru pushed away the brazier.

4

He said, "There's one question I'd like to ask you.

"Amano-san said I will be promoted to a government doctor in March."

"Yes," said Masao and nodded.

"That was my wish. I studied in Nagasaki and mastered treatment procedures.

"If I became a government doctor for the shogunate, my name would rise in the medical field. Eventually, I intended to rise from a government doctor to a court physician.

"But I no longer have that desire."

Masao blinked several times and fixed her pretty, clear eyes on Noboru.

"In short, I intend to stay at the charity clinic.

"Will I ever change my mind for the rest of my life? I'm not sure. But for now, more than honor or wealth, I hope to remain at the clinic.

"I have to talk with Nīde-sensei. If I stay, life will be hard. The connection to fame and money becomes remote. Of course, you'll have to endure poverty, too. Please consider whether that will be acceptable.

"Think about it. You don't have to give me an answer now. I want to hear your honest feelings."

Masao's huge eyes that expressed subtle emotions blinked as

she stared at Noboru. Her pupils were crystal clear as if washed with water. He could see the simple answer meant I have no objection.

"I've thought hard about this," said Noboru like he was trying to remind himself. "A life of poverty may be unimaginable to you. Even if I endure it, I believe it is because my reason for living is my job. When you decide, please send a letter."

"Yes," said Masao seriously. "I'll do as you say."

Noboru felt his chest rapidly heat up. Masao had already decided. She didn't have to think anymore about it and will persevere no matter what. It was not blind obedience with no will but her taking the stance of braving any situation.

Noboru smiled with all his heart as he watched Masao. She smiled back, but the edges of her eyes reddened and she cast down her eyes.

"It's all right. It'll be fine," muttered Noboru, who had said his goodbyes and gone outside before the Amanos. The cloudy night was cold, but that cold felt pleasant to him in his excited state. Noboru walked with a brave, powerful stride.

Immediately after he got back to the clinic, Noboru dropped in at Mori Handayū's room. Handayū congratulated him on his marriage to Masao. He said, "She'll be a fine wife and is a woman to marry if you ask me."

However, he tilted his head, confused about the decision to remain at the clinic.

"Nīde-sensei seems decided," said Handayū. "Tsugawa will be coming here soon."

"Tsugawa?" asked Noboru, looking at Handayū. "Isn't Sensei always talking about needing people here? So that's true."

"Well, yes, but Tsugawa Genzō is a hopeless fellow. If you leave, it's better to have Tsugawa here than not."

"I'm staying," said Noboru quietly. "I intend to stay put even if Sensei tells me to go."

A smile appeared at the corners of Handayū's mouth. This is strange, thought Handayū. When he came here, he only thought about fleeing. That was no mystery and a natural thought for anybody. Everyone who came for treatment was dressed in rags, sweaty, covered in dust, smelly, dirty, half-dead, and near beggars.

Despite being fully occupied with caring for these patients, we had to make house calls to treat patients. On top of that, the salary was a pittance. For the first time, what Noboru seemed to hate made sense. It seemed unnatural for him to remain here on purpose.

"What's wrong?" said Noboru. "Why are you looking at me like that?"

"Oh, nothing," answered Handayū. "It's better not to rush into that conversation with him. I think it's better to wait for an opportunity to bring it up."

"Will you help?"

"I'll try," said Handayū.

The next day while still dark, Noboru opened his eyes to the voices of a noisy crowd. He heard muffled sounds down the hall of a woman seeming to shout, "Let go," and the voice of someone tightly hugging another person. Noboru jumped up, dressed, and rushed out of his room and headed toward them.

The light from the hanging lights along the hall was still bright. The wooden floor under his bare feet was as cold as ice.

The commotion was at the door to a sickroom. As Noboru got closer, he saw four women holding down a fiercely struggling Ei.

"Be quiet," said Noboru. "Seriously ill patients are here."

Ei stopped struggling.

"She tried to escape," said one of the middle-aged women. "When I came back to replace Kawa, she opened that door, and tried to go outside."

The woman was pointing to the half-open cedar door that opened into the courtyard. When Noboru closed the door, he glimpsed the faintly bright sky.

"This young woman is my patient," said Noboru to the women. "Please, everyone, go back to your rooms. Thank you."

The women left for the sickrooms. Noboru encouraged Ei to return with him to her room. As he adjusted her bedding, Mori Handayū appeared. After a brief explanation, he left Handayū and went to consult with Kyojō.

He found Kyojō writing at his desk. When Noboru finished talking, Kyojō put down his pen and thought for a short time. Eventually, he released a low sigh.

"Did you see Amano in Kōji-machi?" Kyojō asked about something completely different.

"We drank celebratory sake in a private ceremony," said Noboru and tried to return to the topic. "How is the young woman? I thought there would be a serious incident, like an attempt to escape."

"That young woman is not an idiot. As she said herself, she only acts like a fool."

After muttering like he was talking to himself, Kyojō abruptly turned and looked at Noboru. "Will you question her for further details?"

Noboru answered, "Well uh, how about Mori?"

"You do it," said Kyojō. "Soon, you'll be married. Maybe you can ask about something helpful. Today, you're excused from house calls, so you can ask her yourself."

5

Nearly an hour passed before Ei spoke.

Both breakfast and tea were brought to Kyojō's room, but she touched neither. She sat on the wooden floor and stared at the wall. She stubbornly displayed denial with her entire body.

Soon after ten o'clock when he was about to give up for today, Ei coughed and talked in a sneering, dry voice.

"Because the cart is broken down."

Noboru quieted his breathing. Ei was quiet again. Eventually, her shoulders shook in a jerk. She turned her back to Noboru and said, "I am going to have the baby. Who's having the baby? I'll raise the baby well enough by myself."

Noboru said nothing. Although quiet, he thought Ei would continue talking, but she stopped and did not move a muscle for a long time. Trying to sound as casual as possible, Noboru asked, "If you want to give birth, this is a good place to have a baby. Why did you try to run away?"

"Because Mother was coming," said Ei. "If she comes, Sensei will abort the baby, so I escaped. I thought I could have the baby somewhere else."

Noboru waited five beats and then said, "But raising a child without a father is not easy."

"Yeah," said Ei. "No father around is probably much better."

"Why?" asked Noboru.

Still looking at the wall, Ei spoke in a droning tone.

Her father's name is Satarō. Now no one knows where he is, but he used to be a performer. He didn't seem to have decided which art but played the shamisen and had a fairly good singing voice.

He performed in small theaters or was called to a guest's formal tatami room and was a traveling performer. He didn't make enough to call it earnings. His contributions of earnings to the household were rare.

Her mother Kane seemed to be known at bars. She was infatuated with Satarō, but they never stopped fighting. This was not the reason life was hard. The source was jealousy because Satarō could get other women.

Kane always said, "I don't talk about money.

"You're an artist. I understood from the start that you'd never earn much money. I say it's the women. You play dumb and find another lover somewhere."

Then there was the wild punching and kicking.

At this point in the story, Ei turned and faced Noboru. Her eyes glared, and she said, "Sensei probably tricked me."

"Tricked you about what?"

"Forget this story. He'll probably trick me and abort the baby."

"Don't say such nonsense," said Noboru. "This place is a government charity clinic managed by the town magistrate. The police are always here on official business. Do you think he could abort a child here if the woman does not wish it?"

"All men are the same," Ei mumbled in her mouth. "Even if she doesn't have a man, a woman and a child do not have to live in hardship."

Noboru said nothing. Ei continued her story.

Kane was infatuated with Satarō and would go along with anything he said, no matter how unreasonable. The husband and wife had six children.

Ritsu, the oldest daughter, turned twenty-three this year; and the youngest daughter Sue, nine. Between them were two boys, Jirō and Kenji. All of them began earning money at seven or eight. They babysat and ran errands. The father and mother took turns borrowing small advances from their children's wages.

Ritsu was eleven when she became a live-in maid at a geisha house in Fukagawa. Since the loans against her wages piled up, in the spring of her twelfth year, a client ravaged her as compensation. Ritsu was so scared she fled and returned home. Then Satarō went to negotiate. What did he arrange? The next time, she worked as a live-in maid at a brothel in the red-light district called Ataka in Honjo.

"This time, she'll be a reliable live-in maid," said Satarō. At first, she only worked in the kitchen and ran errands. Within fifty days, a client attacked her. She thought if she tried to flee and was caught, she'd be punished, perhaps killed. During the fifty days, she took a wage advance worth close to ten ryō for her father and mother.

Ei said, "I was eight then and babysitting at the rice cracker shop in Hachimanmae in Fukagawa.

"While I was babysitting one time, I visited where my older sister was working and heard this story."

Her older brother Jirō was nine and was a live-in servant at a travelers' inn in Bakuro-chō. He also piled up wage advances. This job was his third live-in apprenticeship, but he was dissatisfied with not being able to freely spend even one mon of his pocket money.

While listening to her older sister's story on the way home, Ei realized she had shared some of the experiences of her older sister and brother. Her younger brother Kenji was four years old. Her younger sister Hana hadn't been born yet. Ei thought they all eventually would become victims of their parents. Although young, she felt like her heart froze.

When Ei was ten, she switched employers to a candle shop in Shitaya. About six months later, her older sister visited and announced, "I ran away because working is too hard."

Ritsu turned fourteen but worked for more than two years under extreme abuse. She lost weight and was small, not very different in size from Ei.

When they parted, the older sister said, "Although my body has been soiled and is no good, you need to be smart and not be made a fool."

Ever since then, Ei had been thinking about how this could end without becoming her parents' victim, too. As usual, her father and mother came to the shop to borrow wages. Her mother's reason was "life is hard" after the births of the youngest sisters Hana and Sue. She asked if she could sell me like my older sister. While thinking about this, an unexpected thought arose.

"In the same town as Naka-chō in Ikenohata, there was an idiot named Matsu," said Ei. "He was seventeen or eighteen. His mouth didn't work well. He always wandered around town while snot and drool dribbled down. He had no companions other than children. I watched Matsu-san."

When Ei was ten, she concluded, if I'm stupid, they can't sell me. Then one day while helping with baggage in the storehouse, she fell off the ladder and hit her head and back. That wasn't on purpose. She missed a step on the ladder and lost consciousness for a short time.

6

Ei said, "They made me drink water when I came to, but I thought it was over.

"It hurt like my head split open, and I couldn't bend my back for a few days. I started acting like I was batty.

"I watched and thought imitating the idiot named Matsu-san would be a good idea. My first catch was the doctor. He diagnosed me and said I would recover soon because the cause was the blow to my head."

Ei seemed to recover and acted stupider. The landlord of Chikaroku was neither a good nor bad man and felt responsible for Ei. On the other hand, she worked less, so he refused to give advances to Satarō and his wife.

Because this occurred in her job at the shop, Ei was taken care of, but her wages weren't raised.

If dissatisfied, the loan would be written off. The landlord said, "You can go and take her with you." Satarō tried to take her back three times, but Ei clung to a pillar.

"I'm not going back."

Her crying shout was so loud the entire town could hear her. She sunk her teeth into her father's hand.

As he listened, Noboru slyly watched Ei's demeanor. He thought, her story made sense. Her behavior was normal. However, she slurred her speech and constantly rubbed the palm of her hand beneath her nose and around her mouth. She noticed dribbling snot and drool and looked like a fool wiping them away. Those repeated actions became a habit and a part of her. Noboru was surprised by the deep-seated single-mindedness of a human being.

Ei said, "If my parents were normal, I wouldn't behave like this. But my parents are different. They exploited their children one after another. They do nothing that looks like work, drink sake, eat good food, and leisurely wander around.

"Looking around at the world, poor households are more or less the same. Even parents who love their children have no choice in a life of poverty.

"They'll put their children through few and many hardships.

"Men, especially, are no good. I studied them. A man gets wild a little after he turns thirty. He starts down the road to a wild life with sake, women, and gambling, and stops thinking about his wife and children. I don't know about wealthy people and can't say all poor people are like this, but eight or nine out of ten people always do this.

"The time comes when a man becomes a broken-down cart. If

the cart carries a load after it's broken, the burden carried from the beginning is enough.

"That's why I don't have a husband. The mother and child together. Two people. I can raise one child and work as a live-in maid. If a mother is alone, she will spare the child from hardship. I will have this child and raise it wonderfully."

Noboru asked, "But isn't your mother saying to abort the child because she intends to keep exploiting you?"

"Yes," said Ei, bowed her head and wiped around her mouth. "After my father died three years ago, she drowned her problems in sake and sold my younger sister Hana to a geisha establishment. She's even going to sell nine-year-old Sue."

"So you faked being stupid and were overlooked?"

"No, that's not it," said Ei, vigorously shaking her head. "If her body is good enough, it's not unusual to see customers buy a dopey woman."

Noboru was silent for a short time and then said, "That's horrible. It's awful those sorts of clients exist. They're the broken-down carts."

"Will you let me have my baby?"

"I can't see why not," said Noboru, looking like he was testing Ei. "But what about the father?"

"What about him?"

"You said you don't have a husband, but the child in you has a father."

Ei grinned. "Don't worry about that. If I say I'm pregnant, he'll disappear."

"Did he work at the shop?"

"Did he?" Ei asked vaguely and sneakily shook her head. "I wanted only one child. If I stupidly got pregnant, my mother would give up. In the future, no man may be interested in me.

"I might not live a long life alone, but if there's a child, it'd be worth the trouble. I only wanted one child. I've forgotten what that man looks like."

"My older sister Ritsu escaped once but was caught right away.

She's twenty-three. She moved several times and ended up working in a brothel in Senjū.

"My older brother Jirō, who's twenty, fell into a construction crew somewhere and went bad.

"I'm worried about my younger brother Kenji, who's turning fifteen, and my two younger sisters. But when my baby comes, I will use all my power to protect my own life."

Noboru said, "I understand perfectly. You'll stay under our care until the baby is born. So behave and return to your room. All right? If you run away, you'll only cause trouble for yourself."

"Yessir." Ei nodded. "I won't try to run away again."

That night, Noboru waited for Kyojō to return from the house calls to discuss Ei's case. Kyojō listened to Noboru and said nothing after he finished.

Noboru asked, "May I care for Ei until she gives birth?"

"Until the child is born ..." Kyojō sounded doubtful and looked at Noboru but then gave a quick nod. "Of course. We'll care for her here. What else can we do?"

Noboru stuttered, "I think her mother is going to be a problem."

"I will speak to that woman. Has the young woman calmed down?"

"Yes, she's calm."

"Tomorrow, please meet with the proprietor of Chikaroku," said Kyojō. "Explain that she will stay here until the baby is born. Ask him whether she can return to her job as a maid after recovering from the birth."

Noboru agreed.

7

The next day, Noboru paid a visit to Chikaroku in Ikenohata Naka-chō and spoke to Ōmiya Rokubei, the proprietor. He never believed Ei was the idiot she pretended to be and agreed to keep her on as a maid.

Rokubei said, "I'll clean up the storeroom, and she can live there. Whether Ei is stupid or not, she's a hard worker and helpful. Of course, I won't let her mother get close."

Noboru stressed, "I'm asking a lot of you."

When he returned to the clinic, a person with a serious wound was being carried in. Noboru and Handayū had no time to rest for an hour.

Eventually, the treatment ended. The injured patient's condition stabilized, so they went to the dining hall for tea. There, a message came saying a woman named Kane was waiting. Noboru was astonished. A messenger hadn't come. It was Tsugawa Genzō.

"Aren't you Tsugawa?" asked Noboru.

"I'm so happy you remembered me," said Genzō, smiling sarcastically.

"Yasumoto is always the substitute. The reason this time is I've come back."

Noboru looked at Handayū, who frowned and looked away.

Tsugawa asked, "What is that woman doing?"

"She's here to see Nīde-sensei," said Noboru. "She said she'll wait until he returns."

"She's drunk," said Tsugawa. "Is it okay to shout in the waiting room?"

After a little thought, Noboru said, "Well, I'll go see. Please take her to my room."

Arms folded, Tsugawa said, "To your room. Of course, young doctor."

Handayū clenched his fists. Noboru watched Tsugawa leave and then said to Handayū, "Pay him no mind."

"Pay him no mind ..." Handayū turned and said, "Yasumoto, you're lucky to be leaving. Me and him together ..."

"Oh," said Noboru while standing and waving his hand. "Please don't get mad. It's good that he's here. Didn't you say that?"

Handayū relaxed his fists, tightened them again, and asked, "Have you decided what you're going to do, Yasumoto?"

Noboru kept quiet and lowered his head. He wanted to say, That's true.

From the time she was ten, Ei was determined to protect her

body. She would bear a child. Even amid the severe hardships of the world, she would try to raise the child properly.

Kyojō's way of life was the same. From the appearance of the effects seen, will the hopes of humanity bear fruit in places where efforts that come to nothing seem to accumulate?

Kyojō said, "I bet on myself in situations where my efforts appear to be fruitless."

Noboru thought but didn't say, What kind of sprouts will grow in a hotbed? Even ice contains a passion that will grow sprouts. Isn't there a genuine way to live?

Noboru answered, "I will stay here. Because Red Beard-sensei placed me here. I have that responsibility as a doctor."

Then he went to the dining hall. In his room, Tsugawa Genzō was talking to Kane. Rather than talking with her, he was making fun of her. While Kane wiggled her body, she told a lewd story in a loud voice. Tsugawa boldly prodded her to keep talking.

"Oh, it's you," said Kane when she saw Noboru. "I remember that face. Yuck. The doctors here aren't good at all, are they? Stop acting like you don't hear me."

Noboru didn't speak as he sat at his desk.

"Well, I'll be going," said Tsugawa and stood. "My job is done. Excuse me. Is that all right, young doctor?"

Noboru didn't look at him or speak. Tsugawa Genzō left. Like she was very drunk, when Kane adjusted her sitting position, her legs spread apart showing something turquoise blue below her.

"What have you decided to do about my stupid daughter?" asked Kane. "There's nothing to discuss. Please get rid of it."

"Your daughter says she wants to have the baby."

"That's ridiculous," said Kane and waved her hand like she was swiping away a spider's nest. "A clinic doctor shouldn't take seriously what a dummy like that says. Please fix this quickly. I'm not rich like you and can't be so carefree."

Suppressing his anger, Noboru said, "It would be best if you drop that subject. Your daughter says she will have the baby. We intend to help her give birth. You should stop exploiting her."

Noboru finished but thought he had said too much. Kane stiffened. Her face relaxed by her drunkenness hardened like a taut string. Her expression contorted grotesquely like she was biting down hard.

"You're saying I exploit my daughter," said Kane. "When did I exploit her? What right do you have to say something like that? Let me tell you, I've never, not ever, been a person who talks behind someone's back. When someone like you says that sort of thing, I can't show my face in public. When did I exploit my daughter? Can you show me proof?"

"What is your daughter Ritsu doing?" asked Noboru in a whisper. "What about Jirō and Kenji and Hana? What is your daughter Sue doing?"

"Hmph!" Kane looked away. "You don't know anything about them. I gave birth to those children. I raised all of them. What a mother does with her children doesn't have to be explained to a stranger like you."

Noboru said, "In that case, don't ask for proof."

Kane huffed and puffed and then turned to stare at Noboru.

"I am their mother," she said in defiance. "Isn't it natural to use a child to benefit the parent? As their mother, I've suffered cruel hardships because of those children. That's how it is between parents and children."

She drew herself up to her full height like some thought popped into her mind and said, "If you are devoted to god, won't you be rewarded? If a child's devotion to his parents comes first before all other pious acts, won't everything in the world be settled peacefully? Am I right?"

8

Noboru shivered. The upbringing and experiences of the forty-year-old woman were completely different. He knew he couldn't argue. He thought he wanted to say something to eviscerate her. While shivering, he thought, Should I say something? In the short time before he could speak, the sliding door flung open and Kyojō entered.

Kane was startled and sat up straight. Kyojō sat in front of her, was silent for a moment, and stared at her face.

When Noboru got up to close the door, Kyojō shook his head no.

"Leave it open. It stinks in here."

Noboru sat down.

"It stinks in here?" said Kane. "Are you talking about me?"

"No, that's not it," said Kyojō. "Your rotten character. This room stinks enough to make one vomit. Take a long sniff of your body."

"What's wrong with my personality?"

"It's not only your personality. From the top of your head to the tips of your toes, your entire body is rotting from your bones," said Kyojō. "A mother has a hard time making a living, forces her children to earn a living, and takes it easy despite being healthy. A mother is not soaked in sake and does not sell her children. That sort is neither a mother nor a human being.

"Listen carefully, a lowly beast will sacrifice its life to protect its child. It will not eat to feed its child first. That is a parent, even if it's a beast. You are less than a beast."

Kane looked about to talk back.

"Silence," Kyojō shouted. "Your daughter will be admitted to the clinic and you will be delivered to the town magistrate. If you exploit your children in the future, I think you will be dealt with appropriately."

"Are you threatening me?"

"Go home," said Kyojō. "From now on, if you take advantage of your children, you'll be arrested."

"You're threatening me with that?" asked Kane as she stood. "Hmph, the town magistrate."

Kane paled and stumbled.

"Oh, the town magistrate. You're scaring me. Does he walk around Edo's towns? Don't tell me I'll be dragged off to jail like a wandering balladeer. That's hilarious. I'm gonna die laughing.

"You can't scare me into thinking the town magistrate will get a gang together and come here to get me," Kane said as she staggered from the room and went down the hall.

"Stop it," Kyojō grumbled to himself. "Lately, my tone has been strange. I never yell at or demean others. That woman is only ignorant and foolish. That is not her crime. Poverty and her surroundings are the causes."

Noboru said, "I don't think so."

Kyojō looked up at Noboru and said, "You don't think so."

Noboru said, "The quality of her poverty and circumstances are not related to the true nature of a human.

"I accompany you on your house calls. It was for less than a year, but I've come into contact with a variety of people. While some were raised in comfort and received satisfactory education, others were inferior to the lowest caste of people. Despite growing up in an unbearably poor environment and not being able to read kana characters, how many people have I met who are so elite I have to lower my head?"

Kyojō said, "If you cultivate a poisonous plant, does it remain a poisonous plant?

"You see, Yasumoto, people create effective medications from poisonous plants. That woman Kane is a terrible mother. Screaming at and demeaning her only makes matters worse. Just as medications are produced from poisonous plants, hard work is needed to pull goodness out of a bad person. A person is a person."

Noboru said, "I think I understand what you're saying," then he lowered his voice, "Was that a consideration in calling back Tsugawa this time?"

"Why do you mention Tsugawa?"

"I want to hear your thoughts."

"Do you want me to yell at you?"

"I think that may happen," said Noboru coolly. "You don't have to call back Tsugawa because I intend to stay here."

Kyojō narrowed his eyes. "Who gave you permission?"

"You, Sensei."

"I ... I allowed that?"

"Yes, you did."

"No, I do not give my permission," said Kyojō, shaking his head.

"Yasumoto Noboru will become a government doctor. That has already been decided."

"This clinic needs decent doctors. That was the first thing you said to me," Noboru said without yielding. "My life is here. Medicine is a healing art."

"What are you saying?" asked Kyojō. His voice became harsh. "Medicine is a healing art." He was defiant but aware of his fury. He breathed heavily and quieted his voice. "Saying medicine is a healing art is nonsense. Some quacks will set up a practice with the goal of profit and specialize in earnings from medical fees. It's drivel because they conceal unfair profits."

Noboru was silent.

"Far from a healing art, medicine still does not satisfactorily cure a cold. Correct medical decisions are not made.

"Most are fake doctors who don't try and only muddle through by relying on the patient's vitality. They only blunder even if they work hard."

Noboru said, "Nevertheless, are you saying I will go and Tsugawa will return?"

"Those are two different discussions."

"Sensei, you know they are not different. I'll state it clearly. I will use all my strength to stay here. I've seen your physical strength, but I won't easily lose to you. If you wish, you'll have to toss me out by force."

"You're an idiot."

"Thanks to you, Sensei."

"A fool," said Kyojō and stood. "You're speaking from the enthusiasm of youth but will feel regret."

"You gave me permission."

"I regret that now."

"Let's try," said Noboru, lowering his head, and then said, "Thank you."

Kyojō slowly walked out.

ABOUT THE AUTHOR

Yamamoto Shūgorō was a Japanese novelist, essayist, and playwright. He was born Shimizu Satomu, the oldest child of Shimizu Itsutarō and Toku, on June 22, 1903 in Hatsukari-mura, Yamanashi Prefecture, Japan, and died February 14, 1967 in Yokohama, Kanagawa Prefecture, Japan. After graduating from school, he became a live-in apprentice at Yamamoto Shūgorō, a pawnbroker's shop that closed in the wake of The Great Kantō Earthquake in 1923.

In 1924, he joined the clerical section of Teikoku Koshinjo, a credit agency, and later became an editor at the employee magazine *Nipponkon* of a subsidiary company.

His debut literary work *Suma-dera Fukin* was published in the April 1926 edition of *Bungei Shunjū*. The magazine misunderstood his address at Yamamoto Shūgorō Shimizu 36, resulting in his pen name.

In 1943, he declined the 17th Naoki Prize for his work *Nihon Fudōki*. He published over twenty novels over forty years. Many of his stories, including *Red Beard,* were adapted to film and television.

From the Japanese Wikipedia page about Yamamoto Shūgorō. (Accessed March 26, 2023)

https://ja.wikipedia.org/wiki/山本周五郎

CREDITS

Japanese Text

Yamamoto, Shūgorō. 赤ひげ診療譚. *Akahige Shinryōtan* (Red Beard's Clinic). *All Yomimono* (March 1958 - December 1958).
Aozora Bunko file accessed April 1, 2023.
Input by: Harukaze Non-Profit Organization
Revised by: Kitagawa Matsuike
https://www.aozora.gr.jp/cards/001869/card57841.html
https://www.aozora.gr.jp/cards/001869/card57840.html
https://www.aozora.gr.jp/cards/001869/card57544.html
https://www.aozora.gr.jp/cards/001869/card57842.html
https://www.aozora.gr.jp/cards/001869/card57838.html
https://www.aozora.gr.jp/cards/001869/card57843.html
https://www.aozora.gr.jp/cards/001869/card57542.html
https://www.aozora.gr.jp/cards/001869/card57839.html
(Accessed April 1, 2023)

Cover Image

Ichiyūsai, Kuniyoshi. 難病療治. *Nanbyō Ryōji* (Treatments of Serious Illnesses), Enshūya Matabei.

NDL Digital Collections. https://dl.ndl.go.jp/pid/1307674
(Accessed April 10, 2023)

Chapter Background Images

Sugita, Genpaku. Minami, Yasuichi, copier; Nakai, Saburō,
engraver; et. al. 解体新書銅版全図. *Kaitai Sinsho Dōban Zenzu* (New
Anatomical Illustrations - Copperplate Etchings). Edo: Suharaya
Mohei and three others, 1826.
NDL Digital Collections. https://dl.ndl.go.jp/pid/2537534
(Accessed April 10, 2023)